I0525211

Cirsova®

P. ALEXANDER, Ed.
Xavier L., Copy Ed.
Mark Thompson, Copy Ed.

A New and Thrilling Novel of the Wild Stars®

An Exciting Novella of Earth's Secret War

Suspenseful Shorts Set Near and Beyond Our Star

Poetry

Spring Issue
2023

Vol.2, No 14
$15.00 per copy

The Unshrouded Stars

By DAVID SKINNER

When an astronaut confronts a lamia, she has a proposition for him: she will refrain from eating children for an entire year...if he will take her into outer space!

Hatcher dropped his keys beside the kiosk. The snow absorbed them without jingle or jangle. As he dug up the keys with his ungloved hand, his fingers were chilled. Barely a crystal melted. He clicked open his mailbox, bundled a week of neglected mail under his arm, and restored his glove to his hand.

Most of his neighbors were quite asleep. Few had lit their porches. Their windows were dark behind shadowing trees. A half-moon loitered in the near-winter sky. The snow reprised the half-given light. Hatcher could see perfectly well. As he left the kiosk to cross his street, he saw a lamia assessing a house.

The house belonged to the Carters. Hatcher didn't know the Carters well. Mr. Carter had tried to make friends with Hatcher, who was a slightly famous astronaut, but Hatcher wasn't one for friends. He knew, however, that the Carters had two children, both under six, and the lamia was at their window.

Intent on her hunt, the lamia didn't notice Hatcher. Her halves spiraled languidly, pulsing apart and together again, two fragments of a waterfall—a sandfall, really—a fall, in fact, of stringy and sieved flesh, dried and fluid. A lamia is not actually half-snake, but folklore does tend to misremember its monsters. Nor is a lamia a woman, despite her feminine pieces and voices—although this one, like all her kind, exuded something female, a muffled cry of barren wombs, consuming children in a perversely maternal fashion.

Come to my many breasts, my sweety morsels.

Hatcher was unflappable. Nothing frightened him. His adrenaline rose only as a practical matter, to focus his body on some urgency. This had served him well on his orbital journeys. It also meant that monsters never dwelt in the corners of his eyes. There was never a terror in Hatcher to distort the monsters into fugitive nightmares. He saw monsters as he saw trees or buses. He feared monsters no more than he feared tigers or bears.

But neither was he indifferent. He wouldn't let a lamia eat the Carter children. Full of practical adrenaline, he lit across the snow and, within range of the oblivious lamia, hurled all his mail at her—not to harm her, as such, but to confuse her with a flurry of twisting fliers and envelopes. Then, in his momentum, he crashed into her. Through her, actually. She was not confused by the volley of mail, and her halves parted before Hatcher. He tumbled into the snow.

He was about to rise when he realized she wasn't joining the fight. From his rump, he watched her. She was unperturbed. Her faces intertwined in a stare. A twitch of her lips danced on her oscillating mouths. A squint bobbed on her eyes—eyes now numbering two, now three, now four, now one. The fleshfall was calm. Her voices, aging and youthful, soothing and cold, echoed each other in a whisper: "What is it, Man?"

Bluntly he said, "Don't eat these children."

"Why not? I'm peckish."

"Leave them alone."

"Ah, Man. Do you have *authority*? Do you have *power*?"

He frowned.

"You can't strike me. You can't command me. I suppose," her voices wafted, "you hope to *persuade* me. Are you girded by your *morality*, Man? But you misunderstand the case. By the Scheme of All Things, I and my sisters naturally long for the offspring of men. Children are delicious. There's no moralizing against the Scheme of All Things."

"Just go. Now."

"No."

"Yes."

"Is your plan to *irritate* me? You could say *please*."

He stood; brushed off the snow. He had no idea what he was going to do.

"Or you *could*," she drawled, "make me an offer."

Hatcher sensed the danger. He was not naive. Still... "A deal?"

"Of course! Deals are the currency of the Scheme."

"What do you want?"

"What do *you* want?"

"Stop killing children."

She sniffed. "I don't 'kill.' I eat. Death happens." Her smiles were crooked.

"Stop what you do, then."

"Stop being what I am, you mean."

"Would you starve?"

She eyed him for a moment. She admitted, "No. But truly, the Scheme would not allow me to..." She shivered. "*Convert*. I must be what I am."

"Then a respite."

"Eh?"

"A year. No children. You can do without children for hours, right? For a day? A week? Make it a year. Ten years."

She snorted in contempt. Then she was silent. Thoughtful. She approached him. He didn't flinch. She circled him, fingers flowing on his neck and ears. Softly she said, "Within you I see. You visit above."

"Hm?"

She faced him. Her eyes rolled upwards. "Above. You work in the far above."

"I'm an astronaut, yes."

"Take me with you."

"What?"

"My price. When do you travel again?"

"You want *me* to take *you* to outer space?"

"Yes. When is your next visit?"

He hesitated. "Are you serious?"

"Entirely. When can we go?"

Suspiciously, he asked, "And you'll stop eating children for ten years?"

Her guffaws echoed around them. "No, no, no. You live above for only a while, do you not? That is not worth a *decade*. But... I do feel generous. A *year* will I abstain from sweets. So, Man. When do we go?"

"I haven't agreed."

She sighed. "You will. Think of the *children*."

Hatcher paused. His heart slowed. The winter night marched upon his warmth. His breath clouding before him, he muttered at last, "Preflight quarantine starts Tuesday."

"So soon! Then we go?"

"We go."

Did she squeak in excitement? Hatcher imagined so.

In any event, the lamia turned to the window and, hands waving and fingers overlapping, murmured, "Stay plump, my darlings." To him she cooed, "For now, I am your consort," and wove into the shadows around him.

Hatcher was numb.

The moon and the snow were gaping at him.

O Man! What have you done?

The days until quarantine were uneventful. Hatcher kept an eye on the Carter house, and the children were untroubled and lively. The lamia was visible to him, now and then, quietly lingering in his rooms, as if she and he were casual roommates, without overlapping interests or schedules. His house was *dissonant*, though. An itch; a slit; a wilt. A smell that crackled and a taste that pushed.

His time on the Station was to be forty days. More than a month of dissonance, then. For him *and* his crewmates.

He reminded himself: *With scores of children safe for a year.*

At the quarantine facility, the lamia was unobtrusive. She kept to herself, breaking no veils, whispering nothing, prodding no fears. Her restraint was surely practical. Disturbing anyone *now* would jeopardize her journey. With luck, her practical thinking would persist for the coming weeks.

Hatcher's companions did, however, remark on the uncomfortable *air*—which, curiously, lasted only a day.

For as soon as the lamia realized that the activities of quarantined astronauts were *tedious* and that Hatcher, being essentially imprisoned, could easily be found again, she left to do other things. Hatcher could hardly stop her. He sternly reminded her to eat no children. Taking offense she replied, "You and I have dealt. It is *your* ilk who defy the Scheme. *You* remember to welcome me when I return, William."

His given name in her mouths annoyed him. "Call me Hatcher," he grumbled. Then he felt at a disadvantage. "What's *your* name?"

"Tepinassa."

He blinked.

She wryly asked, "You expected me to withhold it?"

"Sort of."

"*Feh.* And have you hail me as 'Monster'?"

She slipped away.

Early on, in the remorseful light of day, Hatcher had thought to turn their peculiar alliance to a diversion, a way to lull the lamia while he found a way to end her—thus making her year-long abstinence eternal. Early on, however, she had warned him: "I recognize, Man, that I am submitting to *you* in this venture. The setting is *yours*. Do not contrive my death, however. That would be an abrogation of our deal. The Scheme is not lenient to deal-breakers. Nor would I be, should you fail to kill me."

Resigned to playing out their deal honestly, Hatcher still wondered why there *was* a deal. Tepinassa could come and go, unseen by men and devices. She could stow away without him. There was nothing for him to *do* on her behalf. Perhaps he could be her guide to things astronautical—but that was a petty service, hardly worth a year's suppression of one's deepest craving, and in any event she had requested no knowledge or training. When he asked her if she needed his *permission* to stow away, she sneered, "Am I a vampire that needs invitation?" What, then? Obviously, Hatcher was required in a way that entailed himself—and especially his agreement; his *will*.

But she was evasive. "You'll see," she said.

On launch day, he saw.

Tepinassa returned to the facility and woke him before the morning alarm. She beckoned him away from the others. Normally, he and she talked in tight whispers, his head merely turned to a corner or to the ground; but now, she wanted them both out of sight. Unflappable though he was,

Hatcher experienced an animal trepidation. He wished he were wearing more than his shorts.

Barely louder than the hum of the darkened room, she began, "How long have the veils of my kind been nothing to you?"

"Since I was born, I guess," he answered.

"How much do you know of the Scheme?"

"Not much. I found a few books. I overheard things—from your kind."

"You never really... *investigated* any of it?"

"Why would I? I'm not a crackpot."

"A *crackpot*? But it's real."

He sighed. "Somebody else can convince the world. I just wanted to be an astronaut. I ignored you all."

She floated before him, her faces blending in bemusement.

He asked, "Is that why you need me for this deal? I'm special because I can naturally see you? How does that fit in?"

"Oh, no. That's irrelevant. Any willing Man would do. It's just that... Your indifference is fascinating."

"I'm not indifferent. What am I willing for you?"

"Hmph. This." An arm coalesced before him. "Take a bite. And swallow."

He cringed. "What the f—. *Why*?"

"Had you done more investigating..."

He glared at her.

She explained, "Man's place in the Scheme is unique. You are under jurisdiction, and you are not. The Earth is where you live. The Earth is what I *am*. The soil fiercely holds my kind. Were I to go far above, where all is dead, I would wither. Not die, not exactly. Go mad. Succumb to the distance. The parting. The *exile.* Man is of the soil, but you can depart the Earth. The soil goes with you. By eating of me, you erase the distance. You anchor me."

He stared at the fluttering flesh. "This is my role?"

"You can be my guide, too."

His bile rose. "I do this and... you're good?"

"Well. Every few days, you do this. Nothing you eat... lasts.''

He inhaled. "So you'll be at my mercy."

"Yes. True. But we have a deal."

"We do. It's such a risk, though. Why would you do this?"

Her eyes and her noses and her mouths collected to their proper counts, on a single face, intent and whole. She answered him: "I want to see the unshrouded stars."

Yes, she was a monster. Her desire, though, was keenly familiar.

With not a little revulsion, he closed his eyes and anchored her.

Tepinassa knew about the Madness of Exile because she had heard tales of other monsters who had hunted men at altitude, following their prey ever farther above, in zeppelins, jetliners, and suborbital spyplanes. A few had even been orbital. The instinctive longing of monsters for the depths was revealed to be a necessity of the body.

Tepinassa's remedy for the madness was her own, and untested. The binding of man and monster through the sharing of flesh—via hands, genitals, or teeth—was an ancient practice, yet whether a piece of herself in Hatcher's soil would truly anchor her, she could only hope.

And then there were the mundane effects of nature.

A monster is not a figment. It can hide, conceal, deceive, delude, blend into cloud or wall, but it is ultimately *matter.* It has its tricks, its skills, its evasions, but is not immune to forces, whether chemical, centripetal, angular, or gravitational. Physics is prior to the Scheme.

Tepinnassa could not stow herself in the trunk of the Capsule. For one thing, the trunk was unpressurized; for another, it would be discarded on the return trip, before atmospheric re-entry. Nor would her pride let her be placed with the crates. Fortunately, the seven seats of the Capsule were not always filled. Today, only four were needed, to hold Bergamo and Whitney (joining the Station for a long-term expedition) and Johnson and Hatcher (joining for short-term support). Veiled, Tepinassa followed the crew through the access arm and took to an empty seat. She was not sitting, as such. Lamias don't sit. At most, they congeal in a spot, especially when they sleep. But she was positioned to be caught, like a ball in a mitt, when the acceleration struck.

She was naked, though. More to the point: *unsuited.* She had inadequate solidity to support a suit. She could conceivably pour herself into a suit that was already resting in the acceleration cushions, and Hatcher could lock the umbilical and seal her in; but an apparently empty yet weirdly inflated suit had no mission justification, and Hatcher could not concoct any sort of rational excuse for such an oddity.

She had asked, "What is the suit for?"

"Emergencies," he replied, disregarding the functions irrelevant to a fiendish stowaway. "Protection against fire or depressurization."

"Are such things likely?"

He shrugged. "No. But..."

"If they happen, I die."

He nodded.

There was no helping it. "Then I die."

Hatcher hadn't been sure if she was being stoic or fatalistic. Either way, as he now watched her settle into her seat, naked against her fate, his empathy for her was limited. His gut was still bubbling from the fiendish *hors d'ouevre.*

The launch routine continued. Communication with the ground was confirmed. Integrity of the suits was confirmed. The state and location of the Station were uploaded to the Capsule computers. Fuel-up was a go. Despite the weird dissonance in the air—so like that first day in quarantine—the crew kept on. With shakes of their heads and great inhalations, they steadied themselves and did their jobs.

Ignition and liftoff cracked Tepinassa. For an instant, her cry and gasp were heard. Anxiously the crew checked their boards; but nothing was amiss with the ship. And no one would admit an unprofessional moment of dismay. After all, they were used to this sort of painful crush. They decided it was just the stressful air. Just a noise, among many noises.

Just their imaginations.

Once the ascent was complete, the crew removed and stowed their suits, remaining in their cotton shirts and pants. The trip to the Station would take several hours. They'd suit up again at the next critical phase, the docking itself.

With everything in free-fall and gravity disguised, Tepinassa had escaped her seat. She acclimated quickly, given that floating was her usual mode. With no concern for the bustle around her, she went to a porthole, seeking the stars. She fixed herself before the sight. From his position Hatcher could not see her faces. Her unmoving silence could be construed as awe. Everyone who first saw the sight was awed. Everyone got used to it, too. He wondered if Tepinassa's awe would last forty days.

The Capsule was not cramped but neither was it spacious, and Tepinassa created an obstruction at the porthole. The crew became bewildered as they bumped against a thing not there. Tepinassa had the sense to move aside, to give no evidence to curious hands of an invisible body. She stayed ahead of outright discovery, and fixed again at a porthole whenever she could.

Hatcher supposed she was annoyed by this shuffling about. It was hard to tell. The flesh of her faces was capricious. Of course, he couldn't just ask her, not about that nor about her celestial mood. The Capsule was too small for their whispers not to be overheard.

She at least seemed to be sane—although her exile *was* fairly fresh.

Dull hours later, the Station was near and it was time for their approach. Hatcher hissed and caught Tepinassa's eye. He nodded her to her seat. She understood and, perhaps regretfully, left the porthole. Meanwhile, the crew suited up and began the docking routine.

The Capsule and the Station were crossing the Earth at seventeen thousand miles an hour, but relative to the Station, the Capsule was only a car leisurely rolling to a stop. Tepinassa was undisturbed by the rare and rhythmless puffs of the thrusters. The final hard capture was barely a bother.

The crew stowed their suits again and drifted through the docking vestibule into the Station. Tepinassa brought up the rear, behind Hatcher. There was the usual congestion once inside, as the new arrivals tumbled through a zero-g gauntlet of hugs. Hatcher disliked this custom. He couldn't imagine Armstrong liking it. Maybe Gagarin; the Russians did love to embrace. Even so, living on the Station was intimate enough. Hatcher saw no need to exacerbate things.

As put out as Hatcher by the hullabaloo, Tepinassa impatiently flowed around everyone. There was already so much bumping and knocking that her own contributions weren't especially noticed. She surfaced from the crowd and headed into the Station. Hatcher stifled a cry to call her back, too aware of all the ears around him. When she disappeared into an adjacent module, his heart sank, and his guilt rose, as if he had loosed something terrible into the house of his fellows.

Because, of course, he had.

Every wall was a ceiling, every floor a wall, every surface a tiling of panels and doors. Wires and tubes joined this point with that. Patches of velcro secured a flea market of tools and packs. Laptops dangled like weeds. Experiments lived in windowed drawers: a portioned menagerie of ants and mice and infant squids.

For all the cloistered density of the Station, for all the modular tunnels and cul-de-sacs, there was an openness at the center of things, a clearing-back towards the bulkheads, in which one could freely rotate and glide. And the shadows were meager, as there was never not a light nearby.

Hiding was not really possible.

So when Tepinassa again failed to meet him at 19:30 in Node 1, Hatcher went looking for her and, without much trouble, found her in the Japanese lab. She seemed to be... *relaxing*. Her fleshfall, these days more akin to a pool, was not so turbulent. Her eyes were looking nowhere. She lightly bounced off an experiment rack.

Since it was the start of scheduled downtime for the crew, no one was at work in the lab; and since no one human was near, Hatcher was not limited to gestures and terse sounds. He and Tepinassa could talk, albeit in whispers.

"It's nineteen thirty-eight," he said.

"Eh? Oh, the time." She didn't look at him. "Clocks are for Man."

"Uh-huh. So you've said. You sound rational. Are you?"

"Would I answer 'no' if I were not?"

They had already had to replenish her anchor twice, pretty much when expected, about three and six days in. She hadn't started going nuts, but she had sensed a *disorder* inside herself and had prudently called upon his teeth. Toppings of antacid tablets had helped him endure the foul nibbles.

"So you're rational."

"Yes."

He looked around. "Why are you here?"

"Bergamo was here."

It was unlikely that Tepinassa was attracted to Bergamo's study of protein crystallization in microgravity. Hatcher asked, "Why Bergamo?"

Airily she replied, "There is a skein in his mind, reaching to his conception, a dread of *being consumed*. The zoo, for little Luca, was a place of waiting mouths. Even now, there is a tingle in his torso, an intimation of being torn." She giggled. "I don't eat adults but I'm already his worst nightmare. I'm... *tickling* him. It tickles me."

She had been tickling others. On top of the peculiar dissonance to which all were subject, Volokov and Johnson had reluctantly reported a lack of proper sleep, an onset of uncomfortable dreams. They had withheld the specifics, but Hatcher had surmised the source. Though Tepinassa was often at a porthole, and at least once every day was lounging—Earth and stars below her—in the observation Cupola of Node 3, she could only gaze for so long; and in her boredom otherwise she was doing what a monster did.

It wasn't helping the crew's morale that mechanical troubles were piling up. Before

Hatcher had arrived, there had been a failure of the #2 Main Bus Switching Unit. After that, the temperature sensors had malfunctioned on an assembly for carbon dioxide removal. Then there was a significant pressure drop in one of the service modules.

These three troubles were not the only ones. Hatcher naturally wondered if his stowaway was to blame. But even leaving aside that some of the troubles had preceded her arrival, none were so simple that they could have been caused by an untrained lamia with a malicious hammer. Besides, much as Tepinassa was slowly peeling the minds of the crew and arguably reducing their competence, she was not so foolish as to sabotage the Station outright.

"Well," said Hatcher, "I'd ask you to lay off Bergamo, but you won't. Just don't overdo it. *Pace* yourself, Tepinassa. You've got weeks to go."

"You're so practical, Hatcher."

"What else can I be? I know I can't suggest *compassion* for Bergamo. Or Volokov. Or the rest."

"You can *suggest* it."

He snorted. "And you'll reject it."

"Correct."

There was nothing else to say. Having confirmed that Tepinassa was not stark and raving, Hatcher spun around and left the lab. He almost said good night; but stopped himself. His unthinking politeness rankled him. He was getting too comfortable with his stargazing monster.

Two squids went missing.

A mouse had vanished earlier. That

was Tepinassa's doing, as Hatcher already knew. She had admitted it. She had seen how to open the mouse's cell and had purloined herself a warm and bloody meal. She had taken only one because there weren't that many. "I'm not a *glutton*, Hatcher. Must save some for another day."

In a tumult, the crew had searched for the mouse, and now the squids. It made no sense. Where could the animals have gone? The losses were a disturbing addition to all the mechanical misfortunes. Without meaning to, Tepinassa had increased the unhappiness of the crew.

Otherwise, she ate what the crew ate. She had been surprisingly amenable to eating foods from pouches. In a truly practical mood, she had also agreed to use the toilet. Hatcher didn't know quite *how* she used it, but she did; for which he was grateful. Nobody needed lamia scat on the Station.

Hatcher went to ask Tepinassa about the squids. He found her in the Cupola.

She had opened all seven shutters. The shutters were operated simply and manually, each with a crank. Every window—the six of the hexagonal sides and the center circle—shone with a part of the day-lit Earth. Tepinassa was curled along three of the side windows, upon them like a contemplative cat, her faces at the edge of the circle, watching the cloud-covered continents pass.

Tepinassa's voices would fluctuate with every syllable, an erratic harmony, an ebb and flow of timbres—Virgin, Mother, Crone—twisted together and inside out, the repulsive allure, the painful comfort, the vi-

tal decay. There in the Cupola, her voices were curiously weighted to the Virgin sweetness, yet unperverted, very nearly innocent.

She noticed him and whispered, "Hatcher. I have to tell you. The Scheme never gave my kind an inclination to *making things*. We don't have books or machines. Those are things for Man. *You* drew the maps. You took the pictures. You went beyond the clouds and filmed above. I looked over your shoulders and watched your movies... yet even movies are just another kind of shroud." She lay a hand on the center window. "There is glass between, but the light is fresh. The depth is real. I came up here to see the stars truly. I hadn't expected to see my home *like this*."

He stared at the voluminous Earth below her hand. Her wistful oration had disconcerted him. As man is midway from animal to angel, it had always seemed to Hatcher that monster is midway from animal to man. *Perhaps a few monsters were creeping towards the angels.* To be sure, he suspected she was manipulating him. Nevertheless, he was made speechless, and disregarding the missing squids, he joined her in a moment's adoration.

External cameras showed something flaking away from the P6 truss. The flakes had since been identified as ammonia coolant leaking into space. Being a flight engineer, Hatcher was tapped for the EVA to investigate the leak. He was EV2. Reynolds was EV1.

During suit-up, Hatcher was sealed into

his upper and lower torso components and hooked to a wall of the equipment lock. Reynolds was opposite him and likewise sealed and hooked. Takeuchi and Whitney, dressed casually in shorts and socks, were assisting the suit-up, swimming around the boulders of Hatcher and Reynolds, attaching their gloves, Snoopy caps, and bubble helmets.

Whitney was distracted. Her eyes flitted from whatever she was looking at, as if gnats were popping around her. She fumbled with Hatcher's gloves, cap, and helmet. On a laptop suspended near Hatcher's head, she couldn't land rightly on the trackpad and keys, and lost her place in the suit-up checklist. When she noticed Hatcher's concerned glance, she stared at the laptop display with the intensity of a drunkard and positioned her index finger with a comical precision.

It was then that Hatcher saw Tepinassa. She was right outside the lock and peering in at Whitney. She caught Hatcher's eye. A grin echoed upon her flesh. She slithered down and along, rising towards Whitney's stockinged feet. The fleshpool ringed Whitney's bare calves and rose. Whitney tensed. Her finger lost its way. Tepinassa lingered at Whitney's thighs. Whitney inhaled. Sharply. Her eyes drifted up.

Despite himself, Hatcher hissed, "Tepinassa!" She *may* have heard him through his helmet glass; but she didn't react.

"Say again, Bill?" radioed Collins, who was the CAPCOM down in Houston.

"Nothing," grumbled Hatcher. "*Nothing.*"

"Um. Guh. Guys." Whitney's voice cracked. "I'm—not. Feeling right. Can you get. Uh. Kalagah... Kalagin. To finish." She tightened an arm across her belly, trying to hold herself in, and all but kicked on Hatcher to launch herself out of the lock.

There had been a lot of this lately. Every day, some crew member was overcome by *something* and could not fulfill the task at hand. Each tried to persevere, to grit his teeth; but sometimes he simply couldn't.

Whitney was not crucial to this critical EVA, so Houston did not call for an abort. Takeuchi said, "I can finish for Sarah." Reynolds lowered his eyes in sympathy for Whitney. Tepinassa, dispersed by Whitney's kick, gathered herself and rapidly followed, salaciously cackling; while Hatcher glowered in the cage of his suit.

Yet that was not the only baleful turn of the EVA.

Two hours later—having passed through a full night, as the Station orbited the Earth every ninety minutes—Hatcher and Reynolds had removed the modular box of the Pump and Flow Control Subassembly from the Integrated Electronics Assembly, which enabled power generation from the solar arrays on the P6 truss. Their progress had been slowed by a care not to get any ammonia on themselves, since that would create a hazard for the Station when they returned through the airlock. As it was, they had seen no leaking ammonia, not even as the Station had passed orbital noon—the peak time of heating and the likeliest time for any creation of flakes.

Reynolds held the PFCS aloft. It was a third his size. Hatcher took images of its underside. Nothing broken or out of place; no "anomalous conditions," as the engineers put it. Reynolds secured the PFCS to the side, on a stanchion. There was a little cloud of tethered objects around the worksite, including the spacewalkers themselves. Hatcher then rotated himself to inspect the IEA bay.

It was natural for the CAPCOM to confirm periodically the well-being of the spacewalkers, but given the recent troubles on the Station, Collins frequently checked in on Hatcher and Reynolds. Houston was of course frustrated by the peculiar distress of the crew. Since no one could be sent home or sent up—not easily nor soon—Houston could only monitor and advise. Collins was calm and amiable, however, and betrayed none of Houston's frustration. Hatcher and Reynolds reported that they were both fine. Hatcher bitterly thought: *And why wouldn't we be?* Tepinassa was busily concentrating on pitiful Whitney.

Fuming at Tepinassa beneath his methodical manner, Hatcher took images of the bay, which, like the PFCS, was undamaged. In the bottom of the bay were two cutouts for access—holes into the recesses of the IEA. Hatcher retrieved an inspection mirror (a smallish mirror on the end of a stick) to poke into the holes. Collins stopped him and read him a standard warning from the engineers not to touch the mirror to anything inside the IEA. Hatcher acknowledged the warning and lowered the mirror.

Orbital twilight was advancing. Sunlight was angled unhelpfully. Hatcher turned the mirror slowly in one of the holes, this way and that, lowering and lifting. He saw nothing useful. Then the mirror caught. He stopped and sighed. The engineers would not be happy. As delicately as he could in his gauntlets, he tried to withdraw the mirror. It stayed. He could not see any wires or tubes or whatever clinging to the mirror. He shifted himself. He let out an angry breath. Then he saw what was fighting him.

Silver fingers curled to the front of the mirror. They were tiny and thin, these fingers, and nailed in black. A hand appeared and tightened. Startled, Hatcher released the mirror. Having won, the hand let go. The mirror bounced up and out of the hole, flying away until its tether caught.

Hatcher glared at the hole and cursed.

Reynolds and Collins, each in his turn, worriedly asked Hatcher what was wrong. "Nothing," spat Hatcher, "I slipped," as the hand's owner emerged from the hole, twitching its head and assessing its situation, before it sprang across the vacuum at Hatcher's chest, to latch its nails on his DCM. The thing then scratched at the displays and tugged at the controls—*patiently*, as if it couldn't be seen. It was a hideous homunculus, its hide a mottle of stubby spikes and wiry hairs. Hatcher swung his arm inward like a club and knocked the thing into a tumble; and though Hatcher couldn't be sure, the thing's pea-eyes seemed to widen in astonishment as it entered the void.

So the anomalous condition was removed. Hatcher knew, however, that gremlins never wreck alone.

The rest of the EVA was ordinary. He and Reynolds found nothing obvious to explain the ammonia leak. Out of prudence, they replaced the PFCS with a spare. When the spare at first resisted insertion, Hatcher searched for tiny obstructing pseudo-men; but he saw none. Still, he kept an eye out. He also kept himself steady. Collins had no reason to suspect that Hatcher was even troubled.

Later, Hatcher and Tepinassa *discussed* the situation, his whispers charged like shouts. He asked her, "Did you know there were gremlins aboard?"

"Oh. Them. Mmm, not at first. I *might* have pegged the scent immediately, if not for your irritating 'scrubbers.' The air is *dead* up here."

"Uh-huh. So you've complained."

"Hmph. But yes, I have spied a few of the foul things, skittering about. I gather you've seen their race before?"

"Yeah, messing with an F-22. But tell me this, Tepinassa. How are they even up here? You said none of your kind can stay sane in space. Not without... *anchoring*. Did you lie to me?"

She bristled. "Mind yourself, Man. I never lie. There's nothing in a gremlin *to* anchor. Gremlins aren't sane to begin with. They aren't rational. They leaked from the Scheme after Man became atrociously technological. They're not of the soil. They're barely of life. They're—uh..." She waved a hand in a fluster. "*Mindlessly clever rust.* They are decidedly *not my kind*."

"So they can go wherever a man goes."

"Ehh, wherever a *machine* goes."

"And it's just a coincidence they're here *now*? When you're here?"

"Yes. Insofar," she drawled, "as there are any coincidences."

Hatcher desired to sit, to be *placed* for a moment, to think without drifting like some dehumanized dust mote. The best he could do was grip a handrail. With his other hand, he rubbed the bridge of his nose. Amused by his weariness, Tepinassa watched.

He finally said, "I can't clear out a gremlin infestation. I'm the only one of the crew who isn't slowly crumbling. If I left my responsibilities for a madman's hunt, Houston would despair. Make yourself useful, Tepinassa. Get rid of these things."

"Useful!" Her eyes burned. He held his ground—as convincingly as he could with a handrail. She smoldered. "*Feh.* Am I your slave?"

"No. You're also not stupid. This Station goes; you go with it. Think of it as recreational. Hell, even *I* might enjoy ripping their little arms off." He exhaled heavily. "No deals. No Scheme. Just do me a solid."

She squinted at him. "You *are* impertinent."

He shrugged.

"And you aren't wrong," she admitted, smiles curling on her faces. "It *would* be enjoyable. All right. I'll do it. It's the *practical* move."

He nodded, not thanking her outright.

She laughed. "Ah, Hatcher. You just want me distracted from your colleagues."

"No. But that is a plus."

"I'll still find time for that delectation. And don't be so glum. It's not always so bad. Talk to Whitney. You'll see." She trilled her fingers in farewell and tittered out of the Node.

Hatcher did talk to Whitney. His ritual words of concern seemed to repel her. She'd had her fill of sympathy, perhaps. She avoided his eyes. Her unbanded hair tangled around her head. She muttered, "I've got work to do, Bill."

Grasping at some means of comfort, he imprudently said, "Sarah. Don't believe the whispers. It's just noise from a monster. Nightmares. It won't be forever."

She turned to him, her face open and weak. "Nightmares? No, it's... *wonderful.*" Bliss welled in her bloodshot eyes. "Leave me alone." She kicked away.

Telling himself *It's for the children* had worn thin days before. Hatcher was flatly complicit in the sacrifice of his crewmates. They might live. They might recover. All might pass. But the meantime would be cruel. The moral balance was unstable, and *It won't be forever* was, he knew, a feeble thing to say.

Tepinassa hunted with gusto. Though hampered by the scrubbers and by the constant drone of fans and pumps, she managed to catch the whiff and patter of the gremlins, to snatch and thump them with a fog of hands, to crack their bones and twist their viscera and, more than once, gobble them whole. Their vermin sentience tagged her as other than Man, as cousin to them, as one unaffected by veils,

and before long the word went out among them—the mindless word of the ravaged pack—to forgo hiding and jump her directly. She didn't really mind. It made the hunt easier, and their bleeding of her only energized her revulsion.

Peculiar whirlwinds appeared throughout the Station, as items were knocked from velcro roots, panels snapped from hinges, and wires batted about. Empty air collided with the crew. Crashes and screeches peppered the hours. Hatcher almost asked Tepinassa to be discreet in her tussling, but then thought better of it.

For a time, the mechanical failures increased, as if the gremlins, beset by extinction, were frantically ensuring their lives be fulfilled. They ceased being rust and became hail. An oxygen generator fumed with potassium hydroxide. Fire alarms went off without fires. The Station was rocked by mistimed boosters during an altitude adjustment maneuver. Computers stuttered on short-circuited RAM. Exercise equipment fell apart. Toilets reversed direction.

Then everything seemed to settle down. The crew was on edge but realized the Station was becalmed. Things were repaired and did not break again.

When current spiked in a motor of the starboard solar array and a rotary joint jammed, everyone was afraid that the curse had returned. This failure, though, was isolated. Nothing followed on it. All else hummed along. In an atmosphere of tentative hope, an EVA was planned to inspect the joint.

The night before the EVA, at the start of

the crew's scheduled sleeptime, Hatcher spoke with Tepinassa.

They were in Node 3. The Cupola was shuttered. Tepinassa's fluidity was subdued, her halves more defined. Even in the striations of her ragged flesh, Hatcher could see the fresh wounds, the tiny rips and scratches, the crusted blood on budding scars. The filth of her fights remained on her; but of course, what monster had ever bathed? She seemed content, however. Robust. A bit too terribly *present*. Hatcher felt that animal trepidation again. The stark Station lighting had never *quite* dispelled Tepinassa's darkness.

Ignoring his niggling discomfort, Hatcher whispered, "So is this another gremlin?"

She sighed. "I couldn't kill them *all*. Three or four are likely outside on the trusses. You dispatched one yourself. They'll wander inside, sooner or later."

"You think you'll get them all eventually?"

"Eh."

"No?"

"They *do* reproduce. Like mold. One could certainly get ahead of that. Eventually." She grinned. "But don't despair, Hatcher. I have lots of time."

"Twenty days, sure."

"Oh, more than *that*."

He narrowed his eyes. "What?"

Her laughter was layered and deep. "I'm not returning with you."

He blinked. "What the hell? You can't stay. We had a *deal*, Tepinassa. Are you... Did you..." He was flummoxed. "Was there a *trick* in this?" He looked away, rapidly thinking, trying to suss out a deception.

She raised her hands as if to placate, to caress; yet her voices were dominated by the rotten Crone. "Hush, hush. No tricks. Am I a djinn? I've merely decided that, for all the silly tedium of your astronautical life, being in orbit is... *amazing*. I like it here, in the far above. You have kept your part of the deal. You escorted me—and haven't killed me. I will keep my part. I would have done so in any event, but every child is constantly hundreds of miles away. Indeed, a year up here will guarantee my fidelity to our deal. And may I not fancy myself the Station's new guardian mother? I *will* eliminate those gremlins."

"But you need to anchor..." He glared at her. "You've recruited Whitney, haven't you?"

The Virgin giggled, the Mother chuckled, the Crone guffawed. "Dearest Sarah has already eaten of me. Enthusiastically, in fact. But of course she, unlike you, gets that spoonful of sugar. Oh, how her ecstasy distracts from my taste! She'll gladly sustain me once you have gone."

"You can't..."

"I have."

He abandoned his whisper and cried, "But why do that to her? Why *seduce* her? If you need her, be forthright. Make a deal. You did with me."

"Oh, poor Hatcher. You think I didn't seduce you? I knew you were an astronaut. I knew how to draw you in. You are not a heroic man, Hatcher, but neither are you an indifferent man. I knew you would try to save the Carter children and agree to a *prac-*

tical solution."

He scowled. There *had* to be a way to kill Tepinassa without incurring the wrath of the Scheme. Maybe he should kill her regardless! His adrenaline rose. *Could she hear his thoughts?* Levelly he objected, "No one will survive a year of you."

"Ah, never fret. I will do as you commanded me and *pace* myself. I will not ruin anyone. For the sake of this Station, I will refrain from *wholly* undermining the crew. After all, I don't know how to keep things running up here..."

She leaned into his face, her expression fervid and unshrouded, his fear of her finally aroused; and in a singular voice she breathed: "But I'll surely figure out how to run things."

David Skinner loves science fiction. He has been writing steadily since he was twelve. Notable novels are "The Wrecker" and "The Giant's Walk." His SF and wonder stories are collected in his "Stellar Stories." He blogs infrequently at www.davidskinner.biz.

Hunger in the Void

By ANDREW GALLANT

Allan Buxley, a daring-hearted Voyager, ventures into an Orion Gate with his robot companion Sigma-6 in the Sagan-12... and finds a black hole on the other side!

Allan Buxley lifted an eyebrow as he examined the dossier that had been issued about the newest Orion Gate, one of those strange confluences of space, time, and human ingenuity that allowed mankind to venture into strange and faraway places both within and outside of our galaxy—one that he was about to explore.

"This is really it?" he asked Sigma-6. "We know that it's in the Draco II Galaxy, and that there is an unusual amount of dark matter?"

"I'm afraid so, sir," replied Sigma-6, his trusty robotic companion. "Due to the sheer amount of dark matter and how faint it is, even Galileo-class telescopes have been unable to glean much information. As a result, it was approved for initial drone exploration. However, none of the eight drones that were sent returned."

The Voyager's fingers drummed upon the instrument panel's surface. "None, you say?"

It wasn't entirely unusual for drones to be lost when investigating Orion Gates. This was due to a variety of reasons. First, there was no way to send signals to command them when they reached the other side, and thus they were programmed with very simple instructions. This meant that their flight path was often just a parabola that allowed them to collect simple information before returning for data retrieval.

Another issue was the Orion Gates themselves. Sufficiently advanced technology was heavily damaged by them if it was not deactivated when it passed through. Therefore, drones were sent through mostly deactivated, save for a system that would cause it to re-activate once a sufficient amount of time had passed.

This meant that during that time any number of things could happen to the drones, whether collision with space debris, unexpected gravitational pull, or any other stellar phenomena. Really, anything that disrupted the drones' predetermined path enough could cause them to be unable to return well before they could react.

It was for this reason that manually piloted expeditions were often necessary to explore what lay beyond the Gates. Hence the need for men and women like Allan Buxley, a Voyager: those who braved the dangers of the cosmos to expand the horizon of all mankind.

And so, it was with a stoic nature that Allan accepted that he was to venture into the unknown, with nothing but his own abilities and those of his robotic companion to ensure the success of their mission and their own survival.

"Well then," he said, "I suppose we'll just have to journey through and see for ourselves just what lies beyond."

"Yes, sir," the robot replied.

He slipped the thin pad of paper into one of the drawers of his workbench, the brief hiss of pneumatic pressure indicating that it was sealed tight.

He then stood up and walked to the pilot's chair next to where Sigma-6 was currently docked to the floor of the vessel.

He first took in the ship's status with an experienced eye: all systems were green. He then engaged the navigational controls and activated the engines of the Sagan-12.

The trusty vessel came to life around the pair of intrepid explorers, and soon it was cruising through the cosmos towards the coordinates of their target, just off the orbit of Pluto's moon Charon. Outside the ship's viewports, the tiny planet passed slowly by, frozen and lifeless, the only signs of habitation being a pair of space elevators that rose from its surface.

That done, Allan began calibrating the ship's Burnell sensors towards the frequency emitted by the Orion Gate they were to travel through. Beside him, Sigma-6 began his shutdown routine, ensuring that the electromagnetic field projected by the Gate would not damage his systems. Soon the lights along the side of the robot's head had gone dark, as well as those on his boxy frame, save for a single blinking yellow light.

The sensors of the ship gave a short beep, indicating that it had locked on, and Allan activated the vessel's Van Gellar drive. The blackness of space opened up in a square in front of them, revealing a riot of greens and blues stretching off into a tunnel.

The Voyager nodded in satisfaction, and steered the ship straight inside. To any outside observer, the ship had just disappeared.

To Allan Buxley, however, the world had just become color: greens, violets, blues, and hues beyond what a human eye or mind could even comprehend flowed past in an ever-accelerating wave. There was a feeling of strangeness, of peculiarity, of reality, space and time itself being twisted and turned, and then they were through.

Immediately upon exiting the Orion Gate, Allan felt the entire ship shudder and buck beneath him. Several different alarms began going off, and every instrument display turned red.

"What the devil?" Allan swore, but he did not panic. He was a Voyager, and he had been through many a scrape and close call before. More to the point, he could not afford the luxury of panic; Sigma-6's reactivation routine would not be completed for at least another few minutes. If they were to survive, it would have to be through his ability alone.

For he could see what even now was pulling the Sagan-12 into a death spiral: asteroids and small planetoids rocketed past him, and light itself was sucked inward as what had to be a black hole devoured everything for light years around itself.

Allan wrestled with the controls, using every bit of power in the Sagan-12 to slip free of the black hole's pull. The Voyager aimed the ship at an angle out of the deadly cosmic phenomenon, using the rotation of the accretion disk itself to attempt to give him more speed.

Everything seemed to slow, and light itself seemed to bend and break. The Voyager could practically feel himself lengthening, contracting, as the systems that the ship utilized to protect its passengers from the harshness of space stretched themselves to their absolute limit. He could hear the screeching of metal, and he grimly hoped that the ship wouldn't tear itself apart.

And then, all at once, the ship went still.

Space flew past him, stars whipping by the viewports, and the Voyager let out a slow sigh of relief as he began slowing the ship's headlong plunge, starting a retro-burn that would gradually bring it to a halt over the next few minutes.

Allan glanced at Sigma-6 to see that the robot was slowly beginning to power back on; in doing so, he saw the time on the readout, and he noted with a sort of macabre amusement that it claimed that it had been thirty minutes since they had passed through the Gate, even though it couldn't have been more than five. No doubt due to the strange temporal disturbances caused by the black hole itself.

Now that the Sagan-12 was safely out of the pull of the black hole, the Voyager turned the ship about to gaze upon the phenomenon.

Despite mankind's advancements in astrophysics and space exploration, black holes still remained a mystifying enigma. When something exerted that much gravitational pull and warped so much of space around it, it was simply difficult to study it in detail. Not only that, the only true thing that humanity had learned about black holes was that black holes seemed to obey very few rules. Presumably due to the influence of the space around them and their own formation, each seemed to differ from all others in many different ways.

There was a mechanical whirring noise as Sigma-6 completed his reboot. "I see that we are going at a considerable speed."

"We are, yes," Allan acknowledged. "We should be coming to neutral within the next thirty seconds or so; at that time, we can deploy instruments and begin scanning the sector."

The robot turned its head towards one of the viewports and then froze. "Is that a black hole?"

Allan took out his pipe and stuffed it with tobacco. "It certainly appears to be."

The robot seemed to consider that for a moment. "I see, that would explain the drone disappearances. Once instruments can be deployed, I shall start calculating the Sagan-12's Dead Man Zone."

The Dead Man Zone was a radius around any powerful gravitational body in which if a craft entered, it would be unable to escape. While the ship might very well be able to delay being pulled in and crushed, it would not be able to pull away from a zone of no return in which the best the crew could hope for was a doomed stalemate.

Allan struck a match and lit his pipe; he puffed on it a few times before extinguishing the match. The ship, he noted, had slowed enough that it was safe to deploy the ship's instruments, and his fingers began flying across the console.

Within a minute, information about the system began coming in. The first matter that Allan observed was that the space around them was nearly empty; presumably, almost everything that had once been there was now in the black hole's accretion disk.

The second was the detection of a signal of some sort: very weak, but definitely present.

Curious, Allan began adjusting the sensors to strengthen it, and soon it resolved itself into an SOS signal.

Instantly, the Voyager became alert; if there was an SOS signal, then it was likely from a ship that was caught in the black hole; if that were the case, then the time in which to effect a rescue would be short indeed.

"Sigma-6, there's an SOS signal, start getting a lock on its location, I will continue to attempt to strengthen it."

His companion gave a quick beep of acknowledgement, and Allan continued to fight with the Sagan-12's instruments, attempting to get as much as he could out of them.

"It's too weak, sir, and there's too much interference from the black hole," Sigma-6 commented a few seconds later.

The Voyager took the ship's navigational controls. "Have you managed to calculate our Dead Man's Zone?"

"Within a 9.54% margin of error. I can continue my calculations to attempt to reduce it."

"No, continue getting a lock on that signal, put what you have up on screen. I'm going to get us closer."

Sigma-6 paused just a fraction of a second. "Yes, sir."

Allan accelerated towards the accretion disk, a single bead of sweat beginning to make its way down his brow. He was a man of action, a man of daring, yet even he could not deny the thrill of primal terror that rotted in his gut as he began approaching the black hole.

The black hole and the various masses that were caught in its pull filled the viewport now, and the ship began once more to buck and shudder as the Voyager's vessel once again entered into its gravitational pull.

The instrument consoles began to emit an alarm, and Sigma-6 quickly withdrew the most delicate of the sensors back into the ship's hull.

"Sir, we are six seconds from approaching the margin of error for our Dead Man's Zone," Sigma-6 warned.

"The signal?" the Voyager demanded.

"Strengthening. We are almost past the majority of the interference."

A few tense seconds passed, and the ship was now emitting alarms from every corner. By this time, Sigma-6 had withdrawn all sensors except those necessary for locating the origin of the SOS signal.

The very ship around the Voyager was

screaming now, with the screech of metal and alarms. His fingers felt like they were becoming sluggish, and he wasn't sure whether it was just his imagination or whether they were beginning to stretch and lengthen.

Any lesser man or woman might have turned back then, but Allan Buxley was a Voyager, and he would not doom a sapient being to the horror of the black hole through cowardice.

A tense eternity followed, with the Sagan-12 dying around the Voyager as he continued to press onward, deeper into the accretion disk.

"We have a lock."

The words came through a strange haze that Allan had fallen under like a whip crack, and immediately the Voyager began fighting to once more extract his ship from the ravenous grasp of the black hole.

"Sigma-6, exit vector!" he snapped.

"Heading 210, 054, 123. Uploading to screen now."

The Voyager clenched his jaw as the ship fought alongside him to escape the deadly clutches of the black hole. Once again, everything shuddered, kicked and bucked, and then the Voyager's heart froze as he heard something begin to tear.

Then they were once more in the clear, the ship became still, and he quickly set a retro-burn to bring it to a halt once more.

"What's our status?" he asked Sigma-6.

The robot examined the read-outs. "We have lost some hull integrity. I am now adjusting calculations for our Dead Man's Zone to match."

"Belay that. Put signal source on screen first."

Sigma-6 gave a beep of acknowledgement, and an image appeared on the screen; it was a ship with its thrusters on full, trying desperately to escape the grip of the black hole... and going nowhere.

"It's caught." Allan observed grimly. "Sigma-6; options?"

"Sir, that is a Marian vessel."

"Noted, what are our options for rescue?"

The robot turned slightly towards the Voyager. The Marian Empire was an expansionist alien race currently in a state of more-or-less open war with the United Stellar Space Command. In point of fact, Sigma-6 and Allan had foiled more than one of their various machinations, and the robot was quite convinced that were the situations reversed, the Marians would not lift a single digit to help them.

Yet, he could see from the expression on the human's face that such a fact would not change the Voyager's mind, so he quickly pulled up the ship's inventory.

"I'm afraid, sir, that we are in a bit of a conundrum. While our ship normally has a deeper Dead Man's Zone than the Marian ship appears to possess, the structural damage we sustained on our last dive has severely impacted our ability to approach the black hole. We can no longer get in range with our electromagnetic couplers."

Allan retrieved his pipe and chewed on the tip. "What of our ship-to-ship grappler?" he inquired.

Sigma-6 performed a quick calculation. "While we can get within range, there are multiple prohibitive factors. The first, of course, is that using it will impart kinetic energy upon impact with the Marian ship; in its current state, any change of momentum, no matter how slight, might be disastrous."

"Can the grappler itself withstand the exertion that this will put on it?" Allan inquired.

"Chances of the grappler being unable to withstand projected exertion is 35.64%."

The Voyager scowled. "Other options?"

Sigma-6 was silent for a moment and then spoke with mechanical certainty, "None."

Allan sighed. "All right then, we will have to fly at an angle towards them so that the grappler impact won't push them back towards the black hole."

"I concur."

"What's the margin of error?"

"Around 0.61%."

The Voyager grimaced. "That's tight… Too tight for a human…"

"Sir, I must also mention that due to my computational limitations, all of my attention will have to be on navigating the Sagan-12 within that margin of error. I will be unable to do that and utilize the grappler."

Allan thought about that for a moment, then nodded. "Then I will man the grappler. Give me a targeting solution on screen."

Sigma-6 complied and took up the navigational controls, while Allan took up position on the auxiliary controls. The human quickly keyed them onto the ship-to-ship grappler as the robot began pulling the Sa-gan-12 towards the Marian ship.

The Sagan-12 once more began to buck and kick, although as the ship was entering the gravitational pull at an angle, the effect was less pronounced than when they were fighting to escape it.

Still, every movement of the vessel jerked the targeting of the grappler, and Allan's teeth clenched around his pipe. There was no telling how long they had; the Marian ship would have been operating at full thrust ever since they had sent that distress signal. The Sagan-12's own fuel supply was already approaching less than half despite their own limited time within the system.

Then the Voyager cleared any such thoughts from his mind; it just meant they would have to get this right on the first try. A second attempt risked failure and the death of all onboard the Marian ship, as well as their own.

Neither the robot nor human spoke as the Sagan-12 shot towards its goal.

The Marian ship continued its futile struggle against the pull of the black hole, and Sigma-6 merely hoped that the foolish, belligerent organics wouldn't attempt to fire on them. If they did, they might not just doom themselves; any sudden loss of integrity of the Sagan-12's hull would mean death for the robot and his companion.

Under the robot's control, the ship dove onwards until they were within range of the Marian ship.

"We are within range."

"Time window?" Allan demanded, sweat on his brow as he concentrated. The targeting solution jumped around as the ship continued to buck and shudder.

"Eight seconds until we are out of range," Sigma-6 answered. "Eight, seven, six, five—"

The human's hands jerked, and for a moment, Sigma-6 thought that disaster had occurred, as at the moment it occurred, the projected trajectory of the grappler was off of the targeting solution.

Then to the robot's amazement, as the grappler activated a split millisecond later, the targeting solution aligned with the human's aim. Whether by fortune, instinct, or brilliant calculation, the human had adjusted his aim such that when the grappler actually fired, it would be right on target.

The grappler shot across empty space, impacting onto the Marian ship and fastening itself to the hull.

Sigma-6 wasted no time, initiating a burn that would pull the beleaguered vessel to safety.

The Voyager calmly took his pipe once more in his mouth, closing his eyes, his countenance composed. There was nothing more that he could do; all that was left was to trust in Sigma-6's navigation and hope that the grappler line would hold.

He opened his eyes and saw that the burn for the two ships to escape the pull of the black hole was around twenty seconds. He closed his eyes once more and calmly waited, counting down the time within his head.

Then, at nineteen seconds, the ship jerked around suddenly, and the Voyager's eyes snapped open. "Report."

"The Marian ship engaged its engines on a different trajectory, the grappler disengaged just in time, but its structural integrity is compromised."

Allan frowned. "An evasive maneuver?"

"Unlikely. There was no debris that was on an intercept course."

The Voyager turned towards the screen where he saw that the Marian ship had slowed itself and was now on a looping trajectory.

For a moment, he was confused until his long experience in space combat gave him a flash of insight.

In a sense, what the Marian ship was doing was an evasive maneuver in case the Sagan-12 was planning to fire upon them.

Allan sighed. "Sigma-6, open a channel."

"Yes, sir."

As the robot shifted towards the console, Allan moved to the navigational controls and set them back into a retro-burn to bring them to a stop. He grimly noted that their fuel supplies were now at less than a quarter.

"Sir, the Marian ship is not accepting our hails."

"Send the next attempt on the same frequency as their SOS," the Voyager suggested.

The robot did so, and the two waited. The Marian ship began to slow, and Sigma-6 spoke: "They are accepting the hail; putting them through now."

The screen flickered for a moment, and then the blocky blue-skinned form of a Marian appeared. The alien's five eyes all narrowed at the human, "I suppose I owe you thanks… to think that a human would respond to an SOS signal."

There was something unspoken there, that the Marian was still expecting the other shoe to drop.

"Happy to help," Allan replied. "Due to fuel constraints, we will likely be leaving the system shortly."

The Marian's suspicious expression didn't change. "You will, of course, notify us of this so that we might know that you will not be available to render assistance should we run into any further trouble?"

It was Allan's own turn to be somewhat suspicious; there were multiple layers to this exchange. On the surface, it was an entirely genial and reasonable request, but underneath that, Allan understood that the Marian suspected that the human would leave and potentially return with reinforcements.

Yet, all of that only mattered if the Marian was planning to stay within the system, a system whose sole feature appeared to be a very dangerous black hole that had quite nearly swallowed both of their ships.

"Of course," the Voyager replied. "You are planning to stay within the system then?"

"We... must conduct various repairs," the Marian replied evasively.

"I see... but I assume that you are fully capable of such by yourselves?"

"Indeed we are."

"Then I see no reason why you would require us to be on hand," Allan concluded.

"We..." The Marian sighed. "These falsehoods tire me. I will speak plainly. We are here to extract an asteroid that contains a significant amount of Geheminite."

Allan tapped his pipe on his chin thoughtfully. "I assume that the asteroid in question is within the accretion disk of the black hole."

"Unfortunately, yes," the Marian admitted. "Our ship's computer was inadequate for calculating a safe approach for extraction, and so my crew and I decided to chance it with what we had."

Geheminite was an incredibly rare mineral that occurred only in places with a high density of dark matter, along with other factors that weren't as well understood. It was necessary for the creation of Burnell sensors in the detection of Orion Gates and, thus, for far-distance space travel. It was little wonder the Marian and his crew had been willing to take such a risk.

"Hmmm..." Allan sat back in his chair. "And you're telling me all of this because you believe my own is up to the task?"

"Your extraction of our own ship proves that point."

The Voyager shook his head. "Why not return back to Marian space for help?"

"Infeasible. The asteroid in question is on an unstable orbit, in the time it will take to retrieve such assistance, it will be lost to the event horizon."

Allan scowled. "Then leave it," he said flatly. "Geheminite is valuable, but your own lives should matter more than a piece of rock."

"That is... also untenable," the Marian replied. "Should we lose this haul, our own lives are forfeit."

The Voyager felt a small pang. "You are... Insalitas?"

"Indeed, we were burdened with that

shame upon being part of the defeated in the battle of Ultara VI."

Insalitas: a state in which a Marian captain and his crew sought to obtain redemption, or face death. Little wonder then, that they had been selected for a mission such as this.

Allan paused, considering his words carefully.

"Might I suggest another option?"

"And that would be?"

"To instead join the United Stellar Space Command."

The Marian's multiple eyes blinked in an expression of confusion. "To defect?"

Allan was silent for a moment. "It could mean the lives of your crew."

The Marian's face purpled with emotion. "And it would sacrifice our honor and that of our entire line," the alien replied and brought a fist down. "My crew and I cannot accept it."

Allan did his best not to show frustration on his face; in his opinion, it was a foolish task. To so risk the lives of sapient beings for a hunk of rock, no matter its value, was anathema to him.

In addition, something felt wrong about this system, even beyond the swirling death at its center, and he knew that the wisest course of action would be to simply leave. To go back and warn others about the perils that lay in wait here and to preserve the lives of himself, Sigma-6, and any other who would venture here.

Yet to do so would be to turn a blind eye to the fates of the Marians. While he held no illusion that were the situations reversed,

the aliens would likely destroy his ship and then attempt to seize their prize, he could not leave them to death.

And so he stood up slowly. "Then we will do our best to assist you."

A few minutes later, Sigma-6 and Allan Buxley stood by, watching the Marian craft once more approach the accretion disk.

On screen was an image of the mineral-rich asteroid indicated by the alien as it circled within the black hole's orbit. Occasionally, it would appear warped and distorted before the Sagan-12's long-range viewers could compensate for the interference caused by the immense gravitational force projected by the phenomenon.

The Voyager chewed on the tip of his pipe, but otherwise showed no sign of his unease. He did not, of course, doubt the calculations of Sigma-6; according to the robot, there was a course that was entirely possible for the Marian ship to take so that they could retrieve the asteroid safely. It was not a particularly precise navigation either, allowing for a moderate margin of error.

Yet somehow, there was something that made the Voyager feel extremely uneasy.

"You are certain they were forthcoming about their ship's limitations?" he asked the robot.

"Yes, sir, the type of ship that they are flying is a model well known to the United Stellar Space Command, and I assured them that they would not be giving away tactical information by supplying some of the figures myself."

Allan nodded. It was something that he

had feared the Marians would be hesitant about, and an accurate calculation with bad information was sometimes worse than just simply a bad calculation.

Maybe it was that thought that prompted him. "Sigma-6, is there any way that you can analyze the Marians' calculation, the one they used previously?"

The robot hesitated. "During the uplink with their computer to give them the navigational data, I... acquired that calculation, yes."

Allan lifted an eyebrow. "Have you been able to analyze them?"

"To some extent."

"Check their veracity."

"Sir?"

"I want you, to the best of your ability, see if their calculations were adequate for them to retrieve the asteroid on their prior attempt."

"There are many variables, sir."

"Noted. Do the best you can," Allan urged. "Be prepared to cancel the analysis should I require your assistance."

The robot's eyes went dark, and the lights on the side of its body began to blink on and off with a yellow light.

The Voyager glanced at the display of the Marian craft and then went to the instrument console. First, he checked the status of the grappler: structurally compromised, but it would be one of their few options if the Marian ship ran into trouble. The next was their fuel supply: barely enough to get the two ships to safety, possibly, but only possibly; the structural integrity of the Sagan-12 itself would be under heavy strain.

And then, for reasons that the Voyager couldn't explain, he activated the Burnell sensors, keying in on the location of the exit Orion Gate.

He eyed the sensor for a moment, and then shook his head, and it was at that point his gaze wandered over the sensor that surveyed gravitational forces. He frowned.

"That can't be right," he murmured, and his hand began to reach towards the sensor to attempt to reset it, when the navigational console began to blare with an alarm.

He shot towards the console and saw that there were now multiple objects on a collision course.

His eyes lifted towards the screen and widened in shock.

Everything that had been caught in the black hole's grasp was now free, hurtling all about the system like in a game of tug-of-war where someone had let go of one end of the rope.

The gravitational sensors had been correct, whereas mere moments ago they had been pushing past their operational limits in order to chart the forces exerted by the black hole. Now, it read that the system was nearly empty of any such forces.

He began to maneuver, desperately avoiding the debris that now rocketed towards them at bewildering speed, slingshot out of the vanished black hole's accretion disk.

It was then that Sigma-6's eyes lit back up, and the lights on his side turned green. "Sir, I have discovered something astonishing."

"Oh?" Allan asked as he positioned the Sagan-12 in a safe location, and then began to search for the Marian ship.

"The original calculation made by the Marian ship should have been correct," the robot said, "at least with the factors that were available; the ship's sensors must have been faulty. Likely they underestimated the strength of the gravitational pull."

"What if the sensors were accurate?"

"The black hole would have to have suddenly gained in the strength of its gravitational pull, which is highly unlikely."

Then the robot seemed to take notice of the situation. "What happened?"

"The black hole suddenly disappeared," the Voyager explained.

The robot went to the ship's sensors. "That's impossible," Sigma-6 protested. "Hawking Radiation is still being emitted; the black hole is still present."

Allan felt the pit of his stomach turn over. "Then what—"

The Voyager finally spotted the Marian ship. It was towing the asteroid behind it as it pulled away from where the black hole had originally been.

Then, like a fish on a line, it was pulled back, and in the time it took to blink, it was gone.

"Sigma-6, what was that?" the Voyager demanded.

"It appears to have been a directed gravitational pull," the robot responded.

The Voyager's hairs stood on end. "Activate Van Gellar drive," he snapped.

The robot immediately set to the task, and Allan turned the ship away, punching the thrusters to their absolute maximum towards the Orion Gate.

It was just in time.

The ship began to buck and jerk, and alarms began blaring as it was once more subjected to the extreme gravitational force of a black hole.

Somehow in defiance of every natural law, the all-devouring cosmic death trap had reappeared, but in an entirely different location, one that meant that the Sagan-12 and its two crewmembers were now caught in a desperate fight for survival.

Allan felt sweat begin to flow freely down the back of his neck as a primordial terror swept through him. However, his countenance remained even and his hands steady on the controls as he fought for every singular inch that he could wrest from his ship.

"Sigma-6?"

"Van Gellar drive activation is nearly complete."

The ship began to emit a metallic screech once more, and this time the hull integrity alarm blared as it stated that within ten seconds it would reach structural failure.

Then the square of an Orion Gate opened up in front of the ship, and with a last final blast from its engines, the Sagan-12 slipped inside.

Allan wasn't sure whether it was his imagination, but he could have sworn he heard an ear-splitting roar of frustrated hunger.

Then they were gone.

They erupted back into Milky Way space, and the ship slowly began to quiet as the Voyager began a retro-burn to bring it to a stop.

Before the burn was completed, the ship gave a sharp squall as the ship's fuel ran out, leaving it to drift slowly through space.

Allan silenced the alarm, sent out an SOS signal before settling back into his chair, and with slightly trembling hands, took out his pipe and lit it.

Everything around him was silent, the only sounds being his own breathing and the occasional click or beep from the ship's instruments.

He removed the pipe and let out a slow breath, watching the resulting plume of smoke drift upward.

It curled and twisted lazily, and then was abruptly sucked up by the ship's filtration systems.

The sight sent a shiver down the Voyager's spine, and he quickly looked away. Beside him, Sigma-6 slowly came back to life as the robot's re-activation routine kicked in.

"Sir."

"Hmm?"

"What was that?"

The Voyager lifted his pipe back to his lips and took a deep puff. "I don't know, Sigma-6," he admitted. "Make a note that I recommend locking access to that Orion Gate."

"Yes, sir."

Allan took another puff on his pipe and stared out into space, and for the first time, he couldn't help but feel like something might have been staring hungrily back.

Andrew Gallant lives in College Station, Texas with his intrepid feline companion, Koko. He discovered pulp by listening to audio recreations of 'The Shadow' by an angry Arizonan and from there it's been off to the stars and fantastical lands.

The Gold Exigency (Part 1 of 4)

By MICHAEL TIERNEY

A race of birdlike alien humanoids are being hunted and murdered for the gems grown in their skins! A cop seeking answers and looking to stop the killings is approached by an unlikely benefactor: Achilles Hister of the Artomique Corporation!

Prelude
The Exodus

75,000 Years Ago

Angor Broadwater had used the interstellar beacon left by the Ancient Warrior to summon a Wild Stars ship, and his people were the very last to leave the Earth during the great star migration to escape the calamitous upheavals wrought by the underworld races of the Isshla.[1] His people were given a choice between resettlement on a world that embraced technology, as the island of Atlantis had before the migration, or life on a more primitive world.

They discovered that the world the Wild Starriors called Miri was even more raw than the one they had left. There were no cannibalistic giants like the Tearers, but there were even worse terrors called Griefs—meat-eating theropod dinosaurs

that came in three varieties: the towering and solitary Brown Griefs, the pack-hunting Red Griefs, and—worst of all—the Dire Griefs.

To survive, Broadwater's people had to learn quickly the habits of these predators. The Red Griefs only seemed to know how to do two things—eat and sing. While they always seemed to be hunting, after a good meal they wanted to sing about it. It was not a pleasant sound—more like the screech of a nightmare made manifest. The solitary Brown Griefs spent all their time hunting on the savanna, and the only sounds they made were grunts at the ice moon whenever it passed overhead. What the sinister Dire Griefs did, no one knew. With their chameleon-like ability to become invisible, stories were told about them taking victims from crowded settlements with no one noticing. Other stories claimed that they could read a person's mind—and even manipulate them.

Broadwater's people were the last of the humanoid race deposited on Miri, meaning that the most desirable locations had al-

---

[1] *See Wild Stars IV: Wild Star Rising for the whole story about mankind's first exodus to the stars! Out now from Cirsova Publishing! – Ed.*

ready been claimed. They could have easily taken any place they wanted, being a tall and powerfully built people. With their dark complexions streaked from the dust of the coal mines that tainted any breaks in the skin and permanently marked them blue, theirs was a ferocious appearance. But their nature was not aggressive.

The tribal leader, recognized by the half-lidded eye that was tattooed on the palm of his hand, found what seemed like an over-looked paradise in a valley with good water and verdant, fruit-laden plant life. But Angor Broadwater saw the scattered bones of other primates and wanted to continue looking.

A schism took place, and the tribe split.

When those who chose Angor as their leader camped that night on the other side of the ridge, they heard terrible screams of anguish echoing up from the valley. By dawn, there was only silence to be heard. Angor went alone to see what had happened. After he returned, his haste to leave the valley was profound. He never discussed what he had seen.

Angor led his people into a sparse land that was moderately safe from attack by Griefs. He stopped his tribe's travels at a small lake in a land near the great desert, guarded against the savannah by a strip of rock forest. The water and the animals that wandered through sustained them, but on an annual basis, the lake would nearly dry out before the rains came again and brought fresh rivers flowing down from the rocky ridges. So they fashioned jugs from the clay bottom to store water before the lake be-

came too low. As the years passed, they pulled ever more clay from the lake bottom not only to give it greater depth, but also to provide material to build shelters.

This cycle continued long after Angor had passed on. Eventually the tribe adopted a name based on his, calling themselves the Brudwata. By this time, the lake was barely able to support their ever-growing community. The clay had hardened into steps that led down into the ever-growing depths, and the rains were no longer enough to fill the growing chasm.

So they began digging for other artificial lakes, and agriculture soon followed. They quickly discovered that this attracted the attention of the Griefs when the rains became unreliable. As terrible as those circumstances were, even more devastating were the attacks by other jungle races of humanoids, who grew increasingly vicious when driven by hunger and thirst.

The Brudwata were forced to change their ways and learn the arts of war. And while they never attacked a neighbor, those charged to become Warlords became obsessive in the refinement of their skills. Having no knowledge of metalworking, their weapons were all gained from the invaders they defeated, and these artifacts took on an almost religious status.

Despite all the difficulties that they overcame, the worst was yet to come.

200 years into the future

After many tens of millennia had passed, other predators had migrated onto Miri from out of the stars—the Black Eyes from Earth and the Brothan. As bad as their distant Earth cousins were, the Brothan were worse. These half-wolf, half-man hybrids became the greatest threat the Brudwata had ever faced. The Brudwata population crashed from predation.

Adding to their troubles, the whole world grew steadily warmer. The surviving Brudwata were forced to migrate as their ancestral lands became unlivable, abandoning whatever they could not carry with them.

Then one day, the golden and silver ships from legend reappeared in the skies and fought great battles of fire and thunder. Soon after, the Brothan disappeared, and the sky ships became fewer and fewer.

But still every year grew steadily warmer than the last. Their lands were devastated, and the people were starving. Even the once lush bone-filled Valley of Death had gone dry, and strange omens were seen in the sky as a new, golden moon with a strange, seedling shape began stalking the ice moon.

The tribal elders were certain that this was a very bad omen, heralding an even worse calamity. There was even talk that another humanoid tribe called the Tiberals had begun worshipping a stone god that walked like a man.

As darkness fell one night, the Warlords of the sixteen clans gathered around the fire built at the edge of the dry lakebed, their wild green eyes flashing in the light as their wives and children huddled with other members of the tribe in the shadows.

Carmdall was the leader of the clans. He and his eldest son were clearly better fed and fitter than any of the thin people surrounding them.

The deaf ear he turned to the wailing of the women was out of necessity, not cruelty.

"Once there was a time when our tribe was everything," he said in a voice that grew louder with each word, "and many cycles of the seasons would pass before we saw the Children of the Forest or other tribes." The volume of his voice fell again. "My son and I have just returned from exploring far beyond the rock hills, where we barely found enough game to survive. But our journey was a success."

"It's time to leave our ancestral home," said Horos, Carmdall's eldest son, who was the tallest in the tribe. "The peoples of the Silver Cliffs were nearly wiped out by the Brothan. We'll learn to be fishermen."

"They agreed to this?" asked one Warlord, who cut his eyes to Carmdall when he answered.

"We did not ask."

"I know that making war has never been our way," said Horos.

"Now our waters have dried and our harvest either parched on the vine or looted by the Children of the Forest," said Carmdall. "Even should the rains return, we have no more seeds, and there are no animals left to return..."

"That's because we ate them all!" shouted an old woman.

"...and even the Griefs no longer harry us because they do not care for how we taste." Carmdall finished his statement. "We have no choices anymore."

"We have to move," said Horos.

"Even if we have to take the Silver Cliffs by force," Carmdall concluded.

"You said that there was barely enough game for you and your sons?" asked one Warlord.

"How do you expect us to march the entire tribe?" asked another.

"We couldn't make it to the hills," said the first speaker, "let alone cross rock hills and forests all the way to the ocean, and then start a war."

"It's suicide," several voices concluded.

"The only way to survive is to do the unthinkable," Carmdall asserted. "The tribe needs sustenance, so we must decide whether we can stomach what the Griefs cannot."

A wail went up from several women, accompanied by a cacophony of children crying. Carmdall held up a hand to call for quiet, with the palm held outward to show the tattoo of a half-lidded eye.

"It is unthinkable," shouted his wife, Khizeff, knowing what came next.

"I have more children than anyone here," Carmdall motioned for his youngest son to stand by him. He placed a firm hand on his shoulder to keep him from running away, then hesitated a moment before speaking again. "Seven children. As your leader, I offer my youngest son in sacrifice."

Sure enough, his son jolted but was unable to escape Carmdall's firm grip.

"Don't hesitate!" several voices called from the crowd, drawing a scowl of recrimination from Carmdall's wife, but she had no effect. Even those who objected slowly relented in their admonishments.

"We're all hungry," shouted a woman holding a crying baby.

Khizeff glared at the speaker, who pointed back.

"Make her take the first bite!"

"Cook him first," someone else shouted from the darkness.

"Excuse me?" a voice no one recognized boomed from the darkness.

The ring around the fire parted as a strange man with a slight angle to his eyes and an unusual tint to his skin walked out of the darkness and approached the fire. He was dressed in odd clothing and carried weapons at his hip that included the longest blade Carmdall had ever seen.

"I don't mean to interrupt," the stranger walked slowly with both hands raised and his unmarked palms out. "But I heard some of what you were saying, and must have misunderstood what was just said."

"He's a nobody," someone shouted. "Don't listen to him. We're hungry! Let's cook *him*."

"Maybe I *didn't* misunderstand," the stranger cut a look at the circle of hungry people who were growing restless. "In that case, I'm glad to interrupt. My name is Montchuhasus."

"You know the language of the Brudwata?" Carmdall showed his palm when several Warlords began to raise their weapons. "You do not come from the Tiberal—or Silver Cliffs."

"I learned an older version," Montchuhasus replied, his attention focusing on Horos, "a long time ago, when I sailed with Angor Broadwater on my ship, the *Sea*

Howler. He was more than a shipmate; he was my best friend.[2] And if I did not know better, I would think that you were him. You must be his descendant?"

Horos nodded.

"Angor Brudwata was our great father, who led our tribe across the river of stars to this place," Carmdall confirmed. "His name will never be forgotten. Why do you come to us? Are you a Star God who lives forever?"

"I live with one, but I'm not one. I sailed on a river where time moved differently." He shook his head and waved a hand at the confusion his statement clearly caused. "Don't worry about that. The important thing to you is that I now sail with an immortal Star God," he nodded his affirmation as he pointed at the golden sprout-shaped object in the sky that Carmdall suddenly realized was no longer dancing with the ice moon—but had become stationary, hovering directly above. "I really do. I have no idea how old she is. She looks younger than me."

"Why would this matter to us?" Carmdall asked. "We've no interest in worshipping gods."

"It sounded like you were deciding to relocate. So my timing is good." He again motioned toward the golden sprout in the sky, from which lights began to descend when he waved his arm. "She sent me with an invitation for everyone here to take another ride on the river of stars."

---

[2] See *Wild Stars IV: Wild Star Rising* for Montchuhasus and Broadwater's adventures together! – Ed.

"Can we eat her?" asked the woman with the crying baby. It drew a laugh, but the seriousness in her expression belied any humorous intent.

"I think we can help with something better than that," Montchuhasus replied.

Carmdall sighed and rolled his eyes, then patted his son on the head and pushed him back to the outstretched arms of his distraught mother, keeping his eyes turned skyward to avoid her look of condemnation. He considered how unlikely an eighth child had just become.

"Why would this immortal woman save us?"

"Her name is Phaedra. When I said that the timing of my arrival was good, I wasn't talking about helping you in a time of need. I was talking about your decision to go to war."

Carmdall contemplated the eye in the palm of his hand, then looked at each of his sons.

"There is a war coming," said Montchuhasus.

"Is that what has been killing our land?"

"No," Montchuhasus replied. "What happened to your tribe was the result of the Dire Griefs manipulating your planet when they botched an attempt to summon the Marzanti. It might take a while, and it will never be the same as it was, but the weather will eventually balance back out. And if I read the Borealis Niget space currents right, any more Marzanti nails that fall will hammer somewhere else next time."

"I do not understand much of what you said," said Carmdall, "but I can see by your expression that those are not the things that worry you."

"Everything is *connected*, but you're right. Something much bigger and much worse is coming. If we don't intervene, all life will be destroyed—not just here, on your world, but everywhere in the stars."

Carmdall looked at his wife, who listened intently. Her harsh expression had changed to one of renewed concern as both of their daughters hugged her and their little brother.

"I didn't come here to rescue you. I came to recruit you."

Chapter One
The Black Star Reavers

Interstellar Space

In the cargo bowels of the space freighter, Mackstar and Akarastar hid from the bounty hunter who had discovered the bio-transit cube where they had stowed away.

"He's coming," said Akarastar, as the blonde-haired twin followed her brother to another hiding space.

"We're going to have to do some things we don't want to," said Mackstar.

Akarastar dipped her chin in acknowledgement.

"Where are we headed?" she asked.

They both fell silent, afraid to even breath as the heavily armed bounty hunter stalked ever closer.

"The next port of call is Trovador."

Trovador

Constable Conrock paced back and forth, blending in with the ebb and flow of the milling crowds along the main thoroughfare in front of Trovador's chancellery building. He told himself that he had good news and bad news.

Half a dozen Black Star Reavers were scattered across the building's front steps, eyeing every person who approached. They always kept their distance when confirming a shake of the head from the one who was obviously their leader, positioned near the main doors at the top of the concrete stairs and trying to be inconspicuous but doing a poor job of it. He held a device in his hand, with which he seemed to be following Conrock's movement along the street, but was unable to pinpoint the constable in the crowd. The many businesses and government offices clustered in close proximity made foot traffic in the area shoulder to shoulder in some places.

No one knew much about these humanoid reptiles from the Black Star system, other than their ravenous taste for flesh and a determination to integrate with Earth populations that had been taken to the extreme of installing permanent breathing apparatuses to their necks to enable them to breathe their air. The high gold content of those apparatuses had sometimes made these notorious predators into targets themselves, but that problem had seemingly abated of late.

The good news was that Conrock knew they were looking for what was in the courier bag he carried in his left hand. This meant they would be focused on him, reducing the threat to civilian bystanders when he crossed the street and started up the stairs. Sure enough, the lead Reaver aimed his device at Conrock and signaled the others to converge. By the time Conrock reached the top of the stairs, he was surrounded as frightened people scattered in every direction.

"You're probably wondering why I didn't bring backup." Conrock smiled, even though he knew the lack of facial expressions in the reptilians probably meant that they had no clue as to his intent. They probably interpreted his baring of the teeth to be a predatory move, which was not far from the truth. He pulled the flap of his jacket back to reveal the plasma pistol he wore on his hip and placed his right hand on the grip. "The simple truth is, why share the fun?"

The universal translator in Conrock's ear reformed the Reaver's snarls and growls into a reply in English. The fact that this one Reaver did not have a breathing apparatus attached to his throat like all the others indicated that he was from the ruling class, and could afford the surgical processes needed to survive in alien atmospheres. Slits in the Reaver's throat expanded and closed in an alternating pattern with flaring nostrils.

"A whole clutch of hatchlings died for that harvest. They broke none of your laws. Give us the bag. There is no need for a confrontation."

"Oh, I disagree," Conrock nodded to the device that the Reaver pointed directly at the courier bag in his left hand. "Because of interstellar treaties, you technically didn't break any Trovadorian laws when an alien woman died in your *harvest*."[3]

Conrock paused, seeing how the red eyes of every Black Reaver were focused on him and judging their reflexes by the manner in which they stood.

"What I want to know is the identity of the person you bribed to plant a tracker in this bag of evidence from when she was skinned alive. Snort and bluster all you want. I'm not intimidated by your show of force. If I was worried about you taking this from me, I could have removed your tracker and walked right past you. You would never have known. But I want that name."

The Reaver blinked rapidly in what was obviously a form of communication to his companions, who all turned and focused on the crowds gathering at a distance.

"Give us what we want," said the Reaver, "or you will not die alone."

When the other Reavers turned their backs to him, and Conrock's translator was still processing the Reaver's last hiss that escaped his forked tongue, the constable pulled his weapon and shot the Reaver dead. Conrock grabbed the Reaver's falling body and used it as a shield when the others turned their attention back to him. Dropping to one knee, he kept his aim high so that any wild shots would sail over the heads of any onlookers. But his every plasma discharge hit its target.

Conrock dropped the smoking corpse when the last Reaver grabbed the fallen courier bag and tried to run for it.

---

[3] *See The Boundaries of Decision from The Multiversal Scribe, also reprinted in the collected edition of Wild Stars V: The Artomique Paradigm, out now! – Ed.*

"Oh, my god!" someone in the crowd gasped when Conrock took steady aim and shot the Reaver square in the back.

"He could have shot me!" complained another spectator who had been in the direct line of fire. "I could have been shot."

Conrock ignored the grumblings of the crowd, retrieved the bag, and then looked about to confirm that the only stray shots aimed at him had impacted the now pock-marked columns and facade of the building.

He picked up the tracker the lead Reaver had dropped. It was Black Star technology, so Conrock decided to collect it for later investigation. He walked calmly past the armored security that rushed out of the chancellery doors; the supervisor following them was already calling Central Command for a cleanup crew.

"Should have known it was you," Nebraski said as soon as he was finished. Then he nodded at the complainers in the crowd. "They don't realize you just saved their lives. That Reaver would have left bodies all over the place to cover his escape. But you better watch your back because their fellow hatchlings will want revenge... but still, good job."

It was not often that Conrock enjoyed any kind of celebratory acknowledgement. Life had taught him that such events were usually followed by an equally opposite counterbalance, so he had a sense of foreboding when he entered the building.

The chancellor was exiting the double doors of his office when Conrock arrived. The constable's extended hand offering the courier bag was ignored by the bevy of assistants hovering around the chancellor, all speaking urgently about overturning long-established laws and the unexpected consequences that might cause. What concerned Conrock was the way the chancellor did not even look his way. One assistant gave the constable a disdainful nod of the head back toward the office they had just left.

Entering the chancellor's office, Conrock discovered three men dressed in matching black leather overcoats waiting for him. One surprisingly young dark-haired man sat in the chancellor's chair, his hat tossed on the desk in front of him: Achilles Hister. The other two flanked him at either end of the overly-large desk. Conrock recognized the one of mixed Asian descent as Genghis Champlain. The other with purely Caucasian features was Georgian Raveling. They were arguably the three most important Earthmen alive.

"What can I do for you, gentlemen?" Conrock inquired.

"Quiet," Georgian hushed as he and Genghis hovered over the shoulders of the seated Hister, his attention on a communication pad.

Conrock stopped and pretended to be looking around the room.

"Why did the message take so long to get here?" Hister asked.

"Look at the router," Genghis pointed to a corner of the pad. "It was sent from outside the plasma firewall that surrounds the galaxy. I'm surprised they managed to find a live socket on their Maglink."

"They probably hooked to whatever Wild Stars link allowed Bullson to teleport ahead," said Georgian. "Right before they exploded New Atlantis. That much is confirmed, but the part about what happened to Bullson afterwards was corrupted. The only thing that could be deciphered after that fragment was that the entire contingent of Dreadnoughts is heading deeper into the intergalactic void."

Conrock tried not to show his astonishment at what he was hearing. Rumors abounded regarding a hidden Wild Stars world called New Atlantis, but he had never had a hint about expeditions beyond the galactic firewall and into the void between galaxies. The historical precedent this would set would be monumental if announced, but somehow he knew the public would never know. What concerned the constable was how casual they were about discussing it in front of him.

"But why?" Hister asked. "And what happened to Bullson? We should have heard something by now." He looked up and motioned for the courier's bag. "District Officer Conrock, is that what the chancellor instructed you to bring?"

"What does the Artomique Corporation want with evidence from a lower levels murder?" Conrock asked.

"You recognize us?" Achilles Hister confirmed. "Good. That saves us from wasting time with introductions."

He opened the bag, pulled out the largest jewel, and held it up to the light. Nodding, he slipped it into a jacket pocket and zipped the bag shut.

"If there's nothing more…" Conrock figured his question would go unanswered and turned to leave.

"Actually," said Hister, "there is."

"We want to compliment you," said Champlain. "We've looked at your service record. Crime in your sector has always remained at record lows for the city. What we found particularly interesting was the way you used a loophole in the statutes to expel undesirables, completely on your own discretion."

"An effective strategy," said Hister. "In fact, I just made the suggestion to the chancellor that he implement your practices citywide."

"This whole business of charging exorbitant exit fees served its function," Raveling interjected, "when Trovador was a growing city. It needed the population. Now the situation is reversed, and it's time to clean house."

"Although I'm not certain that quockerwodger the chancellor agrees," Hister concluded. "Not only is his staff having difficulty processing the concept of doing business in a new way, he seemed completely unaware of what you'd been doing. So, while I applaud your creativity, your former employer was not so enthusiastic."

"Former?" Conrock asked.

Hister shrugged fatalistically.

"People who inspire change are rarely appreciated." He tapped the desktop in front of him. "Take your badge off and put it here."

Conrock hesitantly complied. His fingers felt a shock of static electricity when he drew them back across the metallic emblem.

"I told the chancellor that I'd collect it

for him," said Hister, "but I didn't tell him why. I want you to work for me now. Be my fixer."

Conrock did not reply, looking into the eyes of each man, trying to read their intent. But these were experienced negotiators who patiently embraced the silence and waited for him to react first.

"A fixer? Fixing what?"

"Think of it more as being the ultimate executive assistant, imbued with the police power of the administration. You've got three jobs to start." Hister pulled the ruby-red jewel back out and held it up to the light. "What do you know about this?"

"That's evidence in a crime," Conrock replied.

"That's silicatein," said Raveling. "It's made from an organic protein that creates crystalline fibers. It's a process that cannot be replicated in a laboratory."

"Because it's a hybrid of minerals and proteins in a crystalline assembly," Champlain added.

"I've read the same reports," Conrock replied. "Those crystals form on the skin of only one species, the avian-humanoids from Phileas. It's a world that's part of neither the Earth Unification nor the Wild Stars. As such, it's outside any jurisdiction, and the Phileans are being slaughtered for their personal mineral wealth. Even worse, because their mood prior to death influences the clarity of the gems, they're being slaughtered on the spot, wherever they're captured."

"Like a hawk guts and plucks prey before taking the parts it wants back to the nest,"

said Hister. "I've issued an Interstellar Order #87 to protect them, which orders their immediate rescue, wherever and whenever Phileans have migrated off-world. They're to be gathered into protective custody. There will be no more slaughtering in the streets."

Conrock cocked his head. Everything he had heard about Achilles Hister and his Artomique Corporation belied any philanthropic leanings.

"That's your first order of business," said Hister.

"What are the other orders?"

"There's been a lot of gold coming into circulation of late," said Raveling. "What do you know about that?"

"Nothing."

"We need to know where it's coming from," said Raveling.

Conrock looked directly at Achilles Hister, the president of the Artomique Corporation.

"A man in your position doesn't spend his time hiring investigators," Conrock asserted. "You said three things. What's the third?"

Hister gave a smile that had a twisted look of youthful exuberance mixed with a touch of cruelty.

"You'll think that this is beneath a man of your skills," he said, "but hear us out. I assure you that this is the biggest challenge you've ever been handed."

Champlain pulled a hand-tablet from his jacket. On the screen were the faces of a young blonde-haired man and woman. They looked to be siblings.

"These are the two most wanted people in the stars," he said.

"How come I've never heard of them?" Conrock interrupted.

"Those innocent faces," said Hister, "hide the most dangerous killers you will ever meet. Trust me when I say that the panic they could cause is too great to risk going public."

Conrock shook his head, not even trying to hide his disdain.

"What did they blow up?" he asked in exasperation.

"You got part of that right, but it's more like *who* was blown up," said Hister, "even though it wasn't by them. They're much more dangerous than terrorists. That girl is a mimic. I'm told she can assume the appearance of anyone—and possibly anything. We're not really sure if the boy has the same abilities or not."

Conrock's expression changed to one of incredulity.

"You can see how this could get out of hand if people started doubting each other," said Raveling. "These twins are the two most dangerous people alive."

"And resourceful," Champlain added. "Their names are Akarastar and Mackstar. They're the twin children of the Wild Stars leader Erlik, who was killed in the Ansa Peace Conference blast."[4]

"So they're out for revenge," Conrock surmised. "I've heard that former U.S. President Bully Bravo was responsible. You've got two ghosts chasing a third."

---

[4] *See Wild Stars V: The Artomique Paradigm! – Ed.*

"They've already escaped custody once," Hister asserted. "We want the girl alive. I don't care how the boy is brought in."

Conrock found that last instruction odd. He also found it interesting that the Bullson whom he had heard mentioned before was rumored to be the ex-President's illegitimate son by an unknown mother. How all these different things fitted together was a puzzle he planned to unravel.

Chapter Two
Top Cop

Conrock woke the next morning, but instead of excitement for his first day on a new job, he felt turmoil over the events of the night before. He and Kaylee had gone for a celebratory dinner, and he thought their relationship was about to move into a new direction. As the Trovador's finance comptroller, she had always been concerned about how they were both employed by the City, and wanted their relationship kept secret, even though he had moved into her apartment. His taking a new job seemed to have changed nothing. When she encountered friends from work, he overheard her refer to him as *nothing more than a friend*.

Sliding away from her and rolling out of bed, he looked at his dress jacket and pants still slung on the chair from the night before. They were supposed to be his new look starting that morning. He pulled his old uniform out of his tiny section of the closet.

Pulling off all the Trovador insignia of rank and dropping them into his single drawer of the dresser cabinet, he inspected his weapons and strapped them on. His next action was almost a reflex, without thought. He pulled out the dresser drawer and emptied the entire contents into a courier bag.

"My God," Kaylee sat up in the bed, "you can't forgive a little joke? I'm just not ready to tell anyone about us."

"I forgave you as soon as you said it."

"Well, you really owe me an apology for how you're acting."

He sat on the edge of the bed and took her hand.

"You know, there comes a point in almost every relationship when a person stops loving everything about someone and starts focusing on their flaws. Eventually, they end up hating each other. I don't want to go down that road."

"So you're leaving?"

"While we're still in love."

The look on Kaylee's face told Conrock that she was already well down the hypothetical road. She began shouting and did not stop even after he had closed the door behind him. Some large object crashed against it.

"Get back here and clean up the mess you made me make!"

He shifted the weight of the objects in his bag, giving them a better balance, and walked away.

When driving his skipper through the tollgate leading to the spaceport, he was surprised at the heaviest traffic he had ever seen.

"Looks like dropping the tolls down had quite an effect," he quipped to the attendant, who gave a disgruntled nod as he waved Conrock's skipper on through.

Conrock noticed that immediately after he cleared the tollgate another constabulary skipper began following his and parked next to him when he reached the Spaceport Security building perched on the flattened upper rim of the caldera slope, high above the many-spired city of Trovador. The far wall of the caldera had long since fallen into the ocean, providing a spectacular ocean view.

It was Nebraski who finally emerged from the skipper that had been tailing him.

"Hold on," said Nebraski, "the chancellor announced you'd left the force." He held up a Cuban cigar and a butane lighter. "Thought I'd offer you a retirement gift."

"It didn't take you long to snap up a promotion." Conrock looked at his old badge as he unzipped the front of his jacket and deposited the cigar and lighter into an inner pocket.

"Word is that he's beyond upset with you. I see that you're still wearing all your weapons and your old uniform, you just ditched all your insignia."

"Only thing I had in the closet." Conrock pulled from the same pocket his new badge and certification papers, handing them to Nebraski. "If he's upset with me now, then he's going to hate it when he learns about this. I'm not exactly what you'd call retired, but thanks for the cigar."

"A BHSS badge?" Nebraski scoffed until he looked at the certification level of the Bounty Hunter/Security/Salvage authority. "Whoa. So much for having you declawed. Never saw one with a Bravo clearance before. What'd they do, name it after the ex-President of Earth?"

"I think so. Same guy who laid the first footprints where we're standing."

"This might pull some weight on the backwater planets, but not with civil and military authorities," then he looked at the certification papers, "which these do. Mandated by the Artomique Corporation and the Earth Unification. That pretty much makes you Top Cop wherever you go. You're right, the chancellor *is* going to hate this. But I'm still going to need all your department-issued weapons and the keys to your ride."

Conrock sighed and pulled the courier bag from the rear, and exchanged his sidearm and keys for his new badge and documents.

"I'd heard you'd been kicked to the curb, but now you can pretty much do anything and go anywhere. You're a walking judge, jury, and executioner. I'll bet Kaylee loves this."

"I thought she would," Conrock hefted his bag, "but I was wrong."

"So she kicked you to the curb, too? That girl never respected you."

"Yeah. It got kind of obvious."

"Some women are all about being in control, and when they aren't pulling the strings..." Nebraski's tone changed when he registered the look on Conrock's face. "What can I do for you... sir?"

"You can start by telling me if you're from Nebraska. I've always wondered."

"Keep wondering," Nebraski smiled nervously, unlocking perimeter gates and coding them into the security building. "Unless you plan to arrest me?"

"How about you back me up, instead?"

The bustling building was a clerestory, and Nebraski led the way through the traffic of bodies moving up and down the stairs to the top story that was elevated above the roof of the rest of the building. Lined with windows on all four sides, it provided a 360-degree view of the spaceport and surrounding ancillary buildings.

"Since I was ordered to follow you and shut you down"—Nebraski focused on the public parking area—"I guess I should at least stick with the first part of that." He dropped Conrock's weapon and keys on a table and picked up a baseball bat that had a tightly packed pattern to its wood grain. He handed it to Conrock. "Until you've had a chance to replace your personal protection, this might come in handy in case anybody wants to take advantage of your perceived demotion."

Feeling the weight and balance of the bat, Conrock nodded at the outskirts of the public parking lot, where several other skippers arrived in a cluster.

"I wondered if you'd noticed them," he said. "Where'd the bat come from?"

"Made from Akaran wood," said Nebraski. "Now that they've been outlawed for League play again, they're getting scarce. I confiscated that one."

Controck loudly slapped the thick of the bat into his palm. Several heads turned to see where the smacking noise had come from.

"And they might not be coming back this

time," Nebraski added. "I heard that Tijuana Tanaka got his nickname the *Laser Surgeon* from burning a groove in one. Even his pitches couldn't break an Akaran bat like he did pine. Wonder if now he'll be coming back out of retirement?"

"Doubt that," said Conrock. "I think he died."

"Hadn't heard."

"A lot of circumstances connected to it. It was kept pretty quiet." Conrock checked several monitors until he found what he was looking for. "But this place sure isn't quiet anymore. The port is the busiest I've ever seen it."

"Traffic out had already picked up when people heard that the Grimgrip entered the next sector. Now that the exit tolls have been dropped, there's not an empty outbound seat. Not much coming in other than commercial, with one notable exception. Have you heard that there's an Expert Killer coming through cargo customs?"

"Nope. Zebulon is not why I'm here."

Nebraski looked over a guard's other shoulder at a computer screen that had caught Conrock's attention.

"Then why are you monitoring his ship that just landed?" he asked.

"Let's go welcome him," said Conrock. "Expedite him through customs."

"Think we should take some help?"

"Shouldn't need it."

Nebraski shrugged, and drove a four-wheeler out to the main tarmac, passing the courtesy cart headed in the same direction.

"Most people think the Expert classification refers to his proficiency," said Ne-braski. "But the way I heard it, is he's the go-to guy when someone needs another assassin killed. Wonder who he's after?"

"Don't care." Conrock focused on the cargo coming out of an old freighter in the security zone. Customs officials were scanning the bio-transfer crates being loaded onto transports when a four-legged alien mammal came bursting out of one in a panic.

"I'll get it." Nebraska steered the cart and changed the creature's escape path.

"Ignore it." Conrock waved his bat to encourage the dog-sized beast back in the direction of the pursuing service droids. "Take us around to the other side of the ship... now!"

Despite the confusion that showed in his perplexed expression, Nebraska complied and brought the four-wheeler rapidly around to the freighter's far side, where the emergency command crew doorway was filled with three figures rapidly exiting.

"That distraction was an old smuggler's trick," Conrock nodded at the two female aliens being escorted by a heavily armed man. "They're why I'm here."

"Wow," said Nebraski when he saw the slender and scantily clad humanoid hybrids, with white hair and white feathered wings and pale skin that sparkled and glittered. "Those are some nice little nothings that they're almost wearing. I've never seen anything like them before."

"I have," said Conrock. "Another Philean came through last year. It didn't work out so well for her."

The communicator in Nebraski's badge

suddenly let out several noisy warnings.

"Someone has overridden the security grid, and they're coming in hot," Nebraski confirmed as a military-class STS hopper descended rapidly from the sky. It passed between them and the distant sun, casting a brief shadow as it dropped between them and the freighter. Rather than landing with the slight bounce one would have expected from a hard landing, the hopper's thrusters gave a last intense burst that blackened both the thruster bells and the tarmac as the hopper made the softest of landings. The craft bore the distinctive markings of the Artomique Corporation. "Who the heck are these guys? Someone you're expecting?"

"Nope. I wasn't expecting this. Get ready to meet my new boss."

Chapter Three
Black Gloves and Golden Webs

The first thing Conrock noticed about the woman who exited the hopper right behind a squad of red and white armored Space Marines was her black gloves that went all the way to her elbows, matching her strapless gown embroidered with golden spider webs.

"That's your boss?" Nebraski asked incredulously.

The woman, who Conrock recognized as Nefarimor, the former pirate queen previously known as the Red Queen, strode on the tarmac with graceful steps that gave her the appearance of gliding, which contrasted with the heavy booted footfalls of her leather-jacketed husband, Achilles Hister. His every step was an assertive stomp as he walked close at her shoulder.

"No," Conrock replied. "The man behind her."

Hister was followed by Genghis Champlain, each striding in the same assertive manner.

"I don't know," Nebraski countered. "He looks a little young for her. I'll bet he dances whenever she pulls a string, which means that she's your boss, too."

Hister nodded his appreciation at Conrock's punctuality and motioned for him to fall in behind them. Conrock noticed that Hister was carrying the courier bag from the day before with a white-knuckled grip.

"Bring the batboy with you," Genghis nodded at Nebraski.

"Why all the drama?" Nefarimor motioned for everyone else to stand back when she approached the bounty hunter named Zebulon. Zebulon had a Philean woman on either side, each virtually identical to the other. "You knew we were expecting you."

"But we were only expecting one Philean," Hister interjected. "Were you planning on keeping a pet for yourself?"

Zebulon shifted his feet for a moment before answering.

"I'm keeping them both," he finally answered, jutting out his scarred chin and flexing his jaw muscles.

"Not an option," said Hister, "and against the law."

"They're not animals," Zebulon retorted, looking at the necklaces they wore, the only way to tell the identical twins apart. They were two halves of a broken medallion, one with the broken side down and the other with the break facing upwards. "Sunrise and Sunset aren't animals."

"You gave them names?" Nefarimor's voice became shrill as she stormed forward and snatched the medallion halves, their thin strings easily snapping. "Phileans aren't self-aware enough to understand the concept."

"Take them into custody," Genghis Champlain ordered.

Nebraski started to join a pair of Marines who stepped forward with wrist restraints but saw Conrock's shaking head and stopped his advance.

Zebulon dropped his chin to his chest and glared at the Marines, while his extended arms shielded the Phileans.

"No," Nefarimor chided Genghis, "we don't need to escalate the situation." She ran a finger across one of Zebulon's extended arms, then grasped his hands and slowly pulled them down. "You're hopelessly outnumbered here, but we're not your enemy. You don't want to commit suicide. Besides, you're the one who contacted us about the Philean recovery reward and teased us with some tantalizing speculation about some stowaways you were tracking. That's why I'm here, and we're all finding your behavior just a little confusing!"

Zebulon made no reply, his expression remaining stoically unchanged.

"We only want to help." Nefarimor sighed. "To do what's best for these poor creatures."

"They're people, not creatures. I won't let them be skinned alive."

Genghis snorted with a smirk.

The Phileans cowered and hugged Zebulon when a cacophony of arguments erupted between the Artomiques and the bounty hunter.

"Stop it!" Nefarimor shouted. "Everyone just shut up! Look at how you're scaring these poor things." Her eyes narrowed as she focused on one Philean in particular. "There's something wrong about this one. I'm sensing..."

"That maybe you're the one who should be afraid?" Zebulon asserted.

"Was that a threat?" Hister dropped the courier bag and took an aggressive step forward, but could not draw eye contact with the bounty hunter.

Zebulon was instead focused on the sky when Nebraski's badge communicator released the shrill warning of a perimeter breach.

"Did no one restore the aerial screens when these people dropped in?" Conrock saw the skippers leap from passenger parking into the cargo area—launching canisters that bounced across the tarmac around the freighter. "Everyone! Look out!"

Hister moved first and fast, grabbing Nefarimor's arm and pulling her with him through the freighter's crew hatchway.

"Guard that bag with your lives!" he shouted at the Marines who formed a circle around it.

Nefarimor could be heard fussing with Hister about how he should have left the bag with Georgian as Genghis secured the door. Genghis prevented Zebulon and the Phileans from following as smoke began billowing from the canisters.

The smoke obscured the approaching skippers' landing, but the sounds of them hitting the tarmac made it obvious that they had encircled the freighter. The distinct scratching of clawed feet was mixed with the sound of bootleg lasers rapidly amping up their charge.

As visibility was reduced to only a few feet, Nebraski and Conrock moved away from the Marines as they formed a defensive circle and backed in the direction of where they thought the freighter was.

The Reavers hit from every direction at once. The Marines' formation was quickly shattered in the chaos that followed. Off to one side, Conrock heard a rapid exchange of weapons—he assumed the bounty hunter was returning fire, but it too quickly tapered off.

Armed with only a bat, Conrock tried to stay close Nebraski, but he quickly lost sight of him in the ever-thickening smoke. He caught a glimpse of Genghis, armed with a pair of extended metal batons and moving through the Reavers with a degree of combat prowess like nothing he had ever seen before. Whereas the Marines were being overwhelmed by the numbers and raw savagery of the Reavers, every precision strike made by Genghis disabled another opponent.

Conrock found himself seemingly alone, but knew he was not. Hovering around him were several Reavers with their lasers trained on him, though he wondered why they had not fired. Then he saw a huge shape lumbering toward him and he understood.

Ever since they had joined Earth's Unification Government, unsubstantiated legends had circulated about the Black Star Reavers. One claimed they continued to grow throughout their entire lifetimes. Conrock had scoffed at that idea, until a Reaver over twice his size loomed over him and holstered his weapon.

"You killed my children," the translator in Conrock's ear interpreted the Reaver's growls and hisses. "I'll feast on your beating heart."

The behemoth lunged at Conrock.

While the lawman never considered himself to be particularly nimble, he easily sidestepped and delivered a blow to one of his attacker's knees that was so powerful, he was surprised the bat did not shatter. Then he remembered it was made of densely-grained Akaran wood.

Having had a closer look at his opponent, Conrock realized that this Reaver did not wear a breathing apparatus, and the way the other Reavers deferred to him indicated his opponent was from the upper echelon of their society.

"This is an awful lot of trouble to go through for revenge," Conrock taunted as he stayed out of reach of the Reaver, who repeatedly lunged at him but was hampered by an injured knee.

"You are a bonus." The Reaver signaled for the others to help.

Conrock laid several bodies onto the ground before enough clawed hands managed to get a grip on him. He was thankful that he had elected to wear his old uniform;

otherwise his legs would have been shredded by the claws immobilizing him. But his arms were still free, and when the giant lizard-man closed to grapple, Conrock laid the thick of the bat in his open maw when he lunged to bite.

The Reaver staggered backward as he ripped the bat out of Conrock's hands, the wood firmly embedded in his front fangs. They were still stuck in the wood when the enraged lizard-man ripped them out by the roots and turned crazed eyes at Conrock, blood spurting from his mouth.

The impact of the Reaver's bull charge knocked Conrock out of the grip of those holding his legs, and he was on his back and desperately trying to hold back the bloodied jaws as the crazed Reaver used his weight to make the outcome inevitable.

Then he heard rapid firing from an assortment of weapons and saw the bounty hunter and Nebraski attacking the surrounding lizard-men from either side.

One dying Reaver bit at Nebraski's weapon as he fell, snagging the weapon in his jaws and taking a couple of fingers along.

Nebraski did a brief-but-intense dance of pain as he whirled in agony, blood spurting from his fingertips that he futilely tried to staunch with his free hand. Then he saw Conrock's dire predicament and, with his good hand, grabbed under the massive head where Conrock's hands were pushing and gave him the power to pull the head back in the last instant before the jaws snapped closed on Conrock's face. Nebraski extended his other arm and dagger-punched with the stumps of his severed fingers, the end knuckles denuded from where the flesh had been stripped away, and jammed them into one of the Reaver's breathing slits.

The blood pumping into the Reaver's windpipe instantly changed the look in his eyes from rage to blind panic. The grip between Conrock and Nebraski turned into clamps to keep the Reaver from escaping. Blood spurted from its nose as it exhaled in an attempt to clear the windpipe, but Nebraski's blood instantly filled it back up again. After a series of powerful spasms, the giant's red eyes clouded, and an inner eyelid membrane closed over them. After one more spasmodic surge to break free, the main eyelids remained open as the Reaver's body went limp.

Nebraski kept his fingers in the monster's neck as he pulled the corpse to one side to allow Conrock to slither free.

"It actually doesn't hurt as bad this way," he explained.

As the smoke began to clear away, Conrock saw a tableau of carnage with destroyed men and lizards scattered in pieces all around. The fight had been short but savage. Several delayed sirens began to sound as emergency vehicles screeched in their direction.

"Judging by the number of the dead," said Conrock, "I'd guesstimate that we were attacked by every Reaver in Trovador. I've never seen or heard of them acting in such a coordinated manner."

"That doesn't make sense," Nebraski hissed through gritted teeth when he finally pulled his fingers free. Conrock sprayed his severed fingertips with sealant spray from the constable's utility belt and then pulled medical tape from another pouch to wrap them.

"I thought they were chasing me." Conrock nudged his attacker with a foot to make certain he was really dead. "But you're right; this was something more. This one died as a distraction that let the others escape. He probably didn't plan it that way—but that's how it worked out."

"They were after the Phileans," said Zebulon. "They overwhelmed me in numbers. It was almost suicidal in how determined they were to snatch them. Why?"

Genghis had been inspecting the dead Marines, who had defiantly held their formation to the last man.

"The Reavers concentrated on them"— he pounded a coded pattern on the freighter's emergency hatch—"and they got the bag. That's the only reason the rest of us are still alive."

"The bounty hunter is right." Nefarimor pushed past a protesting Hister to exit first. "The Reavers got what they came for—that bag and the Phileans."

Conrock wondered just how good her hearing was to have heard Zebulon's remark through a sealed doorway.

"And they weren't following you, little man," she glared at Conrock. "They were following me."

"Someone betrayed us," Hister asserted. "Someone who is in league with the Reavers."

"We'll deal with that later," said Nefarimor. "Right now, our priority is getting the Phileans back. You two take my shuttle." She pointed at Genghis and then Conrock, but her finger wavered on the injured Nebraski and then swept in the direction of Zebulon. "You go with them, bounty hunter. You owe us that."

"I don't need their help," Genghis argued.

"Like you," Nefarimor retorted, "those men proved able enough to survive a Reaver attack, where highly trained and armored soldiers died."

Conrock was surprised that Zebulon offered no argument, his attention focused on a nearby ship blasting off despite the blare of warning sirens that protested an unauthorized launch. The ship's distinctive, oversized engines made it easy to identify as a Black Star Reaver ship.

Nebraski switched off the multiple sirens screeching from his badge and watched the bounty hunter drop to his knees in a display of despair that was incongruous with his reputation.

But Conrock understood. He had seen the frozen fright in the eyes of the dead Philean whose skin ornamentations had been inside the stolen bag. Her fate had haunted him, and as much as he had tried to keep his distance when he first saw the other two Phileans, their frightened eyes blended with hers in his memory.

"It may already be too late," said Genghis.

"Their technology is completely alien from ours," said Hister. "They'll be in space before we can even call out an alert to intercept them, and we have no way to track them once they are."

Conrock quick-stepped back to the four-wheeler.

"Need to change your shorts?" Genghis quipped with a sarcastic tone when Conrock grabbed the bag containing his personal items.

After quickly rummaging through the contents, he pulled out the tracking device he had collected from the Chancellery steps the day before.

"I took this from the lead Reaver that attacked me yesterday," he explained. "I'd intended to identify whoever planted a tracker in that bag. Now we can use it for its original purpose—and track that bag again."

"Again," said Hister, "their technology is alien to us. That tracker is useless."

"Unless…" Conrock started to say as he picked up the fallen bat and examined the jagged roots of the Reaver fangs embedded in the Akaran wood.

"You use their own technology," Nefari-mor spoke more quickly. "Go. Now. Take my shuttle and take my ship, the *Merciless*. Hister's ship, the *Godspeed*, will pick us up."

"Where are you going?" Nebraski asked.

"There's only one space junkyard in this sector that handles Reaver wrecks," Conrock answered.

Chapter Four
Rust Bunnies

After their STS shuttle docked inside the Artomique Dreadnought, Conrock was astonished by the emptiness of the bay, hallways, and even the command center

where Genghis Champlain pulled the captain's chair and had a seat in front of the main control panel. There was no crew nor security anywhere to be seen. The massive ship of war seemed to be operating autonomously.

"Where is everyone?" Conrock asked. "I need to visit the armory."

"No armory," Genghis replied as he began activating internal sensors. "Don't need one when there is no crew."

Genghis calculated a destination and course as the *Merciless* slipped out of orbit and then launched into deep space. He kept punching the engines into ever-higher speeds as the exterior monitors turned a milky white.

"Then who's that?" the bounty hunter, Zebulon, asked when an interior monitor showed a lone, white-haired man approaching down a long corridor.

Genghis's slow exhale was audible, but he gave no reply.

"What's his place in the command structure?" Conrock asked.

"I'm still wondering that, myself," Genghis finally replied. "Let's just say Januman tends to dominate a room."

When the doors opened, the white-haired man stepped into the room with a demeanor of authority and irritation. He was powerfully built—stout more than muscular, and the lines on his face were not those of age. At first Conrock thought the man was simply disgruntled about having been awakened from a nap, and then he recognized the lines were from anguish, deeply embedded from dealing with a tragedy so great that he wrestled with it still. They made him look older than he would have appeared otherwise and seemed to have changed recently, as the muscles in his face now shifted to an expression of perpetual anger.

"I close my eyes for a minute," Januman grumbled, "and I find myself somewhere I did not expect to be. This is unacceptable. Explain yourself, Ganghus."

"You know my name is Genghis,"—he sighed even more audibly than before— "and I'm just following orders."

"Hister ordered this?"

"Nefarimor did, and—to no one's surprise—he agreed."

"Hister and I had just joined Nefarimor here," Januman complained. "If I'd known they were leaving, I would have joined them."

"I know," said Genghis, "I was there. That quick excursion back down to the planet changed when we got there. They decided to send me and the *Merciless* on an urgent mission."

"More foolishness with the Phileans," Januman scoffed. "Chasing trivial wealth."

Conrock read Januman's body movements and eyes and felt that his last statement was not entirely truthful. When he had that thought, Januman narrowed his eyes and cut them in his direction.

"We'll rendezvous with them later on Hister's ship, *Godspeed*," said Genghis.

Conrock could tell that Januman's status, whatever that might be, was diminished in Genghis's mind when his superiors were not around.

"You should have gotten off with us at

Trovador," Genghis added.

"Maybe I still should," said Januman.

"How?" Genghis asked.

Januman waved off the question as he looked both Conrock and Zebulon up and down.

"You," said Januman, locking eyes with Conrock, "are the rarest of creatures—an honest man. You do not hide duplicity." He nodded at Genghis and then Zebulon. "Not like your friends. I sense you are what you appear to be, an honest man with only two goals in life—to deliver justice and the search for a good woman's love." His tone then turned sarcastic. "Good luck with that."

"Do you always size up new people when you meet?" Conrock asked.

"Only when I think it will save time later," Januman replied, watching Zebulon take several steps backwards.

The floor beneath Conrock's feet shivered, and stars reappeared on the exterior monitors. The image of a metallic sphere the size of a dozen outdoor stadiums appeared on the command room's monitor wall. The framework of the exterior grid was lined with metal mesh screens that revealed an interior filled with clusters of starship bodies arranged around the gates, and the pieces of those being disassembled becoming ever more reduced as the conveyor lines neared the many warehouses placed all about the massive junkyard. It looked as though it was tied together with giant threads of string that were habitable corridors webbed from the exterior gates throughout the workstations and warehouses.

"This ship is fast," Conrock observed as they made their final approach at normal-space speed.

"Fastest known to man," Genghis replied.

Januman stood over his shoulder, watching Genghis work their approach.

"How am I supposed to park this war wagon?" Genghis began firing the reverse thrusters. "I'm getting no automated docking instructions and can't contact the yard master."

"Out of the chair, Ganghus." Januman forced his way into the captain's chair.

"The *Merciless* is too big to maneuver manually."

"Nonsense," Januman replied. "This ship is nothing more than a toy. I've operated machines big enough fill a whole solar system and move planets about like pebbles."

Genghis rolled his eyes in skepticism as he securely strapped himself into the nearest chair and gravity-locked it onto the floor.

Conrock and Zebulon did the same thing.

"We're coming in too fast," Genghis warned.

The Dreadnaught slowed at the last second, did a sideways shiver, and glided their forward docking hatch perfectly in line with an unoccupied perimeter gate—without so much as a bump.

"How long have you been flying this thing?" Conrock asked.

"My first time," Januman yielded the captain's chair back to Genghis.

Conrock noticed that there was no movement or activity of any kind.

"There is something strange about this place," said Januman.

"No traffic, in or out?" Conrock clarified. "See any Black Star Reavers anywhere?"

"Nothing, no traffic," Genghis confirmed. "Nothing from those other docked ships, either. Just us. Wait, there are Black Star Reaver signals…" Genghis hesitated, "but they're all from the salvaged ships. Not even the rust bunnies are moving in there."

Genghis referred to the salvage robots that could be seen, sitting stationary on the hulls of the many wrecks. Even though there was no oxidation in space, they were called rust bunnies because, like rust, they were known for never sleeping and being constantly in motion as they stripped down the wrecks. Eerily, as soon as Genghis made his comment, every rust bunny in the junkyard turned at the exact same moment and fixed their sensors on the *Merciless*.

"That's odd," said Zebulon.

"So," said Januman, "what's this piece of equipment you need called? How does it function?"

"How could you know that?" Conrock asked. "We never told you why we're here."

"It's a junkyard," Genghis turned to Conrock, "what else would we be here for? So how do I describe what we're here for?"

"How would I know?" Conrock countered. "I've got a tracking device. We need to find a way to expand its range with Reaver technology. That's the plan."

"And you have no idea how to do that," Januman asserted.

"I'm not a tech guy," Conrock countered. "I'm C.F.S. certified."

"What's that?" Genghis asked.

"Can't Fix Shit. I thought a big organization like the Artomique Corporation would have guys who'd take care of the whole *making it work* part."

"There would have been," said Genghis, "if Nefarimor hadn't insisted that the *Merciless* run on full auto."

"Give your device to me." Januman looked at the Reaver tracking device for only a second before handing it back and turning to the command console. "I'll deal with this. Let me talk…"

Januman left his sentence unfinished.

"Still nothing." Genghis shook his head. "I can't establish communications."

"Then we'll do it ourselves," Januman brought up a schematic of the junkyard's habitable pathways between the major wrecks and warehouse structures, all covered with smaller wrecks docked at portals for gutting. "We won't waste time with the warehouses—we'll go straight to the nearest unstripped Reaver remains."

On the wall screen, he brought up the image of a starship with the same distinctive oversized engines as the one they had seen leaving Trovador.

"Ganghus, you stay." Januman put a hand on Genghis's shoulder when he started to rise. "You others, follow me."

In the equipment room nearest to the airlock, Conrock and Zebulon found helmets and suits for extravehicular activities. Januman scoffed when offered a suit, claimed he was equipped with something far more advanced, and instead concentrated on gathering a variety of cutters and other equipment. Conrock brought the tracking device and his bat, while Zebulon carried what weapons he could strap over the suit without interfering with his maneuvering backpack.

When Conrock began to question Januman's sanity when he entered the hatchway's depressurization chamber, the white-haired man waved a large pair of manual bolt cutters and used them to punch the depressurization button.

Both Conrock and Zebulon futilely tried to stop the process, while Januman watched with a bemused expression. He tapped them both on the shoulders before popping the hatchway and passing through.

Genghis's voice began shouting over their communicators for Conrock and Zebulon to pull Januman back into the chamber and repressurize it.

Knowing it was already too late, Conrock backed away and steeled himself for what he was convinced would be a gruesome suicide. The worst thing about dying from exposure to the void was how the lungs would involuntarily attempt to breathe at some point. In that moment of reflex the void began freezing a person from the inside out. Unless the person passed out from shock, their contortions were a horrid sight to see.

Januman's chest expanded somehow, without repercussions. He seemed completely unaffected by exposure to the vacuum and showed no need for magnetic boots.

"As I explained to the others," Januman communicated to Genghis, "I'm equipped with an advanced system. Don't ask about it. It's complicated."

Januman had parked the *Merciless* perfectly next to a hatch, enabling them to walk across the docking sleeve's outer ring to reach the hatch that normally would have opened to connect with theirs.

"What do you think happened to those other crews?" Zebulon looked at the ships occupying other gates along the sphere's exterior.

"That's why I left Ganghus behind." Januman forced the lock with surprising ease and opened the gate.

Conrock looked around for the nearest rust bunny.

"There was a recent report about a service robot going berserk on a space station," he said. "I wonder if whatever virus caused that might be at work here?"

"A Saturnian Protocol would be another explanation for this kind of lockdown," Genghis's voice sounded.

Conrock knew the Saturnian Protocols were an old Earth reaction to the Saturnian-Eybontic war, where cyber-entities were known to seize control of automated systems and turn them against their owners.

"Then it is a good thing that I switched the *Merciless* to manual when I docked the ship," Januman replied.

The moment they stepped through the gate, Genghis's reply was lost and another voice began to crackle across their communicators.

"There you are!" said the mystery person. "I've been trying to reach you. For some reason, I've lost the ability to communicate outside the sphere. But don't worry about it. It's a minor problem."

"Who is this?" Conrock asked when he saw that Januman would not.

"Use the tube right in front of you and come on down to the nearest warehouse." The voice ignored his question. "We'll get you fixed up with whatever you need."

"We can handle this ourselves," said Januman.

Instantly, every rust bunny in the junkyard took a synchronized step in their direction.

Januman continued to confound Conrock by rising from the platform and somehow managed to maneuver through the void without any apparent equipment.

"I can see that you're a do-it-yourself group," said the voice, "so stop by the warehouse to settle up after you find what you're looking for."

Zebulon shook his head about the repeated lures to the warehouse and followed Conrock when he maneuvered his backpack to follow Januman around the massive engines on a Black Star Reaver starship. By the time they arrived at the nearest docking port, they found that the ever-mysterious white-haired man had already forced the lock open and entered inside.

"How does he do all this stuff?" Zebulon asked on a private channel. "Who is this guy?"

"I have no idea," Conrock dropped a hand to his utility belt tether where the Akaran baseball bat floated at his side. "About him—or you."

Chapter Five
The Barter

The outer hatch closed behind Conrock and Zebulon when they entered a small cargo bay and found that Januman had already restored power and gravity to the Black Star Reaver ship.

"That's not going to do us much good," Conrock observed as the lights flickered and ventilation fans created a sudden surge of air, "since the Reaver's atmosphere is toxic to us."

"You're not going to need the bat," said Zebulon, even though his back was turned to where he could not see Conrock loosening the tether loops to the bat's handle. "I'm not your enemy."

"Then tell me the real reason you came to Trovador," Conrock demanded. "You're an expert killer class BHSS agent—a professional assassin. Why would you worry about the safety of alien refugees? Who were you sent to kill?"

"You're also BHSS now," Zebulon replied, "and I can tell you have a soft spot for those Phileans."

Conrock pulled the bat loose.

"How could you know either of those things?"

Zebulon turned slowly, with his arms spread wide and hands open as he took one step backwards, and then another.

"I told you, I'm not your enemy. I'm only here to recover the Phileans."

The two men stood ten feet apart, motionless and unspeaking for some time, as Conrock waited for Zebulon to make a move for his weapons. When that did not happen,

he debated his next action until distracted by Januman's return with a strange mass of wires and parts that he was rapidly assembling into a handheld device.

With no apparent notice of the tense situation he had walked into, Januman held out a hand for the Reaver tracking device. Reluctantly, Conrock tethered the bat.

Waves of green light filled the bay as a holographic display briefly fluttered in the air around them. It flickered several times and faded away, leaving Januman uttering untranslatable words that Conrock had never heard before, but his tone indicated that they were curses.

"That's the first time I haven't seen you able to work magic," Conrock quipped as he started to look around at the materials scattered about the room. The whole design of the place looked alien, but the cargo crates were universal squares suitable for stacking.

"Give me a minute," Januman replied. "Got to make certain this is going to work before we leave."

"How did you find that stuff so quickly?" Zebulon asked.

"I told you earlier that I'm beyond your technological skills."

Keeping one eye on Zebulon, Conrock looked into several crates that had already been partially emptied. From one, he pulled a pair of semi-clear spray bottles filled with colorless liquids. The bottles were constructed from malleable hemp, so he assumed the liquid was also from Earth. From another crate he pulled a similarly sized canister with symbols he recognized.

As Januman continued to work, Conrock

opened one of the spray bottles and poured out a bit of liquid. He then added in a small amount of yellowish powder from the canister.

"What are you doing?" Zebulon admonished. "Do you even know what you're mixing?"

"Actually," Conrock replied, "I do, and just confirmed it."

He poked his finger deep into the bottle, causing the powder to cluster around the glove, but it did not mix with the water. He pulled his finger out and the glove was completely dry.

"Water sprays from other worlds are prized by Black Star Reavers," he explained, "like certain spices and scents are for humanoids. This yellow stuff is a kind of gunpowder. Very flammable and explosive, but hydrophobic."

He drained the contents from the opened spray bottle and refilled it with gunpowder. Once he found a normal lid for it, he unrolled a mesh net from his utility belt and slipped both the spray and the sealed bottles inside, sealing the Velcro top.

The green holograms once again appeared from Januman's device, but this time they only flickered once before stabilizing. A strange, undulating hum rose and fell with varying degrees of pitch and intensity.

"What's that sound?" Zebulon asked, futilely holding the sides of his helmet over his ears.

"Your Earth technology tends to use sonar-based pulses to track an object," Januman replied. "But the Reavers have a more organic system, like a low-frequency whale song."

Januman attached the tracking device and switched it on. The undulations of sound quickly intensified. Conrock found it extremely discomforting when the sound coalesced into a steady hum. His vision blurred, and he began to sweat as his hair stood on end.

Januman pointed at a pulsing light in the hologram of stars.

"We have their course," he announced and switched the device off, much to the relief of a slightly disorientated Conrock and Zebulon.

"I keep asking, how did you know that was what we were trying to accomplish?"

"You told me," Januman replied in a matter-of-fact tone.

"No," Conrock countered, "we didn't."

"Yes, you did."

Januman opened the cargo bay door to be greeted by a wall of rust bunnies, which immediately extended their mechanical arms and seized all three men with their clamps.

"I see you have finished shopping," the mysterious voice returned on their communicators. "Time to pay up."

Januman looked like he was debating taking some sort of action. Then he relaxed, nodding for Conrock and Zebulon to do the same.

"I'm curious to see what's really going on," he explained.

"I thought you already knew everything," Zebulon quipped.

"Why does this have to be done in person?" Conrock asked as rust bunnies moved in the direction of the nearest warehouse's pressurized dock. He felt a twinge of anxiety in his stomach when he noticed how, in a place with no apparent biological life, all the bio-waste containers lining the lower levels appeared to be filled to capacity.

"We operate on the barter system here," the voice explained, and then went silent to all further inquiries.

Only the three rust bunnies clamped to the trio entered the warehouse through a pressurized cargo bay, switching from aerial locomotion to lumbering on their short, mechanical legs. Their grips loosened only when they approached an unusual ship situated near the center of the otherwise empty warehouse floor, directly below a pair of overhead hangar doors.

Conrock recognized the vessel as a scout class Wild Stars ship that had undergone significant modification. Regardless of what Genghis had said about the Artomique Dreadnoughts being the fastest ships known to man, these scout ships were generally acknowledged as the fastest. Yet someone had tried to improve that speed by adding a variety of instant acceleration devices that would kill any passengers should they ever be deployed.

"Keep your suits on," Januman advised in a low voice when the rust bunnies released their clamps fully.

Zebulon loosened his helmet and proceeded to lift it slightly off the clamps.

"Do you hear that?"

"What?" Conrock asked.

"It's like something you'd hear at a stadium event," Zebulon replied. "An echo of a huge group of people somewhere nearby, all talking at once."

"There is no one here," Januman asserted. "Now put your helmet back on."

The rust bunny that had controlled Conrock motioned for him to enter through the scout ship's open side hatch, while Januman and Zebulon were blocked from joining him.

As he reached the hatchway, Conrock pretended to stumble and fall to one knee. He was back up quickly, but in that moment he had unhooked the Akaran bat from his side and left it blocking the hatch from closing behind him.

He heard voices having a conversation, coming from the very front of the ship. At first, he saw no one, but once he had fully entered the compartment, he saw a severed head wired into a mechanical table where the co-pilot's chair should have been.

"I saw them," said the head, somehow supplied air for his vocal cords, as its wandering eyes focused on the ceiling, "there are immortals coming into our galaxy from the void outside. They've just arrived."

"Pay no attention to his ramblings," said a disembodied voice coming from the command console's speakers. "Take a seat in the pilot's chair."

Looking at the array of surgical devices arranged across the ceiling directly above that chair, Conrock knew that if he took that seat, he would never rise from it as a whole man.

"I want to know more about what the head said," a third voice sounded behind Conrock. He turned to see that Januman and Zebulon had entered behind them and heard servo-motors straining in a futile attempt to close the sideway hatch he had blocked. Zebulon nodded toward Januman as if to answer Conrock's unspoken question about how they had escaped the rust bunnies.

"Pay no attention to what he said," said the voice they had previously heard on their communicators. "How did you get in here?"

"Answer my question," said Januman, "and then I'll answer yours."

"Space madness is an affliction suffered by star explorers with improperly shielded spacecraft," said the voice. "Their brains are bombarded by cosmic rays that destroy their nervous system and impair cognitive function. Now answer my question."

"I asked them nicely," Januman replied.

Through the side window, Conrock saw the rust bunnies standing with heads resting on their chests and arms dangling by their sides.

"That's…" the voice hesitated, "not possible."

"Then you explain it," Januman countered. "Who are you?"

"Someone who only desires an exchange by barter."

"Here." Zebulon continued to ignore Januman's instructions and opened up the front of his pressure suit to pull something from inside. "I'll barter this for what we need. Now let us go."

He held up a very large, uncut blue diamond.

Even Januman had a look of surprise.

"Where did you get that?" asked the voice.

"It's a common pebble where I grew up," Zebulon replied. "But everyone I've ever met wants them. Do we have a bargain?"

"Nice try," said the voice, "but no. You described it yourself—a colored pebble. It's worthless to me. I only barter for information."

"Fine," said Januman, who proceeded to introduce himself and his companions. "Now, tell me more about these immortals. Were they from the Wild Stars?"

"No!" the severed head stated emphatically. "They weren't from our galaxy. They're Extragalactics, and they're looking for immortals from the Wild Stars—specifically the women."

The head's words piqued Januman's interest.

"I didn't think there were any immortal women," said Conrock.

"Oh, there are," the head insisted. "But they're rare. Those other immortals want to kill them all!"

The head's last statement piqued Januman's interest, which turned to anger when the clamps securing the head all released at once and the table beneath it suddenly dropped away as vacuum pressure sucked it inside. There was a series of noises from the head rattling through pressure locks and exterior plumbing in a nearly instantaneous process.

"Bring him back!" Januman ordered.

"Sorry," the voice replied. "I couldn't listen to his ramblings anymore. I only kept him around for the company. Nothing he said was worth retention."

"Who are you?" Conrock demanded.

"I've been known by many names and have been many people. What remains today is mostly a construct of my original self, Dalucar Zonderman, and the best parts of a fellow named Carthage."

"What are you?" asked Zebulon. "There's no one else here."

"Earthmen once called me a Saturnian." Dalucar referenced the race of cyborgs who took that description because they typically regenerated into new bodies once every 30 years, the amount of time it took Saturn to circle the sun. "But now I'm afraid that I've also had to infuse myself with one of my hated enemies, an Eybontic, to survive."

"A Saturnian-Eybontic hybrid?" Conrock asked more than confirmed. "I've never heard of such a thing. But I did hear rumors about a war crimes prisoner escaping a secret prison on Venus."

"Tell me more about the Extragalactic immortals," Januman demanded.

"I can't," Dalucar replied. "I deemed his mind unfit to be absorbed into my consciousness. Now, I did use a bio-energetic formula to keep him alive, so to speak, and you're welcome to go sorting through the bio-trash. But be warned, I used it on all of them. So you're going to have to talk to a lot of heads to find the right one."

"You've got a mass of conscious beings stacked in the trash?" Conrock instinctively reached for weapons he no longer carried.

"They're not conscious in the manner you think," Dalucar replied. "They're able to do basic functions, as long as you don't carve out too much of their brains. But they have no real higher brain functions. People don't really need those to talk, as you've seen."

"You're mad!" Zebulon said angrily.

"No," Dalucar replied, "that would be the severed head."

"Let's go," said Januman. "I've heard enough."

"None of you are going anywhere," Dalucar replied as several cargo doors began opening. Standing on the other side were masses of more rust bunnies.

But before the doors opened fully, the floor beneath their feet jolted as the whole facility was struck by some powerful force on its exterior.

"That was by my order," said Januman.

"That's impossible," Dalucar asserted. "You have no contact with your ship."

"I have skills you cannot comprehend," Januman countered as Zebulon nodded his agreement.

There was a fresh shudder from another exterior blast, which Conrock figured came from the *Merciless*. Genghis had evidently seen their capture and was operating the fire controls manually, which caused a severe reduction in fire rate, but Januman played that off as though it were by his design.

The cargo bay doors began closing as the rust bunnies reversed direction to head back outside, their base programming to protect and repair the junkyard's structural integrity overriding any other input.

"Fine," said Dalucar as the scout craft's main console lit up and the severing of exterior links with the hangar could be heard.

"I'd exhausted this place anyway."

"Get out!" Januman pushed both Conrock and Zebulon to the hatchway.

As he stumbled through, pushed by Januman and a sudden burst of air, Conrock saw the wood of the bat blocking the door was beginning to crack along the grain. It snapped into splinters as his feet barely cleared the doorway before it closed.

Thrown onto the hangar floor next to Zebulon, they both watched as the Wild Stars scout ship rose upwards through the overhead hangar doors that revealed a clear path straight through the heart of the junkyard and into the stars.

"Januman is still in there!" Zebulon shouted as the craft instantly accelerated out of sight, seemingly pulling the atmosphere with it and leaving the bounty hunter frantically working to reseal his suit.

"I told you to keep that on," said Januman's voice behind them.

They turned to see the white-haired man standing there with folded arms.

"But you were on that ship?" Conrock asked.

"That's what Dalucar thought," he replied.

"How?"

"That's my business."

"You saved our lives," said Zebulon.

"Remember that," Januman replied, "should I decide to spend them later."

Wild Stars VII: The Gold Exigency continues in the Summer 2023 Issue!

This seventh entry into the Wild Stars marks the start of the second half of Michael Tierney's 12 volume science-fantasy space opera, as he builds toward the epic finale. For all of the details, see www.thewildstars.com!

Quicksilver

By J. COMER

Cartmill Station has an outbreak of a deadly virus! Can a daring rescue mission to deliver nanomedicines using a dangerous experimental rocket reach them in time?

In the chat window, Jamie Hsu saw that Dan Ngobi's face was incredulous. "Mercury? What do you mean, mercury? How is there mercury here?"

"I don't know, and Nancy doesn't know, but Parmenides thinks it's a large-body impact from the bombardment era, one that differentiated into plutons." Parmenides was the moon-study AI. Jamie Hsu, who had found the mercury, was a small middle-aged man who wore a hand-knitted sweater and a cap, and sat at a cluttered mess of a workstation looking at too many screens. Dan Ngobi, who was in charge of shipments from the mine, was taller, narrow-faced, and wore a company jacket. Outside, the volcanoes of Io made it worth ten years on a Jovian moon, since they supplied both minerals and the energy to move them.

"Plutons? What's a pluton?"

"Metal melted under gee and flowed into different layers. Like gold in the Sierra Nevada, back home." Jamie was from Porterville, California. "Anyhow, what it means is that we have about two thousand tons of mercury in a vein under the chlorinated ice you were looking at." MusCorp had decided that the cheapest way to support settlements in space was to use local resources.

The International Science Council had agreed since this also funded a lot of scientific research. Everyone benefited. "The bots are bringing out the ore right now." He hesitated. "That's okay, right?" He saw Dan consulting a HUD.

"Yeah... hey, this mercury stuff is poisonous. We'd best be careful. But the Hung Seng rates it as... Nice. Very nice." Peak production of metals had made Earth hungry for them, and space settlements needed everything they could get. "Sure, pull out some more mercury. We'll let Maria Elena at MusCorp know when we put the next shipment capsule together. Um, I've got a voice-em; see ya at dinner."

"All right." Not exactly a gold rush, but his mining bots could make them a little cash here on Io. He needed a commendation on his MusCorp dossier, and this might do it.

Jamie followed the bots on cameras. Human labor was not worth shipping out here, but human supervision of bots, leavened with scientific work, was the compromise between the unions, the scientists, the space-enthusiast crowds back on Earth, and the corporations that owned settlements and bases. The bots all had cute names, just like the rovers who crawled all over the worlds and moons and sent back cool pictures and sometimes were followed by human crews, and they all had feeds back on the WorldNet where they posted quotes and jokes and chatted with their fans via media tools... Jamie shook his head over the bots' social lives and opened a screen to his friend Karen. He got her 'busy being a mad scientist' answer, which usually meant she was out firing rocket motors after her work was done. He shrugged and finished four more hours of moving drones and survey cams and then getting the bots to where they needed to be.

Over dinner with the station's main day shift, Karen told him all about a hydrazine motor she'd test-fired: if the higher-ups approved, she wanted to put a sat into orbit with one. They were eating dessert when Dan cleared his throat for their attention.

"Hope everyone ate well." They had. Then he spoke the code phrase that made sure everyone not on sleepcycle heard him. "All Hands, All Hands." The station's comms carried his voice everywhere. "I got an em today that worried me a great deal. Some of you got it as well. Those of you that read them."

Quiet laughter.

"Cartmill Station"—on Callisto, the great ice moon—"posted today that they're quarantined." His face was drawn, lined. People looked at each other. "It's Kratmann's." There had been news posts about outbreaks of the virus. "There have been

fatalities." Karen gasped. "Please, hold off on eming people until we're done here. I know that a lot of us have... friends and family, loved ones, up and down the Network. But I wanted to speak to you all in person. MusCorp has—has assured me that they will do all that they can to speed medical care to Cartmill."

He drew a deep breath.

"Jamie, Naran, they know your work with bots and nano. They asked me to share the medical protocols and to ask you to see what you can do." Santino and Chatmann were weeping silently. Their kid was on Cartmill doing an apprenticeship. Chu-li Wen had come in from the kitchen and sat down, whispering in Benson's ear, Benson shaking his head.

Jamie's heart thudded. This was bad. He nodded, thinking already how to use bots—Cartmill had fewer than they did, he knew—to work with a retrovirus that destroyed the nervous system. Naran, sitting across the table, said, "We'll get on it tonight. Our game tonight can wait, right, guys?" Nods. "I can do the nano half. Jamie's on the bots; he's got bigger fingers." No smiles or laughs. People that they knew and loved were locked in a space station with a monster.

Benson's face was in his hands, his shoulders shaking. Chu-li put her arms around him.

"Why us? Why ask us?" Chu-li frowned. She was the hydroponics specialist, cook, and all-around favorite. "Why not work out a cure on Earth? They've got all the computing power." Sour face. "And all the money."

Dan answered her, somewhat more in control of himself. "They do, and they're sending updates as their medical AIs spit 'em out. But we're closer; a ship from Earth would take too long to get there. Even sending messages takes hours." Speed of light was the ultimate limit. But ships went much, much slower. The Solar System was a big place. Clumsy chemical rockets could take you to the Moon of Earth, but the solar sail and gravity whips had made the outer planets accessible, and inertia had made them desirable.

"Kim, you're the closest thing to a medical officer we've got." Which meant a degree online, atop her degree in planetology, and juggling two jobs. "You can 'face our copy of Paracelsus—into the work that Naran and Jamie are doing." She nodded, clear-eyed.

"Paracelsus is a pretty good medical AI, for the problems we have here. I might need to sit in for a while as well." Ngobi nodded.

"Sleep's not on the agenda, is it?" Naran said.

Dan Ngobi shook his head.

"Then let's get to it." Work would distract them, if nothing else.

The Solar System is a big place. Every schoolchild (who paid attention) learned that if Earth was one cm from the Sun, then Jupiter was five and a half cm, that Neptune was thirty cm, long as a man's foot. The stars were whole klicks away and not easy to get to. But the Solar System could be navigated, as kids learned in their ed-groups and ed-games. Gravity was the key.

Planets circled the Sun, and made Lagrange points along their orbits; matter accumulated around planets and their Lagrange points. Journeys that would take years were speeded up by using the Interplanetary Transportation Network. Granted, a low-energy trajectory wasn't a fast one, but space habs grew their own food in CELSS modules and crew—families cared for each other.

It wasn't that different from living in a science base on Earth. Get to your destination and loved ones, and work out however many years. Already children had been born as far off as Toronto Base on Titan. The Brackett-Mkuma radiation shielding, embedded in HDPE polymers, made space a great deal less dangerous. And humans, inured to living in habs surrounded by vacuum, made putting on a pressure suit no more unpleasant than their Earth-bound forebears had found being laced into corsets and submerged in powdered wigs.

So. Jamie was six hundred million klicks from Earth, four astronomical units, and poring over the information that had been gathered when the virus devastated an old-age home in Costa Rica. The virus was transmitted by droplets or direct contact; it attacked cells directly, as retroviruses often did, and made them produce a brain-wrecking protein similar to "huntingtin" ...a short search turned up information on Huntington's chorea.

Naran emed him. He opened a chat window and saw the brown-faced engineer in his office with a slowly changing parade of nanomachinery in the background. "How's it looking, Jamie?"

"The disease mimics—oh, let's get Kim in on this." They opened another window. Kim was in a fog of medical imagery screen projections, including what looked like a protein-folding problem-solver. She spoke, graphics illustrating her words as she cued them.

"We have a lot of information on what the virus did in this one well-documented outbreak. And a nanobot was used to contain it."

"So, send Cartmill the nanobot plans; mischief managed," said Naran.

"Can't," said Jamie, and at the same time Kim nodded.

"Tanenbaum's Law," she said. No transmission ever had the bandwidth of packing mem-diamond into a truck and driving to where you needed to go.

"Right, right, an electruck, or a cargo-cap full of nano-bubbles—" Nanoshad solved some of the problems caused by the disastrous rise and fall of antibiotics, but nano wasn't magic. It needed an energy source, and it could do one thing at a time, if you were lucky.

"Could one of you explain? My ears connect to one brain," Nara said.

"Uh, you—"

"—you go first, Jamie. You're the engineer." Jamie nodded, and so did Naran.

"Cartmill Station says that they don't have the nano design capacity that we do, because they don't work with nanos as much, mostly just use designs that come

down the Network." They nodded. "We can't send the plans, and neither can MusCorp back on Earth because of bandwidth. The plans are published; they occupy 47 yottabytes of data, with the documentation. The antenna at MusCorp would be tied up for—"

Kim interrupted. "Three years, it says here." She made a face. "So we have to do it another way."

Naran ventured, "The electruck way."

Jamie nodded. "Pack 'em all into a truck and drive it. We have to figure out how to get the plans and the fabber to build the nanos there. Cartmill Base's fabber isn't as good. Kim can have plans made up in a couple of days for a nanobot that'll maybe read and eat the protein, the troublesome protein, and for another that will find the virus and virus particles and then lyse 'em up."

They worked on the nano designs and ended up with three huge files, one for a diagnostic nano for the proteins, one for the virus, and one to process infected cells. It would be a destructive, harrowing experience for the infected brain, but it would be better than dying.

They hoped.

The prototypes worked well in the virtual tests, but there was no way to tell short of injecting them into an infected person whether they'd work or not in 'real life.' There remained the question—"We can load them onto one of Karen's old messenger rockets and get them to Cartmill in under... seventy hours," Jamie calculated.

Kim and Naran were writing a manual to go along with the package when Ngobi emed them.

"Jamie, Naran, Kim, Karen?" The faces appeared, with Karen represented by an animation of her own face. She was busy.

"Cartmill emed me, and their medic is down with the virus."

Oh, shit.

"What does this mean?" Karen for-real appeared.

"It means," Ngobi said, "that there won't be anyone to administer the nano cure, if you get it there. I'm sorry, and I appreciate the work you've done, but—"

"What?" Kim said. "We give up and watch the whole station go mad and die?"

On live cam.

"I am sorry, Kim. I know you're working on something that can get there on a messenger rocket or something—" Kim interrupted him.

"We're done with it. It cost Jamie and Naran some tool time, and me two sleepcycles, but it can go. Karen can launch it next time we're in position." Io's orbit made this easier than it was in some places; Jupiter could give them a boost.

"But they can't use it. Even if you got it to them now. Someone would have to go there." Ngobi was a good administrator, and he clearly disliked this.

Karen spoke, twisting her unruly mass of brown hair into pigtails as she did. Emergencies did not magically make your hair behave. "Dan. What if we could go there?" She had the shade of a smile on her full lips. "What then?"

"What do you mean? The shuttle can't manage that kind of delta-vee," said Jamie.

Dan Ngobi asked, "What do you mean, Karen?"

"Well, I, um, had been working on something. Something I wasn't ready to tell you all about."

"What? Zero-point energy? Cosmic space warp? What the Hades are you talking about?" asked Jamie.

"It's a rocket," she said, confident now. "In my test firings, I got a specific impulse of nine thousand."

"Huh?" asked Kim. "What is that?"

"It means that the shuttle"—their old surface-to-orbit workhorse, retired after a mold infestation—"could get ten tons of stuff to Cartmill in about seventy hours, two long burns and some coasting. About the same as if we could burn at .01 g, the whole way there." Silence. "It means we can do this." She seemed to expect comments. "We can go and take the nano-thing you made and save these people." She took a breath. "Right?"

"Right," Naran said, "if your lash-up rocket doesn't kill us in the process."

Jamie said, "How soon can you have this whatever-it-is ready to fly? Preferably without it killing us?"

"Two days." Living underground, they used the Earth calendar. "With the bots helping me."

"I need the bots. Income, remember? We have ore capsules to fill and send down the Net." The system had little slack built in. Gravity made the rules.

"We can send more next time. The mercury's dense, right?"

"Mercury?"

"Um, never mind. And I need the chemical separator and the Sabatier reactor, Dan." She smiled. "Is that okay?"

"Uh, sure, if it's just for two days. We do have orders to fill." As the one moon with metal deposits in the mostly-rock-and-ice Jovian system, Io supplied materials that otherwise would come from the asteroid belt or distant Mercury. It wasn't the amount of fuel required since Earth orbit was halfway to anywhere. It was the time—closer did mean sooner.

"Then thanks. And I need more coffee. And some help, Jamie?"

"Sure. I'll come on by."

They got down to work.

The bots helped center the clumsy rocket on the launch track. "Fuel loaded, oxidizer loaded," messaged Chun-Woo, who'd run the bots. The flight plan was a complex one: the catapult could send them out, and they'd burn there to send them to Callisto, which was outside the deadly radiation belts and the site of fascinating surface-and-interior science; Cartmill was there on a ten-year mission before going on up the Network to some more ice-moon work. The station was resting on the moon's surface, not buried as Binder was, and did little mining, mostly for their own needs. Their CELSS was terrific, and there was a permanent colony over at Valhalla Basin (which also lacked the needed fabber, sadly; they'd asked).

Karen had loaded the fuel herself and run

the synthesis to produce it with the help of one bot, an older one, Tasha, which she retired afterward. The oxidizer (amazingly, she said she could do this with a chemical rocket) she had kept away from everyone and commandeered the spare glass tank for it. "Not something you want to fool with," was her description.

They met one last time, bags packed, work shouldered onto the remaining members of the crew and the long-suffering bots. The four crew who were going wore pressure suits, with Brackett-Mkuma coveralls over them for radiation shielding, helmets off, of course.

Dan Ngobi was insistent. "I am not chopping the launch permit," he said, "until I know the fuel and oxidizer mix."

As if he knew anything about chemical rocketry. Jamie respected the man; keeping a group of scientists on track was like herding mercury... on dry ice. "She filed the document," he said, "with the Solar Aeronautics and SpaceAdmin," with an effort at a smile. "So what's the problem?"

"Karen," Dan repeated, "what's powering that thing? I am not a rocket scientist," he said, which was true, "but I can't expose you four to danger or death in the hopes of getting a lash-up spaceship out on a mercy mission, no matter how good-hearted you might be."

Cover your ass, why don't you? Jamie thought.

"All right," Karen said. "Here it is." She shared chemical formulae and said, "Jamie's mercury deposit made this possible. I reacted the mercury in an off-site tank with methane and got dimethylmercury. It's—" They consulted their personal information systems, as people did when an unfamiliar term came up.

"Insanely toxic and banned in one hundred and eleven jurisdictions, even in transit!" Ngobi was furious. "Just touching it with gloves on will kill you!" He turned to Jamie. "Did you know about this?"

"I knew she had a formula that was toxic. That was why she thought she could get us there, with a burn in open space, not on a planetary surface, not near anything alive. Dan, hydrazine is toxic as hell, and drinking liquid oxygen will kill you—like that guy on Le Guin Station who killed himself. We have to get there. And this lets us do it."

"You can't have this stuff on my station, on my moon. You'll poison us all! You are not going—we can send a messenger rocket, period."

Karen replied, quietly, calm. "Dan, I had a bot make it. Then I recycled the bot—" That was what happened to Tasha. He could download her software into another bot. Silly to mourn a machine, but he felt bad about it.

"—and the mercury went back into Jamie's ore tanks, to sell. Dan, every drop of the dimethylmercury on Io is in that fuel tank, on a rocket about to leave. We'll come back by sailing ship—" a solar-sailor made the rounds of Jupiter's moons, slow and sure, "—and drop the lash-up into Jupiter's atmosphere if you want us to. I know how toxic it is! I made it! But I did it to save the crew on Cartmill. And we do need to launch now."

"I'll let you do this. But on your own heads be it. I'm registering this as an 'extreme sports' activity and permitting it," he said, touching his chop to the screen of the handheld. "I pray you get there. I pray you return."

Jamie smiled.

Kim picked up the nano kit and her rucksack of spare clothes. As they walked down the airtube, Jamie heard Dan Ngobi calling up a pray-app.

They boarded the improvised spacecraft and then remembered that there was no name attached. "We do need to name this beast, don't we?" asked Kim.

"Don't spaceships always have names?"

"They usually do, sure. Even just numbers in a series," said Naran. "How about *Mercy Flight*?"

"Maybe," said Kim. "Or *Clara Maas*?"

Karen strapped herself into the pilot's couch and lit up physical and virtual controls, with layers of menus visible to her and Naran, who was the co-pilot.

Kim and Jamie took the other two couches in the refurbished shuttle, where soap and water had almost eradicated the black mold and the sulfur stench that was everywhere on Io.

"Let's call it the *Quicksilver*," Naran said.

"Why that?" asked Kim.

"It means mercury, or it used to."

Jamie had never done a catapult launch. He'd come and gone using the new shuttle, which was off at Gish Bar Mons doing prospecting. Nice olivine there—

"It'll do," Karen said. "As First, I'll approve. *Quicksilver* calling Binder Station, requesting permission to launch. Come in, Binder Station."

"Binder here. Permission granted, launch window open for two more kSec." Twenty-four minutes old-style, and they went through the checklist twice, at Karen's insistence. The catapult was warmed up, since after launching them it would send a load of magnesium out to Ganymede for transit to Callisto, then a load of nickel-iron to Europa. The capsules could do a little steering and course correction on their—

"Ten. Nine. Eight. Seven." The voice was Parmenides', the AI, quietly androgynous. "Six. Five. Four. Three. Two. One."

Then Jamie felt a mountain on his chest. He couldn't breathe. Then he couldn't see. Then—had the launch gone—

Black.

He felt a gasping cough, his lungs inflating. Pain, lots of it. Hands on him.

Darkness again.

Jamie woke, really woke, to see the scared faces of the crew, and felt freefall. OK. The launch had—

He didn't know. He tried breathing in and found something in his mouth and nose, some medical something, and tried to reach up, and found pain in his chest and down his left arm. Why? Fifty was too young for heart attacks; this wasn't the nineteenth century or whenever. Kim said, "Jamie, can you hear me?" His vision was blurred. Why?

He nodded. "Can you breathe okay?"

If this crap weren't in my mouth, I'd be fine!

He nodded again. She went on, "I can take the venter out of your mouth and nose, and see if you can breathe. The launch was pretty hard on you."

"Thought we'd lost you for a while," said Naran. Kim looked hard at him.

The breathing mask and tubes came off, and he realized that he was bare to the waist. After coughing and some water, he managed to speak.

"How'd it go?" He coughed again.

Karen spoke, still in the pilot's couch. "We're on course, Jamie. You took four gee for an hour and fifteen minutes; we all did, but it messed you up. Relax for a while." Kim brought him a t-shirt.

"We're on course?" He closed his eyes, opened them. It helped a little.

"Next stop Ganymede," Karen said and turned back to the lash-up control board. "We're doing a course correction burn. I hope you can take it. The final burn at Callisto is going to be rougher." The lash-up shuttle could brake using Callisto's gee, and then land on cold-gas jets to avoid trashing the landing site with dimethylmercury.

Kim spoke to him, quietly. "You have a heart problem?"

"Yeah. How'd you guess?"

"You know you could be sent back to Earth."

"I know. Io's gee is lower. Haven't had problems."

"I'll fab you some pills, okay? But you gotta take 'em."

"Thanks, Kim."

He floated. They ate, meals that Chu-li had packed for them, and napped in turn. Everyone who has been in space learns that sleep is much easier there than on Earth; the Freudians argued that it was the return to the womb. (Jamie didn't care; it was comfy, and he liked it.) Karen did the course calculations over and over until Kim distracted her with a game of pyramids on the mag table they'd snatched from a storeroom.

The course correction came. "Strap in, crew," said Karen. "Burn for fifteen seconds."

A giant sat on Jamie. Rattling all through the ship. He felt his heart strain and couldn't breathe.

Heart conditions are easier in lower gravity. Until it isn't lower anymore.

Couldn't breathe, couldn't breathe. Time stretched, and vision greyed. He felt the shaking and trembling. *We didn't plan for this spacequake: is something wrong? What if this kills me?* He didn't know. He'd been raised Reformed Buddhist but wasn't sure what he believed anymore.

The shaking and trembling.

They needed him to run the machinery. His death meant no repairs. He—

Rattle and thutter.

Did everyone die worrying about the next life? Or just hurting a lot and wanting it to be over?

He didn't know.

Brenschluss. They floated, strapped to couches, in sudden freefall. His eyes still blurred. Kim swam out of her couch and checked him over with her medical kit. "You'll live." A smile. "Now rest a while, listen to some music, and we'll be at Callisto in no time."

"What was that rattling noise?" he asked. Naran frowned.

"Karen, look over the board," Naran said. "Anything that explains the shaking? I felt it too." He smiled. "Nothing serious. This flying science-fair experiment is going to shake anyhow."

Karen paged through layers of consensual imagery, virtual toolbars and dashboards, like harem screens in a hundred colors, and shook her head. "The ship felt it, but I'm running diagnostics all through the systems. It felt like fluid moving." She shook her head, looking worried. "If we have an external leak, we might lose oxidizer, or fuel. Hope you guys like the Kuiper. If it's an internal leak, it's worse."

"A lot worse," Kim said, as she collected some loose pieces from the boardgame. "That stuff's much more toxic than you told Ngobi." It seeped through latex and fabric and leather, and killed by rotting the brain...

"I had to get us there. I had a plan Z that involved using just the catapult, but we couldn't take anyone who wasn't certed for a high-gee launch."

Like me, thought Jamie. "And Ngobi told me he would throw me into a volcano if I touched his reactor." Nuclear rockets worked well for space travel, but Earth (and even the Moon) didn't allow them to be fired too close-in, out of fear of radiation.

There were no laws against chemistry-gone-crazy rockets because few DIY enthusiasts liked working with hydrazine or dioxygen diflouride. The Network was slow, but it sufficed.

"Cartmill called. Another ten staff are down. They're trying to isolate as much as they can. But each compartment doesn't have its own recycler. So it's not easy." Ideally, every hab off Earth would have a fully independent air-water-waste cycler, but in reality no one wanted to pay for it. Binder got by on four "house-rated" units, which in a pinch could keep it going for twenty years, depending on how much the crew liked soybeans. The deep-black explorers who were going to Sedna and Quaoar had much more powerful equipment.

"We need to get there. How is their medic doing?"

"The em we got before we launched said she's down with the virus, and no more news. I think that if she had died, we'd know," Naran said. "And we can't get there any faster."

"Fifty to a midcourse correction, so be strapped in then," warned Karen.

They nodded and went back to running another sim of the nanos and their effect on the virus. All of them took shots of the nano; it would be easier than wearing isolation suits when they dealt with the patients, for psychological reasons.

They ate; they slept. The midcourse correction came, skewing them a little more onto a flyby of Callisto. Again, the ship vibrated scarily, audibly. Again, an endless series of diagnostics showed them nothing, save that the vibration was happening in the pumps above the rocket nozzle, as far from the cabin as one could get and still be on the ship. "Can we get someone back there?" For weight's sake, they only had one repair bot. "Can you pilot the bot?" Jamie asked Karen.

"I can steer a bot, sure. You do more work with them than I do, though. Want to take it out?"

He rolled the bot sternward along the hull of *Quicksilver*, and near the rocket nozzle, he found hull panels that looked stained. He asked Karen if it was related to the problem. "It might be," she replied. "We might've had some leakage when we were loading, or during the burn. Can we get in?" He tried, but the bot's arms didn't have the leverage, he thought. Karen took over and said that the problem was that the magnetic tire chains on the bot's wheels didn't grip the hull hard enough.

"Could one of us go out there suited up and try to get to the pump?"

Naran had drifted over to their conversation, away from the sim tank where he'd worked with Kim. "I could try it; I've evaed some with my club at Bangalore Tech."

Jamie had no experience working on a spacecraft's hull. "Well, Karen built the pump. She could guide you. Mercury is toxic. But—" Kim was still frowning at the tank.

"I can go," said Karen. She was not looking at any one of them. "It's my ship. I built this crazy rocket. I can fix it."

Naran spluttered, "And who is going to

fly it, then? If something happens to you?" He took a ragged breath. "You're out of your mind if you think I'm going to let you go out there. I'm going." Kim came up to where they were arguing in the small cabin.

Jamie countered, "Naran, you've done eva, but Karen built the—"

Kim broke in. "Why don't you all three go out and get killed by the space monsters and stop *ARGUING*?" her tone exasperated, her voice flat.

They all looked at her, surprised.

"I notice that no one wrote an equation that requires the woman to jump out the airlock to get the medicine to the space colony, but I've got about one nerve left, and you all are getting on it, and I'm the reason you're making this trip, so shut up and fix the problem!"

Karen said, "Sorry, Kim. Look, guys, she's right." She laid a hand on Naran's chest. "Naran, go out, with the bot. Jamie, pilot the bot. I'll fly us, and you'll have my schematics as you go. And Kim can work the nano sims in peace and quiet. Okay, everyone?"

Jamie helped Naran suit up over his t-shirt and boxer-briefs: the breathing-corset, the relief tube (yuck), the skinsuit, then the heavy, insulated coverall with the Brackett-Mkuma layer, necessary in Jupiter space, the magboots, the snoopy hat, the helmet, and the heaviest gloves that fit. He hugged them and went out through the portalock that Karen had midnight-requisitioned from a storeroom on Binder. Jamie and Karen followed, huddled in the cockpit, on helmet cam fed to heads-up displays.

Jamie watched through the cam as Naran walked out and clink-clanked along the hull to the rear. On the way, he stopped for a moment and stared, and those inside were stunned by a view exotic even to Io's station crews, whose sky swarmed with worlds. They saw Jupiter half-surrounded by its ring, visible as a near-full circle, and around it, the great moons, as *Quicksilver* streaked out to Callisto. The smaller moons were only sparks, and Callisto was near eclipse. Persoftware found them the great yellow star of Saturn, and, near the Sun, the double point of light that was the Earth-Moon system. Here and there were slews of spacecraft rolling up and down the Network from world to moon to Lagrange point, round and round, visible through software tags. Onward, then, to the tail of the ship and its rocket motor.

The bot showed Naran the relevant panel, and they worked together to open the casing, balanced on emptiness in the cold realm of King Jupiter. Inside was an assemblage of pumps and filters that sent the mercury; a thin spray of liquid, freezing into a spray of ice. Hampered by the gloves, he worked on patching the pipe. The bot held—

Jamie shouted as the patch failed and a gush of liquid-and-frozen dimethylmercury splashed onto the bot and onto Naran. "Oh, Ram," they heard him say.

"Come back inside!" said Karen.

"No!" Jamie shouted. "This stuff is toxic, but it takes megasecs to do something to you. You can finish the repair."

Biomonitors showed Naran panicking

wildly. "Stay on it, man. Remember, you have replacement parts."

Step by step, they took him through the pump repair with the extra parts carried by the bot, which was also covered in a mess of methylated mercury liquid frozen in the vacuum. Jamie agonized over the job, and when they had to do one whole valve replacement over because he couldn't see it, he felt like screaming. The cam was blurry from the spew of poisonous liquid, and wiping made it worse.

The bot's cam wasn't much help either. "Is it done?" Jamie asked after what seemed a kSec.

It was.

They coaxed Naran back inside, his voice near a sob when he spoke to them. "Wait, Karen." Kim said. "His whole suit is caked with this evil crap. He can't come inside, can he?"

"He... it's gotten frozen all over him. So it's not as though it's liquid and going all over the place. Is it?"

Jamie rejoined, "But it's ice. It'll flake off, and..." he consulted a database. "This stuff will melt at the cabin temperature. And a drop of it will go right through your skin and kill you." He paled. "This is serious, isn't it."

"Yeah, the brown guy dies first," said Naran, still outside. "What are we going to do? I just float out here till my air's exhausted?" Jamie smiled. Humor was healthy. He hoped.

"No, no. We can..." Karen had a dangerous smile on her face. "I know what we can do. How brave are you, Naran?"

"Huh?" He seemed more bewildered than ever. "Um, I eva into radiation, riding a rocket that burns mercury, and fix the goddam pump, and save your asses, and get lethally poisoned, and who was the brave one, again?"

"Okay. Here we go. We're all going to be exposed, but less this way, I hope. Kim, put this rope into the lock." She did, coiling it swiftly where the door would dilate.

Before Naran stopped being mad. Good. She touched controls that locked the bot into place on the hull. "Take off your suit as fast as you can."

"What?" he said.

"Take it off. You can live ten seconds in vacuum."

"The radiation—"

"We're outside the belt. There's a line in the airlock. Grab it. We'll pull you in, and leave the suit outside."

"But my suit—"

"Doesn't matter. We can get you a new one. Take a deep breath. Another. Mouth open. Okay? Move!"

They heard a slither of zippers, a slide of clothes-off noises, and last the puff of air as the helmet went, its alarm fading into the silence of vacuum. The lock opened, a residue of air carrying the rope out with it. Suddenly, Naran was in the lock, they saw on cam, and Karen pressurized it as fast as she could without killing him. He still wore the skinsuit and his boots. "Open it." They felt the ship's air thump into the still-thin air of the lock, and Naran floated half-conscious in the ship's cabin, unhappy and alive, blinking to rewet his eyes, swallowing over and over to balance the pressure in his ears.

"Hold still," Kim said, "and I'll wipe you off. Guys, look the other way, will you?"

"Crap. We'll help you." The crew held the man while she wiped him with the chelating pads from her medical kit. She helped him put fresh clothes on and said, "Just rest, okay? We'll need you when we get to Cartmill." He nodded.

The radiation dose— Well, they were headed somewhere safe.

The braking burn was coming up. Kim went over the medical protocols and tested their blood for the presence of the nanos. "You've got a healthy dose, Karen. Jamie, I'll load up another syringe. As for Naran… I'll run a diagnostic suite when we get to Callisto." Naran was dozing in his couch, oblivious. "Karen, how long till we brake?"

"I'll do it slowly. Three kSec till I start the burn."

"We should be fine. Did you hear from Cartmill?"

"Their AI sent a message. The comms crew are all sick."

"That isn't good news. We may have more work than we thought."

"Maybe so. Well, police up the cabin, and we'll get ready." They cleaned up the airswarm of kipple that freefall always seems to produce; gee has its uses.

They strapped in, and slowly, Karen opened up the throttle.

At once, Jamie felt the shuddering that had racked the ship before. "It's the same problem," he said. Karen nodded. She cut the motor and sent the bot rolling back to the tail, where its cam showed a healthy spray of liquid into the black, freezing into ice crystals. "Shit!" Karen said when the geyser showed on their HUDs. "We gotta go back there again?"

Kim suggested, "Can't we just brake and hope we get enough thrust? You designed some slack into the system, right?"

"I'd like to think so. But we don't get a do-over in this one; we're way past solar escape, and our insurance does not cover an out-of-ecliptic rescue run." Being at solar escape velocity meant that the final burn had to go right, or they'd be on a one-way trek to the Oort. (Some decent science that way, surely, but crew liked to survive their missions.) She took a deep breath. "So. Jamie, you're the best bet. Think you can make it out there and back?"

"And get mercury poisoned too?" He grinned madly. "Naran will have company. Do we have a suit?"

"Yeah, yours. Is the Brackett-Mkuma layer current?" Swimming back to the suit locker, they found it was. He hurriedly changed, the two women aiding him, and slipped into the airlock.

"Wish me luck," he said and walked onto the hull.

Dizziness, disorientation, crazywhirl. He saw the empty black, the weightlessness worse on his inner ear than when he had a room with walls and a floor to steady him. He had no eva experience, and even the chatter of Karen and Kim in his ears did little to reassure. "We have half a kilosec to do this, if you want to do any braking at all, ok?" He nodded, realizing how ridiculous it was.

"I can get it done. Um, don't brake while I'm out here, right?"

"We are gonna brake when we have to brake." They could delay, but it meant firing the motor harder, at higher gee. Twice as fast? It took four times as much gee. To divide braking time to one-third? Nine times the gees. He hurried, clank-shuffling down the hull, minding the mag-boots and his safety line, the same one Naran had used. The bot was there before he was; his HUD showed him the globe that was Callisto, where Cartmill had set down for 300 mSec, ten years on old Earth. Almost one J-year. He was babbling. Inside his head.

"Yeah, I'm here." Heave! "We got the panel open, I guess you can see. And I don't think the stuff got on me."

"We can see it okay," Karen said. "Now, take out the tube of sealant."

"Where...Huh?"

"It's in the leg pocket of the coverall; I put it there," said Kim.

"Oh."

He applied the sealant, and the spray of dimethylmercury stopped. "It's stopped. Is it time to close the panel?"

"Get back into the ship as fast as you can. Please." Karen did not sound happy. "Move!"

He shuffle-clanked up to the airlock, asked if he needed to repeat Naran's frat-boy stunt. Karen told him to come inside now.

"Just lie against—" He felt gee, pulling him down to the back wall of the cabin. "I'm going to take it as light as I can now.

But you won't like it."

"You're burning far out, *Quicksilver*," said a voice on the comm.

"You don't want this exhaust," Karen said. "Trust me." She had aimed them over the great ice moon's south pole, braking where the deadly blast could harm no one.

"Everyone ready?" They said that they were. The dark, icy globe of Callisto came on; at the last moment, they saw the lights of Valhalla Base on the nightside. The *Quicksilver's* engines went into hard burn, a hell-blend of mercury and chlorine spraying across the Jovian system, deadly as a fusion plume. He had time to open his helmet before his arms were pinned to the wall/floor. He felt pressure, then more, then pain, then agony. Then red, then black.

It lasted for he didn't know how long.

He woke in light gee, moon-gee, in a station compartment. Sitting by him was Karen, looking worried. "Well, we didn't think you'd make it," she said, forcing a smile. "Kim had to restart your heart. She's tending the maintenance crew now since we need them; she did the kids first. She saw the Chatman boy—he's fine. Then the science crew, then nav. So far she says it's going well."

I have a heart defect. Which is eased by low gee. Which is made worse by high gee. Which MusCorp would use to deny me duty out in the Black.

"It is?" His mind was muzzy. Then he realized—"We're on Cartmill! We made it." He smiled. She handed him a bulb of water.

"We're here. And you're okay. I'm sorry

for the hard burns, but—"

"We got here. So it's good. How's Naran?"

She shook her head. "Chelating therapy and nanobots. The damage is permanent, Kim says. Maybe on Earth they could fix him. The Network can't get him there in less than fifty-five megasecs."

Almost two years. "The poisonous fuel."

"My fault. I'll go to trial for it, I'm pretty sure. I was talking to a legal AI, named Blackistone, about it. If the Cartmill crew testify, I might get off with a shorter sentence." He fumbled for her hand, held it.

"You did the right thing."

"No, I didn't." He stared at her. "I knew that dimethylmercury was a lot more dangerous than any search of spacecraft records would tell Ngobi. It killed scientists on Earth until no one was stupid enough to use it anymore. I sent Naran out there—I knew." She wept.

"You did," he repeated, "the right thing."

"Did you hear me? If I had told him that this stuff could kill him, and eat his brain doing it, and leave him a drooling cripple, and he had decided, then I could tell myself I was doing the right thing. But I lied to him, to Ngobi, to all of you. Your heart couldn't take the gee. But I had to have you along as engineer. I damn near killed you, and you might still die of mercury, or the radiation, or the virus here. You got radiation out there, and so did Naran." Jamie felt cold in his veins. "I got the *Quicksilver* here, and Kim is out there treating a hundred and twenty crew and their kids, and

they might even all live, and she can repair some of the brain damage. Cartmill can go on. But I lied to all of you to do it. And I can't deal with that."

He didn't know what to say. She went on, "I'm going now. Thanks for listening to me, Jamie. You're a good-hearted man."

"Take care, Karen." She left.

Eventually, he slept.

J. Comer is a writer and a teacher. He lives in California.

Comes the Hunter

By BILL WILLINGHAM

Following the trail of dead, the hunter closes in on his quarry: the last of the wizard knights! His magic exhausted, can he defeat his dastardly foe with his wits alone?!

In the seventh year of Coyote, I came upon Bel Canto, the last of the December Men, in a small town deep in the badlands of the Old Tess. Of his former brethren, Canto left the easiest trail to follow. Riding south, down out of the rolling yellow hills of Homa, all I had to do was follow the bodies—well, not bodies to be accurate. Whatever plague he was spreading reduced its victims down to bare, dry skeletons in a matter of hours.

I skirted around the blackened, deeply pitted bones of what must have been a cow. I'd heard that there were still scattered remnants of this once-abundant species down in the Tess, but I hadn't quite believed it until now. Today, as in ages past, men will boast and exaggerate and outright lie about the deeds they'd done and the amazing things they'd seen. Some human qualities don't change.

I dimly recalled the fat steaks and juicy hamburger sandwiches of my youth, more of a distant dream than a real memory. What a waste. The dark magic that had destroyed its flesh so quickly wasn't done with what little remained of the beast's carcass. Like some persistent acid, it continued to etch and scrape away at the bones while I watched. In a day or two at most, all that would be left was drifting dust. I shuddered to think I might be breathing in microscopic parts of the creature even now.

"Are you certain that trinket will keep you shielded from whatever this is?" my horse Derry said. I touched the pendant hanging cold and heavy around my neck, under my shirt.

"Cauley promised it would."

"You should be okay, as long as it stays in direct physical contact with you," Cauley, the relic merchant, had told me. He'd outfitted me with my magical protections for close to half a century, as had his father before him. "Your horse may be another matter, though."

"Why? It isn't alive."

"Some of its components are close enough to living tissue to worry me. This pestilence you insist on following may be powerful enough to degrade it over time. I'm not sure even this can extend its reach to protect you both. Also, not to split hairs, my sole obligation is to you, my client."

"I'd rather not have to walk home."

"Then I suggest you hurry about your business," he'd said. That was months ago.

I rode on, through dry yellow grass and

low scrub, taking it slowly over the small humps and depressions that wrinkled the ground like an old man's whiskered face. I took a sip from my canteen, but spit most of it back after coating the inside of my mouth, not knowing when we'd next reach a viable waterhole. I hadn't traveled this deep into the Interior in a hundred years. The road ahead was a mystery.

"After all these years, I think we're getting close to him," Derry said.

"Can you sense him?"

"No. Call it deduction. He's on foot, and has been for some days. Any creature he might have been riding will be long dead, a victim of his own plague."

"He could be on horseback."

"I don't think so. I would have spotted a trail sign before now. And at the more powerful epicenter of his spell, his horse would have degraded more rapidly. There would be traces left in his wake. I haven't detected any plastic residue along the way. I'm confident we're finally closing the gap."

As we crested a rise, she spotted the town before I did, which wasn't surprising. When she came off the factory floor, she could track the progress of a specific mote of dust in a hurricane. That was a dozen owners ago. In her current shape, she was limited as to what she could see with the maintenance I was able to afford, but her abilities were still impressive compared to a human eye.

"I don't see him," she said, "but my guess is Bel Canto's still down there, inside one of the structures. There are no signs of life in the streets, but plenty of black skeletons in and around the town. I see some

small living animals some distance beyond the far side of the town, leading me to conclude that he hasn't continued out of it."

"He could have backtracked," I said.

"Not coming back this way. I'd have spotted him."

"Or it might mean that his plague finally petered out before he moved on."

"Yes, that's another possibility. Do you believe it?"

"No."

"Then should we go down there and see if we can't put an end to this?"

"I suppose so."

As I rode down into the valley, I checked the gun on my hip, riding tight and heavy in its freshly oiled cross-draw holster. It was a gesture born out of long habit, but useless in this case, since I'd run out of rounds months ago. Though I'd held onto my expended brass, no gunsmith I'd passed in the past month had been equipped to refill them with the basilisk-tipped reloads I used. In hindsight, perhaps I should've let that one smith in Homa City convert my pistol back to using simple lead and gunpowder when he'd offered. Too late now.

I still had my rapier, though, hanging down along my left leg. It was a good blade that held an edge and had a fine balance. It had seen me through many a dicey predicament. I'm told it had a name once in the long ago and had even been blooded in battle against a real dragon, up in one of those northwestern seacoast towns. If so, any name it might've carried was long forgotten now.

As I approached the dead town, the

blackened bones of foxes and rabbits and other small wild creatures began to give way to human skeletons, adult and child. Most lay alone where they fell, but some were wrapped around each other, in couples or small groups, as if they'd held onto each other, even through the agony of having their flesh reduced to powder over a span of minutes.

"I can hear muffled noises coming from that structure," Derry said. She directed me towards a single-story brick and clapboard building with a wooden boardwalk running its length. Wooden beams coming up off of the boardwalk supported a mesh ramada overhead. It was woven of saplings harvested when they were still wet and limber. They were dry and brittle now. But they still cast a nice shade over the porch. A hand-painted wooden sign hanging down from the ramada showed a picture of a glass mug filled with a foamy, amber liquid. More or less the universal sign of a public house.

"Someone's definitely inside," she said.

"Stay watchful." I dismounted in front of the tavern and stepped up off of the dirt street onto the raised boardwalk.

"Call me if you get into trouble. If I can't fit through the door, I'll come through the wall."

The doorway was an open hole with nothing but shadow beyond. Just to one side of the entrance, the remains of a pair of batwing doors lay discarded on the dusty floor. As soon as I entered, anyone inside would have me at a momentary but considerable disadvantage while my eyes adjusted from the bright afternoon sunlight to the gloom within. But since standing silhouetted in the doorway would give someone the same advantage, I walked right in without pausing.

A few steps inside, I stopped to see what I could see, ready to defend myself if need be. No one attacked me immediately. After a few seconds, I could see that there were more human skeletons on the floor. Dozens of them. There was a polished wooden bar that ran the length of one wall, with a long mirror behind it. Its corners and edges had been acid-etched with decorative filigrees. There was a round brick fire pit in the middle of the room with a large metal tepee tent flue and iron roasting spits secured above it. Big meals were cooked there, providing further evidence that the deep lands of the Old Tess still boasted some of the huge meat animals that had long ago died off almost everywhere else. A dozen small ceramic pepper pots were lined up along one lip of the cooking pit's curving brick wall. Their various colored glazes indicated the thermal severity of their contents. According to the ones laid out here, the former patrons liked their meals spiced in a range that began with merely wicked and extended all the way up to dragon's breath lethal.

Several tables were arranged around the indoor cooking pit, and a man was seated at one of them. He was slim and dressed in segmented black and amber. The armor was finely decorated and looked expensive. It would most certainly be spell-strengthened enamel over paper-thin, molded sheet plast, as light and maneuverable as the simple brown cloth I wore, but impervious to anything short of a high-powered rifle shot. His jet-black hair and beard were cut short and immaculately trimmed. Like me, he carried a rapier as his blade of choice, but his was already unsheathed and lying across the table in front of him. Its elaborate basket hilt was carved in the likeness of entwined rose stems—thorns and all—with each needle-sharp thorn tip pointing outwards, forming a nearly 360-degree circumference of protection around his sword hand.

"I always wondered why they called you Belamandus of the Iron Rose," I said. "Now I guess I know why."

Bel didn't move from his seat but continued to drink directly from a brown ceramic liquor bottle—one matching the dozens that were stacked behind the bar. As he drank, he regarded me with alien eyes that were ochre at their edges and faded to a bright and piercing vermilion in their centers. Any sane man would run from those eyes. I wanted to as well, but didn't have the choice.

"Why aren't you dead?" Bel said, when he finally spoke. "My spell is one of the Nine Terrible Workings. Everything for two miles around me in every direction should be no more than dust and memory."

"What can I say? You have spells, and I have counter spells. That's the way of those in our profession." That was a lie. What spells I once had available to me had been spent long ago in the pursuit of the eight other wizard knights in Bel's order. In killing them, I'd exhausted the powers I'd painstakingly built up over the ages. What few magical protections I still enjoyed were

those lent to me by Cauley's medallion.

"Help yourself to a drink," Bel said with a gesture towards the bar. "These townsfolk are a generous people, and everything's on the house. You might as well join me and refresh yourself while I ponder what to do with you."

I selected a bottle from behind the bar and sat across from him at his table. As I sat, he gestured again in an offhand way, and I felt the prickly sensation of a general interrogation spell crawling over me.

"Ah, I see now," he said. "You're the one, aren't you? When I became aware that someone was following me, I naturally assumed he was no more than a simple bounty hunter, with more greed than sense, or even just an overly curious pest. I stopped here to let you catch up to my killing radius, so that I could be on my way again without distractions. But you're no simple bounty hunter, and though you take pains to appear the ragamuffin, you're more than another itinerant spell soldier. You're the Intrepid Slayer, the doom-bringer of my brethren."

I answered with a small incline of my head.

"Your name is Nemesis."

"Not originally, but it's one of the names some call me now. I find it a touch over-dramatic."

His interrogation spell continued its work, feeding my private and dreadful histories to him as we sat and drank and passed the time. I didn't try to block its progress with any of the non-magical mental techniques still available to me. I wanted him to see the terrible powers I'd wielded in the past and maybe assume I still had access to them. I wanted him to learn as much as he could stand to take in, as fast as he could take it, so that he didn't have time to sift the information and perhaps discover how vulnerable I was, should he decide to make our coming duel a battle of spells rather than blades.

Bel's face, which had before only showed indulgence and confidence, now began to take on an aspect of astonishment.

"And more! I can see that now! You're the original deicide! Long before you hunted us, his most ardent disciples, you killed the First Magus who made the world!"

Now that his fear and passion were up, it was time to turn it into anger.

"You can argue all you like whether or not he was a great magus," I said. "In terms of raw power, I'd even have to agree with you. But he was never a god and never made a thing. Instead, he used his powers to shit all over the Earth, until it ended up in the awful state it's in now. Believe me, friend, he was born into our world and born human, just like you and me."

"Blasphemer!"

"Back in the day, your First Magus was just another asshole, a rude drunk, a moocher, and a card cheat who happened to stumble into a lot of undeserved power. He died last year still owing me the thirty-five bucks he stole from my wallet a dozen centuries ago when I was foolish enough to let him sleep on my couch one night after his girlfriend had quite rightfully tossed him into the gutter."

Bel began sputtering his rage but still issued no challenge. I hoped one more good twist of the knife should do it.

"Your god didn't die well," I continued. "He begged for his life and had pissed himself well before I began to blast and bleed him in earnest. He was right about one thing, though. His moronic followers would try to destroy the world after his death, to make good on his claim that the place couldn't survive without him. Hunting you fools down turned out to be quite a chore. I've never heard such blubbering and pleading as when I'd finally get one of you genocidal nuts cornered. But I should've known. Cowardly, degenerate gods can only breed cowardly, degenerate acolytes."

"Spells or steel?" Bel cried, getting to his feet.

Finally.

It was the traditional challenge between fellow wizard knights, and it saved my life—at least for a few moments longer. His challenge gave me the choice, and since I couldn't hope to survive a duel of sorcery, I'd match him blade to blade.

It was simply a matter of making him mad enough to blurt it out.

"Steel will do," I said and drew my weapon.

"Outside, where I'll have room to kill you with proper elegance, even though you deserve no better than to be chopped down like a wild dog!" Wild dog was a bit of a redundancy these days. Those that survived had long ago lost their affinity for our company and traveled in massive feral packs. Bel took up his sword of roses and stomped out through the doorway.

I waited a bit before following. Let him think I was afraid to rush to my death. I actually took the time to see if there was anything in the tavern that could help me eke out a small advantage in the coming duel. Lacking his magic armor, I was already suffering a considerable handicap. I didn't find any holdout weapons behind the bar— no concealed guns, nor so much as a common burn stick or zap dancer. I searched quickly beyond the bar and reluctantly settled on a thing or two that might possibly come in handy, if everything went my way, the planets were aligned, and the gods were in my corner. By then, Bel was calling for me to come out and face my doom.

I did.

He was in the middle of the street, about twelve feet away and facing me with his sword out. Derry was at least a dozen yards down the street in the other direction, caught within some sort of restraining field. She was held fast, and I could see a wild look in her eyes and a bit of foam at her muzzle.

"I sensed the true nature of your riding animal," Bel said, "and put it in a cage. I make no accusations that it would've tried to interfere, but it's best to be sure that this will remain a private affair between the two of us."

Too bad. My plan was to cheat exactly in the way Bel had anticipated. I'd hoped to circle with Bel until Derry was directly behind him, at which point she could rush up and stomp him to death before he knew it. I tried to think of something else while we took our places opposite each other.

We came *en garde*, and I tapped at his blade's foible a bit with mine, just a few tentative engagements at maximum separation to test the dexterity of his grip and the strength of his wrist. Both were fine. He easily disengaged his tip each time, in small deft circles, without ever letting it wander off target.

He circled a bit to his left, and I followed suit to keep position, but dragged my trailing boot just a bit to see what kind of dust I might kick up. A few dim puffs blossomed about waist high, which seemed promising.

Suddenly, Bel beat hard against my blade and kicked his forward foot forward into a lunge. I let my blade circle and came around in a high outside parry to block his attack, but he'd already anticipated me and dropped his blade into a low attack while continuing his lunge. I responded, parrying low whilst simultaneously backpedaling in an ungainly and undignified effort to restore some distance between us.

It worked—mostly.

Instead of opening me up from groin to belly, his low-line attack simply nicked my forward thigh. He recovered out of his lunge and pressed his immediate initiative. My retreat had kicked up more dust, though, and he stepped forward into the growing cloud. That was a mistake. He should've let the initiative go while he retreated and regrouped. Instead, he fully immersed himself in my dust, just as it rose to eye level, leaving him blind and disoriented, if only for an instant.

One instant was all I needed.

I engaged his blade in a binding parry and rode my blade down his, in a screech of complaining metal, letting its shaft act as a guideway through the concealing dust directly towards his body. I felt my point come up solid against his unprotected chest and stop hard.

Damnation.

I'd hoped the stories about my sword's history were true and that it had enough raw magic in it to overpower the refined magic of Bel's armor. They weren't, and it didn't. I should've remembered my own dictum: men tell tall tales. I had a good sword, but nothing beyond that. I recovered from my lunge and retreated again, further down the street.

Bel followed me, smiling a smile of certain victory.

Though we might be closely matched in skill, I was handicapped by the need to find a vulnerable target between the joints of his armor, where he could cut or pierce me anywhere at all. He'd already drawn first blood on my thigh, and it was beginning to hurt and leak blood, just as he'd expected. He could afford to prick and nip at me all day like this, taking ever-greater advantages as I grew constantly weaker. That was pretty much what he did. After a few minutes, I was bleeding from a half-dozen small cuts on my legs and arms. I'd have to think of something soon.

To buy time, at the end of a small flurry of bladework, when both of us tried to attack and riposte, and riposte again, I suddenly drew my pistol and pulled the trigger. The hammer fell on an empty chamber, of course, but it still caused him to flinch and retreat, giving me enough time to step up and place a thrust between the two plates of his elbow joint.

I missed by less than an inch, but that was enough to count against me. He recovered into his *en garde* stance entirely uninjured. I dropped the useless pistol and continued to look for an opening. Maybe if I could circle him back this way, he'd trip on it. Then again, as long as I was indulging in some wishful thinking, maybe the earth would just open up and swallow him.

Though his armor included a helmet covering the back and top of his skull, Bel's face was left open and unprotected. Call me a cynic, but I was suspicious. I advanced with a few not-too-well-aimed high attacks that were designed to let him parry, but in a way that would keep my point coming back close to his face each time I disengaged and presented the same attack, over and again. Each time my tip got anywhere close to unshielded flesh, some of the decorative overlays around the edges of his helmet would flow out and create a protective armor mesh between blade and face. It happened almost instantly—far faster than I could press an attack.

"Cheater," I said without passion, as we circled some more.

"Not at all," he said. "Had you thought to bring such armor, you'd be better off as well. No steel or stone or any other cutting or bludgeoning material can get past my defenses. You're beaten already and just haven't realized it."

"But it's not perfect," I said. "It didn't

close up to protect against getting dust in your eyes. You should tell the lazy armorer who made it for you that you didn't get your full money's worth."

"I'll consider that next time I see him," he said—rather that's what he started to say, but before he could get the full statement out, I had stepped back again, bringing me temporarily out of range of even the deepest lunge and started violently kicking dirt up towards his face as fast and as accurately as I could.

I have no idea if it worked, because all I could tell for certain that I'd accomplished was creating a much bigger cloud of dust in the middle of the street. Bel had disappeared somewhere inside of it. While waiting for him to reappear, I reached into my pocket with my off hand and drew out one of the small ceramic pepper pots from the cantina—the one with the forest green glaze containing the hottest powder. In another second, I could begin to make out Bel's outline again.

I advanced in a single deep lunge, plunging forward with my blade. Bel parried hard, and I let him carry my blade far off target, which was fine since it brought his blade off target as well. For a single instant, we were staring at each other, mere inches apart, with no steel separating us. That's when I threw the entire pot's worth of bright crimson pepper dust in his face. His intuitive helmet couldn't close up tight enough to intercept it.

Bel went down, on hands and knees in the dirt, coughing and sneezing, spitting and screaming in pain. I stepped up to him and took my sweet time finding just the right opening between overlapping segments of his scalloped armor. Then I placed my blade tip in the breech and drove it home, hard against underclothes, skin, muscle and bone, until it found his vitals.

Later, after the magic fence around her had faded, Derry and I rode south out of the town, which may or may not have had a name. If it did, I never found sign of it. Bel's sword and the dismantled pieces of his wonderful armor were tied in a bundle across the back of her saddle. Spoils of war.

"Why south?" Derry said, after we'd gone a ways. "Our hunt is finally over. At long last we can go home. I'm in need of a thorough refitting."

"Because all signs indicate this may still be cattle country. Once we get forward of Bel's two-mile death radius, we might get lucky and find one."

"To what purpose?"

"If you'd ever had a beefsteak, you wouldn't need to ask."

"This form I've taken is a grass eater. I doubt I'd enjoy the meat of any animal."

"Then we'll find you some grass as well. That's where the cows would be, anyway."

Bill Willingham is an American writer and artist of comics, known for his work on the series Elementals and Fables.
https://nohtsc.square.site/

Starring Hedy Lamarr

By TROY RISER

An alien intelligence on the moon with the ability to possess victims engages in an all out secret war against Earth! It's up to a secret world-wide conspiracy to stop it!

1: THE BLUE DUCK

Fitch and Hargrave left Shepperton Studios in Surrey and headed northwest in a silver-gray Austin 1100 to the submarine base in Clyde. Fitch was annoyed the Austin was a '68, shiny and new. Fitch had specified an unremarkable car for the same reason he wore nondescript gray suits and cheap shoes. No one notices. No one remembers.

Leaving London, Fitch struck up a conversation with Hargrave, the stolid, taciturn former SAS man behind the wheel. The two had never worked together before, and Fitch wanted to gauge Hargrave's responses, get a feel for the man. Topic had turned to The Director, who had delivered that morning's mission brief. Fitch could count on fingers of one hand those few who knew who and what The Director really was and found himself annoyed by Hargrave's blasé reaction: stony-faced, imperturbable, completely unruffled, which had in turn ruffled Fitch.

"So you're saying you truly had no idea who he is? World-famous film director? Cinematic legend? Hollywood genius?"

"I've seen two of his movies," Hargrave said. "I liked the gladiator one well enough—epic sword and sandal, right? Good stuff. But the other one I've seen? His war movie before that? That one I didn't like."

"Not enough 'once more over the top, lads,' Hargrave?"

"You think I don't like it because it's anti-war, Mr. Fitch?" Hargrave shook his head. "Most soldiers are anti-war, at least those I know who have been in one. What sane man can truly be *for* war, the bloody awful thing itself? Or doesn't recognize the occasional necessity of it, if it comes to that. So no, that isn't the reason."

A long minute passed inside the close confines of the car until Fitch finally broke the silence.

"Go on then, Hargrave. Why didn't you like it?"

"You recall the villain of the piece, right? The division commander who called a fire mission down on his own troops?"

Fitch nodded. Fitch's ability to remember was one of the reasons he had been picked as a runner for the organization. Fitch could (if he wanted) play the entire film in his head, from opening title sequence to end credits.

Eyes on the road, Hargrave said, "The general in the movie was right to do it."

"You're having me on," Fitch said.

"I'm serious, Mr. Fitch. If the tactical situation demands it and there is nothing for it, no other options, no other way to get those troops onto the objective, then I would do it, and so would you, most likely. But the general is the villain, you see, shown to us as cold, arrogant, cruel, and unfeeling, while the hero, the man who opposes him, is portrayed as a handsome, brave idealist. Pure manipulation, Mr. Fitch, loading of the dice."

"And you don't like being manipulated," Fitch said.

Hargrave shook his head. "Who does? But yes, Mr. Fitch, to your point: I do know who The Director is; rather, what the public thinks he is."

"And you weren't the least bit taken aback?" Fitch asked, eager to get back on topic. "Not even, oh, I don't know, mildly surprised by the revelation?"

Hargrave shrugged. "That he's *The* Director? Not really, no, Mr. Fitch. Thinking about it, show business is a genius cover. Who can say no to a movie star or a world-famous director? Fame of that sort strikes me as a passport to anywhere, a magic key that opens all doors."

"I suppose it is," Fitch said, allowing himself a smile. "And it's just Fitch, please, no mister."

Fitch saw Hargrave drove never taking his eyes from the road, always aware of his surroundings, not easily distracted by talk, and he found it reassuring. Fitch liked competence in small things. Survival in their line largely relied on the accumulation of small advantages, getting the details right. Fitch didn't believe in luck. Luck in this business is lack of planning that doesn't kill you right away.

"You've worked for The Director before, then?" Hargrave said.

"From the beginning," Fitch said.

"You trust his judgement?"

Fitch lit a cigarette, cracked the window, pitched the match. "I trust his ingenuity. I trust his imagination," he said.

"And The Artist?"

Fitch shook his head. This conversation with the usually quiet Hargrave was making him uncomfortable. Talking about the organization and those in charge was tacitly discouraged. Early on, Fitch had been trained to think of the enemy as a spider at the center of a vast, interconnected web, feeling for movement in its strands, listening for prey. Don't give it that movement. Don't pluck that string. Give it nothing, not a word, not a whisper.

But Hargrave is new, Fitch reminded himself. His curiosity is natural, expected.

"You'll be meeting the man yourself, soon enough," Fitch said. "He's very open. Talk to him. Get to know him. Draw your own conclusions."

It was late afternoon when they passed through Leeds. Both men were hungry and agreed upon a pub called The Blue Duck, a place Hargrave had spotted from the road a few kilometers from town. Inside, the place was empty except for the pudgy barkeep rolling silverware into napkins behind the bar. Fitch made his way to the bar while Hargrave settled in a booth in the back with his back to the wall and his eyes to the door. Fitch slid onto a stool, took off his hat, and made ready to order something cold and quick for them both and then get moving again because time was short.

Dishes crashed in the kitchen. Fitch heard the bang of a swinging door, caught a flash of movement at his left. He started to turn. Things happened quickly.

A thickset, red-faced matron in an apron charged screaming from the kitchen and came hurtling at Fitch, clutching a cleaver high above her head, her eyes rolling in the sockets, her screams not screams but a continuous siren-like wail so piercing Fitch winced at the screechy rawness of it.

Betty at nine, he thought.

Fitch spared a glance across the bar and saw the barkeep mouth *Mum?* as she came on. Fitch slid from the barstool, reaching for his pistol and turning to face the woman now almost upon him, her jaw forced open so wide it had unhinged and distended, her mouth a maw of yellowed teeth and lolling tongue. Suddenly, Hargrave was standing to his front, a burly, broad-shouldered wall blocking her path.

Hargrave stepped deftly inside the arc of the cleaver as the woman brought it down. He drove forward with his arm extended like a rugby fend, taking hold of her throat with one hand while grasping her wrist with the other. He dug in with his thick fingers and thumb around her neck until they disappeared in the folds and dewlaps under her chin. Then squeezing and crushing and pull-

ing her trachea loose from the cartilage like a plumber yanking an old pipe from a wall, he brought her scream to a glottal, gurgling stop.

Hargrave let go of the big woman and allowed her to fall to the floor with a heavy-sack thud. His thick handlebar mustache twitching with agitation, Hargrave stood somberly over the body, slowly shaking his head. The unnatural suddenness and savagery of her attack had dumbfounded him. Hargrave was no stranger to combat, but this wasn't a combat zone. This was a pub in Leeds. This was somebody's mum.

"Nah, man," Hargrave said. "Nah."

Fitch, calm as he was always calm once a fight had started, turned to the shock-stricken barkeep on the other side of the bar, finished drawing the silenced Makarov from the shoulder holster under his jacket, and shot the man twice to the body then once to the head. He did it all quickly, smoothly, as if it was the most natural thing in the world. The popping of the gun was loud, silencer or not, and the barkeep dropped to the floor, the shelf of his chin catching the edge of the bar top on the way down with a sharp, neck-breaking crack.

Fitch leaned over the bar to make sure of his man, as he had been trained. The body had rolled onto its back. He found the dead man's eyes disconcerting.

They always look so surprised, he thought.

Fitch turned away and saw Hargrave still standing over the body of the cook, the barkeep's mother. Holding his pistol loosely at his side, Fitch crossed to Hargrave, tapped the big man on the shoulder, and ushered him aside.

Once Hargrave was out of the way, Fitch emptied the rest of the magazine into the woman's head. He removed the magazine, took another from the inside pocket of his sports jacket, and reloaded, debating whether to shoot her again. The enemy could reanimate fresh corpses if enough of the brain was still intact, making for some nasty surprises in the past, but after a moment, Fitch decided against it. This one's head looked properly obliterated.

"This is not KGB," Hargrave said simply. He gazed pointedly down at the woman's body. "She was not KGB. And no one said anything about slotting civilians."

"KGB? Is that what M-I5 told you?" Fitch gave a rueful shake of his head and holstered his pistol. "You were briefed this morning to expect the unexpected, Sergeant Major. She—this—was the unexpected part." Fitch walked behind the bar, stepping gingerly over the barkeep's body, opened the register, and started scooping up notes and stuffing them in pockets. He took up his short-brim fedora from the bar and walked around to the entrance to prop the door with a chair.

Fitch saw Hargrave appeared immobilized, which sometimes happened to those new to the mission when the gibbering idiot-child truth of things revealed itself. Fitch had been frozen in that same door early on, but there was no time for it now.

Fitch said, "You have orders, yes?"

Hargrave looked up, nodded dolefully.

"Then obey those orders. There are matters to attend. Help me frame the scene."

"No time for a proper job," Hargrave said, surveying the pub.

"We only need to clear the space visible from the outside," Fitch said. "Nothing that can be seen from the windows or the door."

They worked quickly. Hargrave took the cook by the ankles and dragged the body to the kitchen, leaving the barkeep's body safe from sight behind the bar. Fitch was nervous but not showing it. Matters could escalate if civilians came by right now and spotted something amiss. In the event of witnesses, steps would be taken to contain the situation. Containment was key. Finch knew from bitter experience what some of those steps might be.

Leeds would bleed.

2: HARROGATE

Before they left, Fitch used the pub's pay telephone to call his man at Thames House to arrange for a new car. The Austin was compromised. They needed a new car. With his near-eidetic memory, his actor's memory, Fitch had maps in his head encompassing London, Leeds, Lockerbie, Glasgow, and Clyde, and knew the location of every MI-5 safehouse along or near the route.

Fitch considered and disregarded the safehouse in Leeds. They had been seen entering the pub. Local authorities could be a problem. So instead he directed MI-5 to a dot on the map north of Harrogate, where they would make the swap. The MI-5 man thought Fitch and Hargrave were after Russians and wished him good hunting.

Fitch hung up, shook his head. Russians. He wished they were after Russians.

When he got in the car, Fitch saw how tightly Hargrave's hands gripped the wheel, noted the muscles working in his jaw. Fitch gave directions, taking them the roundabout way to avoid traffic and attention. When they were in the country, headed northeast to Harrogate, Fitch broke the silence.

"We've never given it a nickname or a codename, Hargrave. We just call it the enemy, all lowercase. Because of the chatter, you see. People always talk, even in our business." Fitch barked a cynical laugh. "Maybe especially in our business. If we gave it a name, the name could echo and spread. That must not happen."

"What is it, Fitch? What are we talking about here?"

"I'm not Shop, so I can't tell you what it is from a scientific standpoint, Hargrave, but I can tell you what it does: it can think, it can plan, it can read human minds—at least superficially. It can take people over and make them do terrible things—simple terrible things, really, nothing complicated: walk, run, hit, bite, choke, stomp. It can hold and use basic hand weapons—as you saw—but not guns, nothing involving dexterity. It can make a Betty speak but not very well."

"A Betty?"

"A *Betty*. Someone taken—" Fitch stopped, corrected: "A human female taken over. For some reason, it prefers women. More suitable brain chemistry, maybe. We don't know. It can and will use men. Males are *Zekes*."

"Aircraft codenames from the war," Hargrave said.

Fitch nodded. "For whatever reason, it never takes children. Some adults it apparently can't use at all, like us. Something about our brain wave patterns and body chemistry. I don't know. Like I said, I'm not Shop."

"So we're immune," Hargrave said.

"So they tell me," Fitch said. He lit a cigarette and went on. "It gets even worse, you know. Sometimes the dead won't stay dead. That's what it did in Paraguay. They all came alive in Paraguay. It'll use them, if they're fresh, with a nervous system still intact. Dead or alive, such people are called *Taken*."

"The woman in the pub."

"I had to make sure she stayed down, yes."

Fitch continued. "Sometimes it employs a more subtle approach. It gets inside minds, invades dreams, becomes that little whispering voice nudging them along to *do* for it in some way, vex a problem or escalate a crisis. Such people are *Touched*."

"Bettys and Zekes, Taken and Touched." Hargrave shook his head. "I don't believe in devils, Fitch. Or men from Mars, neither. None of that."

Fitch said, "Back at The Shop, Dix called it an *extra-dimensional extrusion*. Before you ask, no. I have no idea what that means. I was an actor before all this, Hargrave. Actors only pretend. We don't actually *know* anything."

"What does it want?" Hargrave said.

Fitch paused, looked out the passenger window at the wooded landscape, said, "Us dead." After a moment, Fitch shook his head ruefully. "No, wait, sorry, that's too flip. You asked a serious question, an important question. We think it wants to nudge us into war, Hargrave. Set things in motion. Blow up the world."

"Can it be killed?" Hargrave said, his gray, expressionless eyes never wavering from the road.

"Very smart people have some ideas along those lines. You'll meet some of them. Killing it would be nice but killing it and stopping it give the same result. Those at the top don't know if it can be killed but do think it can be stopped, possibly captured and imprisoned. I believe them."

"You've said it speaks. You've spoken to it?" Hargrave said.

Fitch nodded. His lips were compressed almost to a grimace.

"What did it say?"

"It said, 'Pretty, pretty Elise waiting for you all day.'" Fitch took a last drag from his cigarette, pitched it out the window.

Hargrave shook his head uncomprehendingly. "Elise?"

"Elise was my wife," Fitch said. He kept his voice flat, without intonation, as if reading aloud a weather report. "It took my wife and murdered my son and waited for me at the door of our flat, holding up my little boy's head in both hands. Like a present."

Hargrave said, "'Angin shite, man."

"Go west at the intersection at Pateley Bridge," Fitch said. "I'll tell you when.

There'll be a farm road on the right. Should be a cottage on the left 200 meters in. Based on location, I'm guessing gamekeeper's cottage, something of that sort. Look for it. There won't be a light. Stop short about thirty meters. We'll make the approach on foot."

"Egress?"

Fitch said, "Only one way in or out. The road dead-ends in the moors."

"This thing, how powerful is it? How many can it take at one time?"

"I've seen it take dozens." Fitch scowled at the memory of that souk in Morocco two years before, when the crowded marketplace had erupted into chaos, and all but he and a few children had been taken all at once. Escaping, Fitch had run down a taken friend he had been using as cover, the journalist Barbara Dane, breaking her back under the wheels of his Land Rover and leaving her writhing in the sand.

Like a bug, Fitch thought. She had been screeching too, screeching his name in the enemy's voice: guttural, mocking.

"Long guns in the boot," Fitch said, forcing himself back to the here and now. "You stand overwatch while I take the door. You've got the SLR. It's modified as an automatic but—"

Hargrave cut him off. "It likes to jam on automatic, yes. I know the model, Fitch. I was on the team what tested it in the field."

"Headshots," Fitch said.

"Always," Hargrave replied.

The lights were out inside the cottage. One car was parked to the side, another in the front a few feet from the porch. As he approached, Fitch swept the beam from his flashlight across the front and saw the sturdy, rough-hewn door was ajar. Fitch grunted softly, handed his flashlight off to Hargrave, and unslung his shotgun, a refurbished Winchester 1897 he preferred for close work because of its slamfire capability that allowed him to keep the trigger pulled and shoot rapid-fire when he slammed the pump. The cottage was small. If the enemy was inside, this would be close work.

The sharp crack of a shot rang out, and Fitch could feel the breeze of a bullet as it sang by his ear. Fitch had time to think *This is new* before Hargrave shoved him to the ground, fired a short burst from his SLR, and threw himself down beside Fitch. The two low-crawled through the sticky black mud to the car on the side of the house and crouched together for cover. Glass shattered as two more shots were fired through the car window above their heads.

Pressed beside him, Hargrave hissed, "The shotgun! Give it!"

Taking the shotgun, Hargrave edged around Fitch and worked his way to the rear of the car closest to the door, rose to a crouch, and fired two blasts at an angle through the cottage side window. Fast for a man his size, Hargrave rushed to the door, kicked it open, and charged inside. The shotgun boomed once, twice. Furniture crashed. Shouting. Hargrave cursing. More shooting.

Now up and moving, Fitch scooped up the flashlight Hargrave had dropped on their mad scramble for cover and went inside, Makarov drawn and at high-ready. He called Hargrave's name.

"We're clear," Hargrave said, his voice muffled by the thick walls.

The beam of Fitch's flashlight fell upon the main room of the cottage. Fitch did a sweep of the room, stepping around a broken chair and the overturned table. Playing cards littered the floor. In front of the ancient stone fireplace, he found a poker lying on the hearth, the blood on its tip and shank still wet. Fitch looked up when Hargrave called his name from the adjoining room, the bedroom.

From the far corner of the unlit bedroom, Hargrave said, "Find the light, would you?"

Fitch found the switch by the door and turned on the light, a naked bulb hanging by a short length of wire from the low timber ceiling.

Fitch saw a man's naked, spread-eagled body nailed to the wall on the far side of the room facing the door, close enough for Hargrave to brush against in the dark. The man's midsection had been split vertically from sternum to crotch, spilling its bowels. For reasons of its own, the enemy had used blood as paint to paint a crude, ragged square within a large, smeary circle on the wall, framing the mutilated body like a ghastly exhibit. Fitch noted the way the body was arranged, all of it somehow familiar. He knew this from somewhere. The association nagged.

Hargrave was standing over the body of the shooter lying below the window from which it had been firing. The expensively tailored suit gave its owner away as a Security Service agent, one of the two who had brought the swap car to the safehouse. Its right hand still gripped an antique short-barreled Webley revolver, possibly an heirloom from the Great War stowed and forgotten and overlooked when MI-5 took possession of the place. Hargrave had repeatedly shot the agent at close range with the shotgun. Brain matter and blood covered the wall and the window in a grotesque abstraction.

"I thought it couldn't use guns," Hargrave said.

Fitch shrugged. "This is a first, old boy. Had I known, I would've told you."

"At some point soon, *old boy*, you must tell me everything," Hargrave said. "I'm no good if I don't know particulars."

"You'll know what you need to know, Hargrave. It's better that way."

"Soldiers soldier, is that it?"

Fitch said, "This business of ours gets complicated. Obedience simplifies."

"Blind obedience?"

Usually outwardly calm, Fitch stepped close to Hargrave and looked up to peer directly into the older man's eyes. Fitch's usually amiable features were hardened into an angry mask.

"Very well, Hargrave, we face—for lack of a better word—a *being* able to warp time and bend space. It shoots a beam of some kind from the moon—from the bloody *moon*, Hargrave—that takes good people and turns them into rabid animals and then burns their brains out. It means to murder the world. So yes, you clod, you brick, we demand obedience, or we're finished, all of

us, everything, everyone."

They stared at each other, both hard men but neither so inured to violence they couldn't recoil from atrocity or balk at the *wrongness* of the mind that devised it. They were still very much human.

"The Vitruvian Man," Hargrave said.

"The what?" Fitch was nonplussed.

Hargrave turned and nodded at the body on the wall. "I saw how you looked at that poor sod. He's been made to look like da Vinci's Vitruvian Man, the Canon of Proportions, the drawing. You've probably seen it dozens of times."

Fitch studied the body on the wall. "So what's the point of it? Is it making a joke?" Fitch screwed up his nose, his mouth twisted with distaste. "It likes its little jokes."

Hargrave shook his head. "It had to wait. Perhaps it grew bored."

Silence hung between them.

"Apologies, Hargrave," Fitch said.

"None necessary." Hargrave drew himself up. His manner was formal. "I am soldier to the bone, Fitch, and I know how to take orders. But this..." Hargrave paused, collected himself. "This is strange country. I need to know more to be effective."

"We'll see. First things first." Fitch gestured at the body nailed to the wall. "First, we take this man down. No one needs to see this."

Perceptive to shifts in moods, Fitch caught Hargrave's expression.

"Problem?"

"Something you said. You said the moon, Fitch. You said it was shooting mind control beams from the moon."

Fitch gave a tight-lipped smile. "Yes, Hargrave, aliens on the moon. Mind control rays."

"*Yer daft apeth, talkin' bobbins*," Hargrave said.

Fitch gave him a puzzled look.

"Something my mum would say, Fitch. This is some unbelievable shite. It sounds even worse when you say it out loud."

"The absurdity of it saves us, Hargrave. Never believe differently."

After they finished pulling the body from the wall, the two men laid the corpse out gently. Hargrave covered the body in a wool blanket he found on the floor by the broken chair in the main room. Both men were smeared and spattered with blood and mud but went outside and washed it off under the hand pump behind the cottage as best they could and donned their trench coats to cover the rest.

Fitch mourned his hat, which had been trampled and ruined in the mud during the gunfight. The fedora had been out-of-fashion, but old-fashioned had been good, since wearing it—along with the black half-framed horn-rimmed glasses he didn't need—lent a sense of substance and maturity to the persona he usually wanted to project. Fitch's tall, lean, muscular frame, boyish good looks, and wavy blond hair worked against him. People remembered him when what he usually most needed was to be quickly glanced at and just as quickly passed over and forgotten.

Since their swap car was now riddled with holes, Fitch decided to use the Security Service S2 Bentley instead. Hargrave found the keys in the pockets of the body of the man he had shot. Getting in, Fitch spotted the bulge in Hargrave's coat pocket as he slid behind the wheel and adjusted the seat to accommodate his legs.

"You took the Webley," Fitch said. "No point. I checked. It was empty."

Hargrave shrugged. "I found more cartridges when I went through his pockets."

"Sentimental, Hargrave?"

"You saw what those lads had? Little Walther PPKs, just like the movies. So no, Fitch. Not sentimental. Besides, I like the feel of it. It has a large grip. Fits my hand."

Hargrave started the Bentley. The big L-series V8 rumbled to life in a way that made Fitch think of a large jungle cat waking from a nap. Whatever its shortcomings, the Bentley had power and speed and, Fitch thought, *We have need of both*. He figured four hours to Clyde. Their window was narrow and closing.

"Straight-on?" Hargrave said, gunning the engine for emphasis. Fitch turned and saw Hargrave was smiling. It occurred to Fitch this was the first he had seen the big man smile. *Better to come at them smiling*, he thought, and grinned a little himself.

"Petrol?" he asked.

Hargrave glanced at the gauge. "Plenty."

"Straight on, then," Fitch said. "Whatever happens, we fight our way through and keep going."

3: CLYDE

A woman in nightclothes stood by the side of the road in Calthwaite and flung a young girl of four or five—probably her daughter—in front of the Bentley as Hargrave and Fitch were coming through. But the Taken thing's timing was off, and it threw the girl too early, giving Hargrave time to swerve. When he swerved, Hargrave didn't turn away. Instead, he went off the road and turned into the Betty, hitting her a glancing blow with the bumper like English on a billiard ball and sending her flying into the woods. Hargrave had barely missed hitting the girl, who was now on her hands and knees and crying in the road. Hargrave saw her, knew she was there, and slowed but didn't stop, wasn't stopping, and Fitch was leaning into Hargrave and shouting, "Stop the car! Stop the car! Stop!" inches from his ear.

"We can't stop, Fitch! You said not to stop!"

"We're not leaving the girl!"

"Not our mission, Fitch! Not our mission!"

"It's a judgement call. I'm making it. Stop the bloody car."

Fitch opened the passenger door, bolted from the still-moving Bentley, and sprinted back to the girl. When he reached her, he wrapped her in his coat because she was clearly going into shock. He was picking her up and readying to move by the time Hargrave had turned around and returned, bathing them in the Bentley's blinding headlights.

Hargrave was shouting something but Fitch couldn't make it out. That's when he heard the dragging scrape of shuffling steps on pavement, the keening moans and wails of the Taken that always—to him—had the quality of a lament. Fitch, in that moment of uncanny calm he always felt at times like this, figured out what Hargrave had been shouting. *A trap*, he thought. *Because of course.*

In the starkly bright wash of the headlights, Fitch could see them coming, blood black-smeared on their clothes, spattered on their wild-eyed, open-mouthed faces. Fitch counted ten, with more shadowy forms looming on the periphery, which meant more on the way.

After that, Fitch's perceptions became jumbled and confused. He heard the rev of the motor and the squeal of tires and felt the rush of air on his face as the Bentley drove by and hurtled through the bunch coming forward on the road, scattering them, hitting them, or running them over with the sickening crunch of bone and the wet-slap thump of meat. Fitch heard the squeal of brakes as Hargrave stopped and then backed up until even with Fitch and the girl.

Fitch had time to open the rear driver's side door and toss the child inside just before the remnants of the mob were upon him, flailing at him with garden tools, grabbing, biting, tearing at his clothes, trying to pull him down like wild dogs on a deer.

Turning and twisting like the dancer he had once been, Fitch managed to break free and fire his gun into the mass of clawing, lurching bodies but without accuracy or effect. He saw the pitchfork propelled like a pike out of the phalanx of massed bodies to his front and was quick enough to twist his body yet still caught two of the tines deep in his side, the force of the thrust slamming him back against the Bentley. He spotted the flat of a shovel coming at his head from his left but was fixed in place by the long, thin tines of pitchfork like a moth on a pin and felt a tremendous blow just above his left temple. A bright white light flashed behind his eyes in a sudden sunburst.

Fitch heard gunshots as if in the distance and barely felt it when Hargrave threw him onto the backseat of the Bentley with the girl. Time skewed. Fitch was six again, sinking to the bottom of the family swimming pool on his father's Los Angeles estate, his place of refuge when his parents would bicker and fight. He would let himself sink to the bottom where it was quiet and warm, weightless and safe. In the here and now, part of him—the part not yet shutting down—wondered if he might be dying.

No, he thought. *Not yet. Not now.*

With a drowning man's desperation, Fitch swam slowly back to consciousness, finally jerked himself awake, grabbed the back of the seat and pulled himself forward with enormous effort until his mouth was a few inches from Hargrave's ear. "*A Lady without Passport!*"

"Jaysus!" Hargrave cried, so startled he nearly lost control of the Bentley.

"Say it at the gate, say *A Lady without Passport!* Say it at the gate or they won't let us through. End of the mission, end of everything. *A Lady without Passport!*"

"Right," Hargrave said, composing himself. "Got it: *A Lady without Passport.*"

Fitch nodded and felt a moment of groggy confusion, that sense of something missing, and when he reached his hand out on the backseat he realized the something missing was the girl they had saved in Calthwaite. His coat was there, wadded into an encrusted, blood-caked ball, but she was gone.

Fitch shouted or tried to shout to Hargrave. "The girl! Where's the girl?" but it came out weakly, a barely audible whisper.

Hargrave had picked up the alarm of his tone and guessed at its meaning. He looked over his shoulder, shouted, "The girl is alive, Fitch! She's alive!"

"Where?" Fitch said.

"I dropped her off at Kirklands on the way. It isn't a hospital-hospital but they have doctors there. I carried her inside, gave her to the first nurse I saw, told her I had found her wandering by the side of the road, and got out fast as I could. I know how it looked. The girl had blood all over her. I've got blood all over me. We're running out of time."

Looking down, Fitch saw Hargrave had tried to pack the wounds in his side with wads of cloth cut from Fitch's shirt but blood was everywhere. He was covered with it, sticky with it, and wondered how much more he could lose. The pain in his side flared molten hot and a wave of nausea came over him with such intensity he thought he would vomit. His head was a drum, *rataplin, rataplan.*

They were expected. The RNP guards at the gate to Clyde HMNB were part of the mission or so heavily bribed or darkly blackmailed the distinction didn't matter.

Fitch faded in and out. He heard Hargrave's gruff, rumbling Sergeant Major voice, the bark of orders, and felt jostled and manhandled as he was taken from the Bentley and placed on a gurney. It was raining. The rain cooled his burning forehead. Maudlin, delirious, Fitch felt so grateful he could cry, and finally allowed himself to pass out.

4: HMS *DALL*

The first thing Fitch saw upon waking was Hargrave hovering over him, stretching his lips and baring his teeth in a semblance of a smile.

"Stop hurting your face, Hargrave." Fitch said. His throat was dry. It hurt to talk. He tried to sit up, failed, and tried again, this time successfully. Hargrave gave him water through a straw, which he sucked greedily. Waving off Hargrave, Fitch winced from the pain in his head, lancing through his side, radiating in pulse-like waves throughout his body. It took him a moment to gather himself, steel against it.

Fitch surveyed his surroundings: arching steel bulkheads around him, cables and pipes and too-bright fluorescent lights overhead, the stale sweat smell of men in close quarters. He spotted a short, ferret-faced medical orderly standing off to the side near the foot of his cot, pressing a clipboard to his chest, nervously shifting his weight. The presence of an enlisted medic made sense since submarines rarely engaged physicians. He also noticed the young man was wearing a ring on the ring finger of his right hand, the hand holding the clipboard.

Not a wedding ring. An ivory cameo of a woman's profile. He recognized the profile. Her profile. The Lady.

He's one of ours, Fitch thought. He felt a measure of relief, even reassurance. Field agents were trained to operate without support of any kind because there often wasn't support of any kind, but Fitch was grateful there was evidence of it here. It was like evidence of God. They weren't alone.

"What do I call you?" Fitch said to the orderly.

"Rupert, sir."

"*Lady of the Tropics?*"

Rupert screwed his face in concentration and then gave the countersign. "Manon DeVargnes," he said, pronouncing it 'Dee-varney.' "Not her best work, I'm afraid."

"I blame Ben Hecht," Fitch said. "My mother knew Hecht, said in those days he was knocking off a screenplay a week and a fifth a night."

Both men ignored Hargrave's bemused expression.

"Your assessment, please." Fitch kept his voice casual but had no illusions. Nothing would be allowed to endanger the mission, least of all the weakness of his own fragile body. It could go badly for him if he couldn't go on. A runner who couldn't run was of no use to anyone, and knew too much to keep alive.

Rupert nodded, stepped close to the cot and produced the clipboard. When Rupert read from it, his vaguely Lancashire accent nearly disappeared.

Training flaw, Fitch thought. *He's forgetting himself, blowing his cover. I'll correct it if*

I live.

Rupert drew himself up. "You were treated by a Royal Navy doctor who asked for and received permission to leave before you woke up; that is, if you woke up, given the concussion. The doctor said he wanted nothing to do with this sneaky-beaky shite. His words. You were mumbling, largely incoherent but some came through. I think he was worried about being compromised, made privy to information he was not supposed to have."

"Smart man," Fitch said. "Get on with it, please."

"You've been adjudged fit to continue, Mr. Fitch."

Fitch nodded, keeping his face impassive so he wouldn't betray the relief he felt.

"Your left shoulder was dislocated," Rupert went on. "That has been addressed. You've suffered a concussion, as I noted earlier. Given you're up and awake, it is unlikely you've taken serious brain injury, but the doctor couldn't commit one way or the other. You also have two cracked ribs, a perforated kidney and—*had*—a partially collapsed lung, but it's been patched and stabilized. There might be other internal injuries, but we can't know without x-rays. You've experienced severe blood loss, too, meaning possible organ damage. You'll be given antibiotics to ward off infection, but if there is infection…" Rupert trailed off, raising both of his shoulders in an exaggerated shrug.

Fitch turned to Rupert. "Time to insertion?"

"Sixty hours. I'll notify the Captain you're ready to be moved."

Fitch and Hargrave were allocated an enlisted bunkroom meant to sleep eight, a wealth of space on a submarine. Rupert, checking in, brought food from the mess. After eating, Fitch craved a cigarette but ignored the craving since he knew breathable air was at a premium on a British Porpoise class. Air came from the outside. He didn't want to sully the air.

"What is it with your man Rupert?" Hargrave said.

Hargrave was in the small open space available in the middle of the bunkroom, stripped down to his undershirt and boxer shorts, and prone on deck doing regulation pushups with metronomic regularity.

"Elaborate, please," Fitch said. With an effort, he swiveled to a sitting position on the edge of his bunk, leaning forward to avoid hitting his head on the upper. His head was a balloon.

"The way Rupert looks at you," Hargrave said, pausing his exercise. "The way he talks about you, practically in whispers. Lad's star-struck. He told me you fought off a dozen of those things in Rome last year by yourself, without a gun."

"People exaggerate, Hargrave, even in our business."

"So what's the truth of it, then?"

"There were five, two Zekes and three Bettys, and I had a very big gun." Fitch didn't mention the fight took place deep in the catacombs, where he was desperate, alone and afraid in the absolute dark, his flashlight gone, knocked out of his hand, with a screeching Betty tearing at him and clawing at his eyes and throat, his ears bleeding from the percussive reverberation of the shots he had to fire by sound and feel.

Fitch shook off the memory and forced a smile. "Did my fan club bring our kit?"

"Over there," Hargrave said, nodding his head in the direction of the racks closest to the bulkhead door.

They opened the heavy sea bags and laid out the contents: weapons, wardrobe, identification, and the usual wallet and pocket litter, as well as a good enough mix of currencies to sell Fitch's Nicky Desmond bona fides.

Fitch was gratified to find the long blond wig he had asked for. He wore his natural hair groomed short, a practical necessity when fighting at close quarters with the Taken, but he was going Mod to this party and needed long hair to make the persona work. The wig would also serve to cover some of the swelling and bruising. Fitch had asked for makeup too, which was thankfully in the bag. Makeup would cover the rest.

"So let me tell the tale, Hargrave: my name is Nicky Desmond. I call myself a star although it's been what? Five years since I've had a decent part. I grew up in show business and starred in a popular western show as a kid. My one lead role as an adult was in a low-budget disaster of a teen dance musical called *Rock Baby Rock,* but—thanks to my parents—I happen to be rich, so my face and name still show up in gossip rags. I bribe editors and publishers to keep it there."

"So who am I, then?" Hargrave said.

"I don't know, Hargrave. My body-guard? My butler? Loyal retainer? Does it matter? I'm rich, remember? People with money always have people."

"Bodyguard works."

Fitch went on. "I'm known for being known, famous for being famous. I'm seen at lots of parties and know lots of people. I drink too much and talk too much and may or may not have a drug problem—but hey, who doesn't?" Fitch caught Hargrave's expression, stopped short, raised an eyebrow. "What is it, Hargrave?"

Hargrave had been doing a weapons check, disassembling, cleaning, and testing the functionality of their pistols from the sea bag, a 9mm Browning Hi-Power and a Colt Commander in 45 ACP, which had been Fitch's choice. The expression on Hargrave's face struck Fitch as sad and sympathetic, Fitch decided, and it smacked of pity, and he didn't like pity. Never wanted it, never asked for it. Despised it.

"Out with it, man," Fitch said. "I can order you."

"All right, then," Hargrave said, putting the Hi-Power's slide aside. "That isn't a cover, Fitch. That's you. You're describing yourself, aren't you? Who you were before all this?"

"I am who I need to be, Hargrave. I know Nicky. Nicky's a weak, dissipated boy-man who never went from Nicky to Nick and never learned how to handle hardship or grief, so now he loses himself in sex and alcohol and drugs. Tragic, really."

"So you play yourself playing yourself playing yourself, is that about right?" Hargrave said.

"I believe that covers it, yes."

"Space aliens on the moon, Fitch," Hargrave said. "Mind control beams from another dimension."

The two men looked at each other and then burst out laughing, making Fitch grimace with pain from his cracked ribs, making Hargrave laugh even more.

5: THE FOUNDRY

Topside, turned away from the sharp, biting wind, Fitch and Hargrave waited for the *Dall's* sailors to inflate the motorized rubber dinghy the two men would use to reach the southern tip of Manhattan, a few miles north from their current position. From there, it was three miles by alley and street to the Decker Building on Union Square.

Fitch didn't know why Liberty Island was chosen as the insertion point for the New York end of the operation. He suspected the British Navy, so proud of its silent running capabilities, insisted on such a needlessly risky drop point as a cheeky swipe at the Americans, and *oh, how these service rivalries among high-level brass grate on the nerves*, Fitch thought. They're still schoolboys on a field playing a game, my side your side, us and them. The Russians and Chinese were no better, even though some of them, a very select and secretive few, had also been briefed on The Director's mission. He had worked with their field agents, liked them, and admired their focus on the objective to the exclusion of all else. But their superiors?

Like all military men, Fitch thought. So stodgy and rigid in their thinking, so narrow in their focus. The Director was right to despise them.

Rupert saw them off, giving Fitch and Hargrave a brief, furtive wave as they got underway, Hargrave in the rear with the oars, Fitch in front with a compass to guide. Fitch worried for the orderly since the boy, so inexperienced at tradecraft, had possibly broken cover. Someone at the top might perceive a containment threat and decide Rupert was a problem to be solved.

Fitch hoped not. He liked Rupert.

After they reached the landfill gravel beach, the two men dragged the dinghy to the treeline east of the ferry terminal and started fast-walking through The Battery. Moving through the area south of the park, Fitch could hear steps, voices raised in argument, a man and a woman, but he hadn't yet registered a threat, and it bothered him because he knew the threat was imminent, waiting.

"Come out and fight," Fitch said softly.

Hargrave reached out and put the flat of his hand against Fitch's forehead, an almost paternal gesture coming from one so reserved. "You're burning up, Fitch. That infection Rupert warned you about—"

"—doesn't matter. Nothing matters but the mission. You know this."

"Yes, Fitch, I know this. If we make contact with the enemy, I'll come to you, right? Don't displace."

"I can go on," Fitch said. "Let's finish this."

They stepped onto Broadway and headed north. They were in the financial district at three in the morning, so traffic was comparatively light. Fitch knew the bustle would thicken and quicken the closer they came to midtown, but for now the going was easy. Fitch watched Hargrave, taking long, loping Infantry strides that seemed casual yet ate the distance like an inexorable machine. Fitch found himself hard-pressed to keep up, but he managed. *Movement is life*, he thought.

Hargrave heard it first. The big man paused, held up his hand at Fitch, his head canted quizzically to the side, listening, and then Fitch heard it himself, at first thinking it was a siren, a faint long-eeeeEEEEEE! Getting louder, closer, coming from above. Fitch started to look up when Hargrave shoved him hard enough to send him staggering back, the falling body a blur until it slammed with a thudding crunch face-first into the sidewalk where Fitch had been standing a few moments before, splattering blood and brain and bits of bone in a spatter-paint starfish pattern extending nearly to his feet.

It's bombing us with people, Fitch thought, had time to think, but then Hargrave was grabbing Fitch by the arm and pulling him along. "Incoming, mate! Move! Move or die!"

Another Taken body hit concrete several feet away, plunging through the canvas awning above the sidewalk just before impact and narrowly missing a man and woman, a couple, the shock of it causing them to fall together. The woman sat up and screamed as shrill and high-pitched as any wail of the Taken. For all Fitch knew, she might *be* Taken. *It would be*, he thought, *a logical next move.*

A third body fell a few moments later, this one even closer, a Betty. Fitch didn't hear the scream. Maybe she didn't scream. She fell at his feet with a wet blanket slap in a splash of blood, the height of the fall reducing her pulverized body to a steaming pile of scrambled hash on the sidewalk. Fitch could just make out a maid's uniform.

Fitch allowed Hargrave to jerk him away and drag him from the scene. They started running, with Hargrave grasping Fitch by the crook of the elbow to keep him up, propel him forward, cutting through the first alley without streetlights off Grand on their way to Bowery, figuring the enemy couldn't hit what it couldn't see. They sought darkness like a friend.

Going through the alley, Fitch caught sight of shadowy figures moving ahead in the cluttered, garbage-strewn terrain and started to reach for his Colt, but Hargrave stayed his hand. Taken attacked on sight. Whatever was moving in the alley wasn't attacking.

Fitch and Hargrave passed through warily. One of those Fitch had felt watching detached himself from the wall and moved to intercept. Two others rose from the shadows to flank him, forming a wedge. The light was dim, but Fitch could see the man's hands. To read intentions, Fitch always looked first at the hands. He guessed their weapons were knives because they seemed to be seeking to close the distance.

The tall, twitchy, sallow one at the head of the wedge opened his mouth to speak, but Hargrave was having none of it.

"You lot don't want a bite out of us," Hargrave said. "Me and my friend here have had quite the night, and I'm short on patience—at the end of it, you might say. You make a go of it, and all of you die. I mean it. I'll hurt you first, and then I'll make sure to end you before we go, no messin' about."

The three men, all of them feral junkies gaunt from malnutrition, filthy from the street, hungry for a fix, exchanged hesitant, nervous glances, and came to a silent agreement. They fell back, stepping aside and fading into the gloom. Fitch and Hargrave hurried on.

Coming out of the alley onto Houston, Hargrave said, "Enough of this, mate. We're cadging a ride."

Fitch caught Hargrave's expression. "What is it?"

Hargrave took Fitch gently by the shoulders and steered him against the wall of a tobacco shop. "I'll find us a ride, Fitch. Don't go anywhere."

After Hargrave left, Fitch remained standing, focusing on staying alert, on his feet, in the here and now.

"Mister? Are you okay? Are you hurt?"

Fitch looked up and saw a young black woman peering up at him, little more than a teenager. He read the concern on her face and realized how he must look. The area was well-lit. She could see his sickly face, his struggle to stay on his feet, the blood on his coat. It occurred to Fitch he was marked and anyone close to him was in terrible danger.

"You're in terrible danger," he said.

Her face registered alarm, then fear.

"This blood isn't mine," he said.

She started to back away.

"Run," he said.

She ran.

Fitch heard the blare of a car horn, saw Hargrove behind the wheel of a red Ford Falcon waiting at the curb. He staggered to the passenger side and slid inside and closed the door. He tilted his head back and closed his eyes as Hargrave drove the last two kilometers, parking the stolen Ford alongside Union Park. When they got out, Fitch found his second wind, and they walked on foot the remaining distance, traversing the northeastern quadrant of the square to the Decker Building, pausing to ditch their bloodstained coats in the bushes along the way. The lobby doors to the building were unlocked as Fitch had suspected they would be. No one in the lobby, either.

Fitch saw Hargrave standing in front of the elevators, eyeing the closed doors with suspicion.

"It can't get to us in this place, Hargrave. Trust me on this."

They took the elevator to the 6th floor and stepped into what The Artist called The Foundry and began wending their way through the crowd, with Fitch counting at least two dozen people visible in the dim purple light, milling clusters and couples and cliques coalescing, falling away. The music was loud but not so loud it drowned the murmur and buzz of conversation and not so good it tempted people to stop talking and listen.

Fitch knew people here, was known, so he ignored the nearly overwhelming nausea and now all-embracing pain he was feeling. By effort of will, he made himself method-act *Rock Baby Rock* star Nicky Desmond into existence: feverish, pale, bleary-eyed and staggering not because he had been stabbed and beaten by a Taken mob a few days before on a nowhere road in England, but because rich and dissolute playboy Nicky Desmond was killing himself with drugs and booze and ennui, the poor has-been bastard.

Still in character, Fitch ran into an actress he knew, whose name his head hurt too much to remember, whose face lit up when she saw him, who said she had a problem she knew only Nicky of all people would understand. She complained she wasn't getting a part (sad frown drama face), worried she was typecast, and Nicky in return could only sympathize, darling. No one in the business likes being typecast or pigeonholed, but there it is. People want a certain flavor. You become that certain flavor and you stay that flavor forever and they tire of it eventually, tire of you: same-old, same-old. It's like a hell, really. Other people are a hell. Hell is other people. Who said that? I did. Liar.

At some point, Fitch and Hargrave had become separated. Scanning the room, Fitch spotted Hargrave engaged with Candy, The Artist's third in command. She had taken Hargrave by the upper arm and had locked eyes with him in a way that signaled her absolute attention to whatever he might be saying. Fitch had partnered with Candy before, on that precious metals deal on the docks with the Chinese envoy pretending to be a Tong lieutenant, and felt a tinge of regret Candy no longer worked in the field. Nobody better. In her way, Candy was as capable as Hargrave and nearly as ruthlessly calculating as Fitch himself.

Not for the first time, Fitch found himself amused (as no doubt The Artist was amused) knowing The Artist's famous Foundry was all so much avant-garde window dressing, existing solely to hide the mission and relay messages to a global network of ruthless agents and deadly assassins locked in a life-or-death struggle with a genocidal alien mind-monster from another dimension.

Absurdity saves us, he thought.

"Nicky! Nicky darling!" It was Jud, The Artist's second, easily one of the most physically flawless men Fitch had ever met, even in a cloistered milieu teeming with physically flawless demimondes and decadents. Jud weaved through the crowded studio and made his way to Fitch, who had assumed his Nicky Desmond face and was smiling broadly, showing off his even, white, immaculate teeth. The two men embraced.

"Message for The Artist," Fitch said to Jud, speaking low in the other man's ear.

"*Dishonored Lady*?" Jud said.

"Madeline Damien," Fitch said.

Jud whispered back, "Blood on your shoes. Yours?"

"Some of it," Fitch said. "We've had some trouble. Could be more on the way. We'll need an out." He broke the embrace. "Our friend throws quite the party," he said.

Jud nodded and laughed. "Oh, but doesn't he always?" He turned and gestured to Candy. "The Artist wants to see these two marvelous gentlemen. Would you?"

"I would," Candy said, and led Fitch and Hargrave to The Artist's office adjoining the studio. They were intercepted on the way by a slovenly, dark-eyed, frazzle-haired woman who sprang at them in a movement so jolting both Hargrave and Fitch reached for weapons, only checking the impulse when they saw she was human.

"Candy! Candy! You going to see The Man?" the woman was saying, her strident tone frantically demanding. "Tell him I'm here, okay? Tell him I'm waiting? He said he'd get back to me, but he hasn't gotten back to me. Tell him it's about the screenplay, *my* screenplay. Tell him!"

Fitch and Hargrave exchanged uneasy glances. The woman was charged with an erratic intensity that put Fitch on his guard and left him unnerved.

She's been touched, he thought. Fitch considered quietly killing the woman then and there and started forward but Candy caught his arm, came close, and whispered in his ear, "I know what you're thinking, lover, and no, she isn't. It's okay."

Candy broke from Fitch and turned to the woman. "I'll tell him, Valerie," she said soothingly. "I'll be back soon. Wait for me on the big couch. We'll talk, just us girls. I promise."

"Okay, okay, but you'll tell him, right?"

"Cross my heart," Candy said.

The Artist was seated behind his desk, the kaleidoscopic panorama of the New York skyline at night visible through the window behind him. The office itself was conventional, even staid, which Fitch considered more telling of the man than the crowded, amphetamine-charged chaos of his studio space. Given the spartan décor, Fitch figured few would notice the absence of a telephone on the desk or wonder at the composition of thin plaster-looking walls or the thin, ordinary-looking glass that still somehow managed to shut out all sounds emanating from the studio or the city outside.

The Artist was striking a thoughtful pose, cupping his chin in his hand, with his thin, angular face in profile, as if he was focused on an empty corner of the room. His right hand—the side closest to his visitors—was out of sight under the desk. Fitch guessed he was holding the Berretta Model 70 32ACP he favored so much. It lacked the punch Fitch preferred, but The Artist was an excellent shot, almost surgical in precision when engaging assassins, usually underworld hitmen whom the enemy paid through wire transfer via anonymous Swiss bank accounts. Of The Three, The Artist was least like his public persona. He was portrayed in mass media as an almost ethereal, fey, otherworldly figure looking down upon humanity from a deeply ironic, sardonically mocking Olympus.

Nothing touches this man, Fitch thought.

Without turning to face them, The Artist said, "*My Favorite Spy*?"

"Lily Dalbray," Fitch said. "She couldn't catch a break. I mean, Bob Hope as 'Peanuts White'? They never knew what they had when they had her."

"They knew," The Artist said, turning to face them. He glanced at Candy, who squeezed Hargrave's arm and walked by in a breeze smelling faintly of lemon grass and peppermint, closing the heavy door softly behind her. After she left, The Artist opened the right-hand drawer of his desk and put his pistol away.

"You have a message for me?"

"Campbell's Soup 1: Black Bean 44," Fitch said. He glanced at Hargrave, whose face was impassive and unreadable.

"So The Director, that impossible man, actually came through," The Artist said. "Building The Lady's device on a space movie set was brilliant, and I love him for it. I'll start work on the new transmission right away. When you see The Lady, tell her I'll need a week, maybe a few days more than a week. Integrating detailed logistical data into the work is no easy trick."

The Artist called all of his coded paintings 'transmissions,' which was, Fitch decided, completely accurate. The Artist's paintings *were* transmissions, the only means of communication The Director's people had found the enemy couldn't—for whatever reason—decipher. Technicians at The Shop had told Fitch the enemy was apparently stymied by art, especially abstractions, perhaps because the concept of art was alien to it, outside its understanding, but they could only guess. No one really knew why. They only knew The Artist's paintings worked as an effective communications channel when little else did, making the true nature of his paintings one of the

most closely held secrets in the organization. It was also a secret, Fitch suddenly realized, his new partner Hargrave wasn't cleared to know.

The Artist read the flare of alarm on Fitch's face and guessed its source. "There are no secrets between any of us in this room." He indicated Hargrave. "We are all of us friends here."

"Not all of us," Fitch said. "I think you've been compromised—"

"—That Valerie woman in the hall," Hargrave said. "She doesn't feel right."

"Finishing each other's thoughts is a sure sign you're a couple," The Artist said in his droll, whispery voice.

"We're not a couple," Hargrave said.

"You are partners in this thing of ours, which means you are closer than a couple ever gets." The Artist rose from his desk, approached Fitch, stared at him intently. "You're badly hurt, Nicky."

Hargrave said, "I don't know what's holding him up."

"I have an idea," The Artist said. "But to your point. We *have* been compromised, but this presents a greater quandary: we can't let it know we know. We'll just have to play along, see what happens." The Artist made a strangely affecting bird-in-flight gesture with his hands that made Fitch think of a magician releasing a dove.

Fitch was feeling faint again, discombobulated. Blood loss, he supposed. Fever. Maybe both. His surroundings had taken on a disembodied, dreamlike air. Even the pain he had been enduring seemed far-off. Fitch felt Hargrave come up behind him and leaned back gratefully against the bigger man for support. He could make out The Artist talking to Hargrave: "Take him out through the service entrance downstairs. A car is waiting. My people will take you to the airport, with my Cessna 411 ready to go. Candy will call ahead. A two-man medical team will be there when you arrive. They can treat Nicky on the way."

"On the way?" Hargrave said. "Where are we going?"

"Florida," The Artist said. "To see *her*, of course, The Lady, star of the show."

6: BIRD ISLAND

Fitch slipped into unconsciousness on the way to the airport. He woke up twice, when the blast of the twin propellers from the Cessna washed across his face as they wheeled his gurney to the plane, and then again when the plane landed roughly on Bird Island's temporary airstrip, a thin layer of concrete poured over the small island's marshy terrain. After that, Fitch felt a dark wave wash over him and knew nothing for a while.

He woke later in one of the guest bedrooms of a lakefront home. A clean suit was hanging from a hanger on a hook, his belongings on the top of a bureau, his holstered gun on the seat of the chair against the wall by the adjoining bathroom. He guessed it was warm outside, but the windows were open, and a large ceiling fan overhead circulated and cooled the air. He could hear the twitter of birds and the hum of insects outside.

Fitch got up slowly, sore all over, and saw himself in the mirror over the bureau. His head had been shaved to a prison camp burr, showing the stitches. His midsection was wrapped in fresh bandages to bind his ribs and protect the wounds in his side. Thinking about the fight on the road in Calthwaite made him think of the little girl. He hoped she was all right, poor thing. Tough break. He felt badly about killing her mum.

Fitch found a razor laid out for him in the bathroom and washed up. While he was getting dressed, he could hear voices in the house, muffled through the walls and floors: a deep, masculine voice he recognized as Hargrave's and another voice, a woman's voice, lilting and familiar, one he had known since childhood. He finished dressing, holstered his Colt, and went downstairs to join them. When he reached the bottom of the stairs, Fitch followed their voices until he found the two of them, Hargrave and The Lady herself, seated in the dining room, sharing breakfast. Both looked up and smiled. Fitch smiled back.

"Lady," Fitch said simply. It was what almost everyone in the organization called her: 'Lady' or 'The Lady.' Only those closest to her used her real name. Names could echo. Names could be dangerous.

"Garland," The Lady said, her smile widening to reveal her beautifully perfect teeth, addressing him by his own real first name—the only person who could since all others who had known it were dead now. She said, "You must be hungry, darling. Come join us."

Fitch smiled in return and strode forward, still smiling, and when he was close, within a few feet of her, his face frozen in a rictus grin, he drew his gun and pointed it at her head and squeezed the trigger as Fitch had been trained to do, as Fitch's muscle memory had told him to do, but nothing happened. He pointed the gun and pulled the trigger again and again. He heard clicks but nothing happened. Why hadn't the gun fired and why won't the gun fire and WHY IS THIS WITCH STILL ALIVE? She wasn't dead, and she was supposed to be dead, and this primitive monkey-made metal wasn't working, and why wasn't it working?

"Right, well," Fitch-thing said after a moment, placing the pistol carefully on the table and slowly raising its hands. "This is awkward." Fitch-thing turned to Hargrave. "Your work?"

"On the *Dall*," Hargrave said. He was standing now. He had his own gun out, the Webley revolver he had acquired at Harrogate.

"How long have you known?"

"That you weren't entirely you? Since Calthwaite, a little after."

The Lady turned her gaze from the alien thing that had been Fitch and spoke beyond it, at a point behind it and to her right.

"Subdue him," she said. "Avoid physical damage."

Fitch-thing registered a *phut* sound from behind, then a stinging sensation in the back of its neck, then nothing. One of the security detail came up from behind and caught Fitch-thing as it started to fall and eased the now-unconscious body to the floor.

"That was bloody quick, Ma'am. What was in that dart?" Hargrave said. He pronounced Ma'am *Mum*.

"A curare derivative," The Lady said. "The trick is in the dosage."

Hargrave and two of his men secured Fitch's body and took it by elevator to the lowest sub-level, which opened to a large, high-ceilinged bay. In the middle of the bay was the containment cell they had prepared for Fitch-thing: a silvery steel box the approximate size and shape of a shipyard shipping container, its walls made of alternating layers of titanium and paper-thin composite—the same composite substance that lined The Artist's office in New York. A large viewing window with automated shutters ran the length of its facing side and resembled in function the one-way, half-silvered surface mirrors used in police interrogation rooms.

Under Hargrave's supervision, the security team unstrapped Fitch's body inside the cell, stripped off its clothes, and placed it on the cot, which comprised the cell's only furnishing. Fitch-thing would eat a protein gruel through a feeding tube extended from the wall. It would relieve itself in a 12-inch diameter hole in the floor. It would wash itself with a shower attachment in the ceiling and drink using the short, nipple-like protuberance next to the feeding tube.

"How long will it be out?" Hargrave asked.

"It isn't out," The Lady replied. "The dosage was carefully calculated. It woke up 10 minutes ago. It's faking."

"With respect, Ma'am, everything this thing says is a lie. Why are we doing this?"

"Because I wish it, Hargrave."

Hargrave, standing at loose parade rest, feet apart, hands behind his back, nodded. "Very good, Ma'am."

"Sound the klaxon, Hargrave. We've no reason to be polite. Electrify the room if it fails to respond."

Hargrave signaled to the technician in blue mechanic coveralls standing post at the central control console, who nodded an acknowledgement and pressed a round, palm-sized red button on the instrumentation panel to his front.

None outside could hear it, but Fitch-thing in the cell spasmed and bolted upright on the cot with its eyes squeezed shut, its mouth open, its hands tightly pressed to its ears. The Lady allowed the siren to go on for several seconds until she signaled the technician, who palmed the big button again, turning it off. Through the view window, they saw Fitch-thing relax and swing its legs over on the cot until it was sitting up with its bare feet on the metal floor.

"Voice, please," The Lady said to the technician, who flipped a switch on the panel. She picked up the microphone, held it close to her mouth, and started to speak but stopped when the speakers gave a feedback squeal. She glared impatiently at the technician, who hastily made some adjustments. Looking through the view window, The Lady tried again, said, "Nod your head if you can hear me."

Fitch-thing stood up with an effort, hindered by Fitch's injuries, and stepped close to the one-way glass. It stared at first and then started making faces in the mirror, not like a child makes faces but like a psychopath makes faces, trying on expressions, practicing emotions that can't be felt: grins, frowns, happy face, sad face.

"We must come to an understanding," The Lady said. "Do exactly as I say or you get the horn again, or worse. Do you understand?"

It nodded. Its jaw was working, its eyelids spasmodically fluttering open and squeezing shut. Hargrave was reminded of manic little Valerie in New York.

"May I speak?" it said, with utter lack of inflection.

The Lady glanced at Hargrave, looked back at the glass. "Speak," she said.

"If you blare that horn at me again, old girl, I'm going to take Fitch's hands—these hands—and rip his earlobes right off. If you flood this cell with an unbearable light, I'll pluck out his eyes. And just for kicks, I'll bite off his tongue, too."

"Go ahead," she said. "Garland Fitch is dead. And you? You aren't going anywhere."

"See now, that's where you're wrong. Your man Fitch is very much alive, and he's right. In. Here—" It tapped its temple with its index finger. "—in here with me. Screaming."

"I don't believe you."

Fitch-thing barked a laugh; rather, what it thought a human laugh sounded like, said, "Believe this, flapping meat: I'm breaking out." It twirled its finger to encompass its cell. "This box of yours can't hold me. I'll find a way eventually."

"Daedalus," she said. "More specifically, the Daedalus Crater. You know it? You may call it something else—or nothing at all, for all I know, but do you know it?"

Fitch-thing froze in place and became motionless. Its eyes were wide-open and unblinking, making Hargrave think of lizards and snakes. It didn't shift its weight or scratch its nose.

This thing doesn't human *very well*, Hargrave thought.

The Lady went on. "In nine months, an Apollo Program spacecraft will be engaged in lunar orbiting maneuvers. While orbiting the moon, its crew will drop a device—my device—into the Daedalus Crater. It is a jamming mechanism, one I invented, and it is meant for you, little thing. When the signal stops—when *you* stop—I want you to know it was me, to know I am the one who ended you."

"You're bluffing. Such a device is impossible..." it said, trailing off as if distracted or confused. Fitch-thing was looking down and to the right, not at its feet but at something else, although nothing else was in its cell.

"It is very possible. I should know."

In a dull monotone, Fitch-thing said, "Cast out this wicked dream which has seized my heart."

The Lady glanced sharply at Hargrave, then back to the view window. "Wait, what? What did you say?"

"Do catch up, you miserable meatbag. I said such a device is impossible. We were eating worlds and draining suns dry while you were crawling out of the sea on your slimy little fish bellies. Nothing you do can stop what is coming. You have no weapon, no ruse, no trick or trap we cannot anticipate and defeat."

"Yet here you are," The Lady said.

Its stolen face suddenly a livid mask of rage, Fitch-thing hurled its body—Fitch's body—against the composite-reinforced glass of the viewing window and rebounded onto its back to the floor. It got up immediately, robotically, and put its face close to the glass.

"I'll get out, out, OUT! And when I get out, I'll find you, oh yes, I'll hunt you down and find you and make you suffer, and oh how you will suffer! And then I'll rip you apart, tear you to pieces, cut your pretty, pretty, pretty face off and wear it and dance—"

"I fear I am about to be bored, Hargrave."

Hargrave caught the attention of the technician, who cut off the audio feed. Hargrave turned to look back at the view window. Fitch-thing had lost control. Spittle flying from its mouth, it raged and pounded against the glass, smearing it with blood and snot and phlegm.

"Shutter it," Hargrave said.

The Lady rose from her chair and draped her scarf across her shoulders, readied herself to leave. Hargrave found himself fascinated by the way she moved. He had never seen anyone, man or woman, get up from a government-issue, gray-metal folding chair with such effortless grace. Every movement The Lady made, no matter how small or mundane, seemed charged with feminine allure.

I am, Hargrave thought, *struck by her beauty*.

The thought embarrassed him. He had read the phrase 'struck by her beauty' countless times in fiction and had passed over it derisively, thinking it just a phrase, a lazy shorthand writers used. He felt heat on his face and guessed he might be blushing.

Like a schoolboy, he thought.

"Walk with me, Hargrave," The Lady said. Something in her voice told Hargrave she knew exactly how she affected others, even now in late middle-age.

Hargrave nodded and followed her to the elevator. They stepped inside and turned to face the doors. The doors closed. The Lady smiled a little. The two had known each other for years, and it was one of the few times Hargrave had seen her smile. He found her smile beguiling—as most men did, he supposed. Sunlight breaking through clouds.

"Fitch is alive in there," she said. "He's aware. He's fighting it."

"*Cast out this wicked dream which has seized my heart*."

"You caught it?" she said. "Good."

They stepped from the elevator onto the first floor of that part of the facility resembling a house. Hargrave was surprised to find it was afternoon. His sense of time had become skewed underground. He went to the liquor cabinet and poured drinks. They stepped out together onto the veranda. The day had turned gray and cool, at odds with

Hargrave's mental image of Florida as perpetually sunny and tropical. He sat on the porch swing. She sat beside him. They didn't speak for a while, both content with the quiet.

"So that line," Hargrave said. "Where is it from, then? A book? A poem? A song?"

"*Sunset Boulevard*," she said. "Cinema."

"One of yours?"

The Lady laughed. "Oh, Heavens, no."

"So what does it mean? If it is Fitch, what's he telling us?"

"It is a message directed at me," The Lady said. "On one level, he refers to himself, held prisoner in his own body. On another, he invokes a famous line about the illusory nature of our craft and our ambitions—our 'wicked dreams'. It was also—I think—an allusion to his mother, an actress friend of mine, part of my circle in those days." The Lady smiled, shook her head. "It gets very complicated. Garland knew he would need to go deep to beat them, to convince me it was he truly speaking."

"Them?"

"You and Garland are wrong to hate that awful thing down there wearing his skin and beating on the walls of its cell. A bad man points a gun at you. Do you hate the bad man or the gun?"

"You're saying the enemy isn't the enemy?"

"I'm saying we have been fighting a weapon, Hargrave, a machine: a very smart machine for all that, but still just a machine. Tomorrow, we receive Dr. Yoojin Lee, a lovely woman who also happens to be among the most intelligent human beings alive and certainly smarter than any machine. There is a strong possibility she will be able to save Garland. If she saves Garland, then after next December we will be able to save every person on the planet we can find who has been touched by this..." She paused, searching for the right word.

"*Evil* works," Hargrave said.

She nodded. "As you say."

"And our real enemy? The ones with the gun? Its makers? What about them?"

"Next year America puts men on the moon. Two of the three men on that mission work for me. While my agents at the television networks play a 47-minute moon movie shot by our dear friend The Director, those two brave and beautiful men will take a short trip to a nearby crater and steal every bit of our enemy's technology we know they will find, all they can carry. Subsequent missions will retrieve the rest."

"Then what?"

"Then we reverse-engineer that technology and hopefully find a way to take the fight to our real enemy. We steal his gun and shoot him with it."

The Lady noted Hargrave's expression, his incredulous smile. "What is it, Hargrave?" she said. "What is so funny?"

"*Hopefully*," he said, unable to hide the sarcasm in his tone.

"All soldiers are cynics," The Lady said, smiling that lovely, perfect smile again, shaking her head, her green eyes flashing. "You misconstrue. Hope isn't the belief all will be well in the end. Even children know happy endings are fairy tales. Hope is something else. Hope is the conviction there is a point and purpose to our lives and work. That is hope.

"I have hope," she said.

Artist and writer Troy Riser's work has previously appeared in Cirsova magazine's Winter 2022 issue with his Halloween-themed horror short story, "Pick Trick". Several of his stories have been published elsewhere. He's working on a novel.

Coming Soon from Cirsova Publishing

The Feast of the Fedai

By JIM BREYFOGLE

Kat is intent on raising an army to reclaim Alness! Can she and Mangos arrange to recruit an elite core of highly trained Fedai in Alomar before her secret gets out?!

Mangos had been moving toward home since leaving Alness a month ago. The familiar stench of Alomar filled his nostrils, wafting up from the docks, the gutters, and the alleys. Alomar—home—the decadent, the corrupt, where every virtue and vice from this world or, it was bragged, any other could be had for a price.

He shouldered his way through Alomar's crowded market, where the smell of sweat and spoiled food mixed with the other odors of the city. He nodded greetings to the vendors, not sure if they recognized him but sure they didn't care. It was just good to be home.

He let his gaze stray on the fruits in one stall and, in consequence, slammed into a man who came the other way.

"Sorry," Mangos muttered.

"You ought to be," the man said, pushing Mangos.

Mangos bristled; he didn't like people pushing him. "I've apologized," he said. "Keep your hands to yourself."

"I'll do what I please with my hands." The man was solid, a bald man without much neck and a thick chest. He looked made for fighting, but he dressed like a dandy—clothes of velvet, and lace, and linen.

Two men trailed behind him, thugs by their look, and not as well dressed. "Hey, it's the Mongoose!" one of them said.

The bald man, without taking his eyes off Mangos, turned his head slightly to ask over his shoulder, "What?"

"It's the Mongoose, you know, the one Bardor told—"

"Shut up!" said the bald man.

Mangos let his hand stray to his sword as the bald man glowered at him.

"Well, Mr. Mongoose," said the man, "it was by good fortune that we met."

"Was it?" Mangos asked. "Whose?" The two thugs started to flank him to either side. The crowd, sensing trouble, ebbed away.

"Mine," said the dandy.

Mangos backed away, keeping all three in view.

"Hey! Stay away from here," said the woman inside the fruit stall. "I don't want you ruining my fruit with your fight."

"Not my fight," Mangos said, but it was, whether he wanted it or not. He thought to put a building to his back, but without looking, he backed right into an alley.

"That's right," said the dandy, following in after him, "let's take this someplace more private."

Mangos drew his sword and hazarded a look behind him. Apart from a rain barrel and a layer of garbage, the alley was empty. An iron gate blocked the far end. "Damn."

The two thugs attacked; Mangos gave ground, parrying. He could beat either of them, but both together… and he needed to keep an eye on the dandy.

He put a wall to his back and held off the thugs. A crowd of people gathered at the opening of the alley, but nobody called the constable; they just watched.

"Gods, two of you, and you can't kill him," said the dandy, drawing a small tube from his pocket. "Step aside. I'll finish him."

The thugs scrambled back. Mangos's heart pounded.

The dandy smiled and sauntered forward. He pointed the tube at Mangos. "It's almost too easy."

A fine mist shot out of the back of the tube. As it spread and enveloped the dandy, it burst into flame. He threw the tube away from him with a shriek and danced back, slapping at his face and shoulders, then his hands, as the fire stuck to him and spread.

Screaming, he turned to his men. With one hand clutching at his chest, he reached out and staggered toward them. The words "help me" emerged from the flaming ruin of his face.

The men shrank back. "Gods, no," said one. "Stay away from me."

As if the words were a trigger, they broke and ran. The slower stopped at the corner and looked back. He doubled over to vomit, started to run again, slipped, and tumbled out of sight.

The dandy fell and dragged himself to the rain barrel. He grasped the rim and, with hideous effort, threw himself head-first into the barrel.

Water overflowed onto the street. Steam rose, but the fire didn't go out. Flames danced within the barrel and the water began to bubble. The dandy stopped struggling and settled in deeper until only his feet stuck out.

"Didn't expect that," Mangos said. He gingerly picked up the fallen tube. "I'm going home now," he announced. Seeing no objections, he strode out of the alley, carefully avoiding the pool of vomit, and turned toward home.

Mangos paused on the portico. He drew in a deep breath, now savoring the clearer air. The mansions of the wealthy looked down on the rest of Alomar, perched on any one of the many hills where the breeze cleared the heat and stench of the city.

Some things are natural transition points, he thought, his hand resting on the door lever; *things you pass through and nothing is the same again. Doors can be one. Questions can be another.*

He snorted. *The world is the same. Only the people have changed.*

He hesitated, stalling, by looking over the city. He would find his answers soon enough and know if the people had indeed changed.

Down in the harbor, almost lost amongst the carracks, galleys, cogs, and caravels, a small fleet of dromonds was tied to the northern quay. *Fedai* warriors crossed the extended gangplanks and formed ranks on the stone quay. Bardor's private slave army; they, too, were returning from Alness, though their journey would have been quicker and, presumably, less eventful.

Enough. Go in. Mangos opened the door and passed into the house.

The sound of voices drew him to the parlor. Kat's, and a man he didn't recognize. The door was open, but again he paused, staying out of sight of those inside as he listened to their conversation.

"You know nothing of war," said the man. "That was a task for others."

"Those so trained can no longer fight," Kat said, an edge in her voice.

"Do not join them in their graves. You have done well in Alomar."

Mangos looked proudly around the entry of the grand home. Alabaster columns, marble floor: yes, they had done well.

"If they even have graves," Kat muttered.

Mangos squared his shoulders and entered the room.

Kat looked up from the table where she sat and smiled, a broad grin of pleasure that he couldn't help but return.

"Who is this?" demanded the man with her, and Mangos turned his attention to him. The man was a bit shorter than Mangos, broad of shoulders but thin. He had dark hair salted with grey, and a narrow face with a worn expression.

"Mangos," Kat said, "This is Grel. At one time he served as assistant quartermaster of the Alnessi army."

"And now a slave," Grel muttered.

"I keep no slaves," Kat said evenly. "Even though I paid for you." Grel lifted his hand to his neck and rubbed a ring of raw flesh where a slave's collar had recently been. He looked down.

His eyes still on Grel, unsure of what to make of the man, Mangos said to Kat, "I delivered your message."

Kat drew in her breath sharply. "I assumed you didn't reach Karn in time."

"The time wasn't right, just as you told him."

"Yet Karn proceeded," Grel said, his voice had a nasal quality that reminded Mangos of a wasp buzzing.

"Karn was already crucified when I gave him the message," Mangos said. "But he was a true prince of Alness; bound and nailed to a timber 'X' in the Grand Plaza of his own city." He looked Kat in the eye. "He was your brother."

"Younger," she admitted.

"He's dead."

"I know. Word reached us nineteen days ago."

"You knew," Mangos accused her, suddenly angry. "You knew he was your brother!"

"I wasn't sure, but I suspected."

Mangos glared at her, and she stared back. "You don't care about your brother's death?"

Now Kat flashed anger. "Of course I care!

But I've known for almost three weeks, and I already mourned him when Alness fell." She looked away. "I find it hard to grieve anymore."

Mangos weighed this. "You never told me you were a princess," he said.

A small smile played on her lips. "You never asked."

"By the gods of Eastwarn," Mangos couldn't help himself; he chuckled softly. "I wouldn't have thought I'd need to." He raised an eyebrow. "What happens now?"

"Now, I take back my country."

"Perhaps you can talk her from this reckless course," Grel said. "She is not prepared for this."

Kat ignored him. "Once the *Fedai* return from Alness, we can begin."

"They arrived today," Mangos said. He rubbed his hand on the back of his neck, his mind racing. "Do you have an army hiding somewhere?"

"Not yet."

"Anybody else know you're a princess?"

"Bardor."

"Bardor?" Mangos shook his head; that was bad. Bardor bankrolled Rhygir's conquest of Alness and sent five thousand *Fedai* to bolster the mercenary leader against Karn's army. They had returned, but he would send them north again to fight any army Kat might raise. "How did he find out?"

"One of his Alnessi slaves saw me and told him. She used to be married to one of the junior officers. The officer was killed, and she was passed amongst the mercenaries before being brought to Alomar and

sold."

"You've no hope if he knows your intentions." Mangos said. He thought of the assassination attempt. "I met some people on the way here." He dug the dandy's fire tube from his pouch. "They offered me a warm reception."

"Yes, those were Bardor's boys. They like those because of the horror they create—a bad way to die," Kat said. "Careful which way you point it. They're tricky and expensive toys."

With a snort, Mangos slid it back into his pouch. "Bardor should hire better people to use it then. Now, about that army…"

"You'll start it for me," Kat said. "If you're willing."

Mangos was stunned she needed to ask, and he realized sometime in the last three years he had made his choice without ever knowing it. "I will stand with you."

A slow smile crept over Kat's face. "Good. Let's get started. Talgon is having a 'Toast the Host' banquet in a week."

Mangos didn't know Talgon, and it must have showed, for she said, "Talgon trains and sells *Fedai*. He is returning to Alomar in a week, and the banquet is his way of announcing he has more *Fedai* to sell."

"You'll buy *Fedai*?" The idea surprised Mangos, and Grel too, by his intake of breath.

"Not a whole army," Kat said, "that would cost too much, and Talgon doesn't have that many ready. But all the easy recruits in Alness are already dead. We need a core of fighters to give ourselves credibility—something to convince prospective recruits we have a chance.

"And no," she added. "I'll not buy the *Fedai*—you will. I have other things to do at the banquet."

"Toast the Host" banquets, Mangos knew, started centuries before when Alomar still engaged in empire building. A particular Prince of Alomar, Mangos couldn't remember which one, celebrated a victory by passing out free wine to the masses and hosting a great feast for the wealthy. The masses, in a gesture of spontaneous glorification, broke into the feast and toasted the Prince with their flagons of free wine.

So began the custom of the wealthy and powerful hosting a meal where the guests were expected to bring their own chalices for toasting the host. Like much else in Alomar, they were an opportunity for both the host and guests to impress each other. The feast was expected to be worthy of acclamation, and guests vied for the most impressive goblets. It explained the unusual number of goldsmiths specializing in drinking vessels.

"We need glassware," Mangos said. They had inherited the house, fully furnished, from the previous owner, and apart from the silver tankards, he didn't know what kind of drinking vessels they owned.

"I had some made," Kat said. She drew a leather box from under the table. It was tightly made, with a leather handle and bright brass clasps. She set it on the table and opened it.

Two goblets rested in red silk. Kat handed him one.

The goblets' bowls were a light and lustrous shade of gold where innumerable colors chased each other too quickly for the eye to register. Carved crystal vines, rooted at the foot, formed the stem and entwined the bowl. Lapis lazuli fruit hung from the vines and, presumably, hid the fasteners that held the bowl to the stem.

"Is this made from the Golden Pearl?" Mangos asked. Awe thrilled through his body. A person drinking from this couldn't be poisoned.

"Honor to our host," Kat lifted the other goblet in a mock toast.

"Indeed." Mangos examined the exquisite craftsmanship. "These are beyond price." He glanced up. "These could buy many soldiers."

"They've saved my life twice in the last month," Kat said.

"Not for sale, then." Mangos put his goblet back into the box.

That evening in the mansion's tower study, Mangos pored over the ledger Kat had given him. He needed to examine the long columns of numbers and know the categories, for the *Fedai* would be expensive.

The numbers represented Kat's share of their treasure—a fortune, and he felt guilty he had so little. Drink, wagers, and pleasurable company had claimed the larger amount of his share. Kat appeared to have kept every copper coin. "This is unbelievable," he murmured. She must have been planning this for years.

"A moment of your time?"

Mangos looked up. Grel stood in the

doorway. Although he asked, it hadn't sounded like a question, more like a demand. Mangos remembered Kat's description of the quartermaster: *a petty mind, filled with nothing but numbers and charts. But he's good at that. He could tell how many daggers should be in the armory and number their nicks.*

"Yes?" he said, beckoning Grel into the room. He closed the ledger he had been examining. If Kat's accounts were Grel's business, she could show them herself; Mangos would be damned if he did.

"Do you even know what it takes to field an army?" Grel asked.

"It takes men," Mangos said. "And nothing else matters if you don't have them."

"And if you have the men, you need to feed them, to arm them, to move them about. It is no small task, and no task for a woman, especially one untrained."

Mangos resisted the urge to strangle him. "Do you even know who you speak of?"

"Better than you, evidently."

"I wonder."

"I'll tell you one thing I do know," Grel said in his rasping, buzzing voice. "Armies need to be fed. Contracts are settled seasons in advance. You cannot buy enough food for an army on short notice."

"The grain merchants—"

"Already have the harvest under contract," Grel said. "If anybody has any grain to sell, you'll only get it at famine prices."

Mangos leaned back. He couldn't argue with Grel's logic.

"Convince her to give this up," Grel pressed. "You don't want her killed."

"No," Mangos agreed. "But she's not easy to kill." Suddenly he thought of a solution. "Fortune has it that I know a grain merchant, and she is in our debt. Contact Polonia."

Grel frowned. "*She* suggested Polonia also. But we shouldn't waste money on a venture so clearly doomed."

Mangos felt his fingers twitch. He really did want to strangle the man. "Doomed?"

Grel snorted. "Even if you can feed the men, without weapons and armor, they're doomed. She doesn't have the knowledge or training for this."

"You don't seem properly grateful to the woman who freed you."

"Free?" Grel blinked, as if the word surprised him. "I carry three years of nightmares, three years of beatings, three years of hunger and loss since Alness fell. I am not free. But please excuse me if I don't care to add to that burden."

Mangos sighed and relaxed his hands. He could not argue with that, but neither would he hold up Kat's plans. He said, "Another thing an army needs is everybody working together. Contact Polonia."

Grel opened his mouth, perhaps to protest, but closed it without saying anything. He nodded once and turned to leave.

"And, Grel?" Mangos said as the quartermaster reached the door. "*She* has a name."

Grel hesitated, but didn't turn and didn't speak.

Mangos glared at the empty doorway; then, opening the ledger, he scanned the columns. There, buried amongst "non-currency assets," were the neatly written words, "125 tonnes silvecite ore—located in Pytheas."

So Kat never sold the silvecite they earned by killing the mine worm; instead she shipped it to Pytheas, where the smiths owed them for defeating the dragons.

Shaking his head, Mangos began to chuckle. Clever, clever Kat. The army would be very well-armed indeed.

If he could get it started with the purchase of the *Fedai*.

Talgon's walled mansion was well-situated, high enough on one of Alomar's hills to lift it above the haze that hung over the slums and workshops. There was very little space between the perimeter wall and the building, just enough for some ornamental trees and a few patches of well-trimmed grass. The house looked like a fortress, as suited a man whose influence came from brokering warrior-slaves.

Instead of gargoyles, a half-dozen *Fedai* perched atop the outer wall: three on each side of the gate.

A doorwarder, dressed in festive red and gold, stepped forward and held up his hand to stop them. "It is the tradition of this home that you surrender your swords," he said.

Mangos looked at him in surprise.

"Your safety is guaranteed while you're a guest," the doorwarder assured him.

Mangos closed his hand on the hilt of his sword as if he would shield it from the man. "This is a unique weapon," he said. "It's Marin's first silvercite sword."

The doorwarder bowed slightly. "I would direct your gaze to the words above the gate." Mangos read the words above the wrought iron gate as the doorwarder quoted them, "This is a house of honor."

Mangos eyed the scrawny man and wondered if he *could* keep the sword safe. It didn't matter, he decided. This was Talgon's house and Talgon's honor, and Talgon's *Fedai* would see to the keeping of both.

Kat unbuckled her sword. With a sardonic smile, she offered it for keeping. Much more reluctantly, Mangos followed suit.

"The words on the gate are true," Kat said, "but misleading. In Hafiz, honor is a way of life; for Talgon it is a front for business."

Two more *Fedai* guarded the house's main entrance, where an old butler directed guests further into the house. He bowed as they approached. "The Mongoose and the Meerkat?"

"Yes," Kat said.

The man smiled and beckoned them forward, then pointed. "Through the hall, dinner will be served in the courtyard." He lowered his voice, now sounding like a kindly grandfather. "You have your toasting goblets?"

Kat patted the box at her side.

"Good, good," the old butler said. "Sorry for asking, but adventurers have a certain reputation." He chuckled, almost to himself. "And it isn't for their manners."

"Thank you," Kat said. She led the way through guests who loitered in the hall, and they emerged under a portico that surrounded the courtyard.

In the center of the courtyard was a green bronze fountain of a dragon, wings unfurled, breathing a jet of what looked like red wine into the pool below.

Mosaics covered the rest of the courtyard, dragons and unicorns and lions, all entwined with geometric patterns. A large urn filled with flowers sat in each corner.

Couches ringed the mosaics, pulled to the edge of the portico where they sat, two between each column, each with its own slave. Another row of couches ran along the walls of the house. These were for less-favored guests, Mangos supposed, because of the obstructed view and only one slave served the many couches.

Though it wouldn't be dark for some time, lanterns hung from the columns, sending light and sweet perfumes into the dark corners under the portico. Musicians on the roof began to play.

Mangos had never met Talgon, but he had a description and didn't doubt he would recognize his host. He saw Hartwick, who sold gladiators and animals to the arenas. Ninix San, the archivist of the alchemist guild, he knew, but others he didn't recognize. He didn't recognize the thick-necked man wearing emerald-studded bracers, or the bald man with a tattoo on his head. While he didn't know the young woman in red, he wouldn't mind meeting her. Her dark hair hung over one eye and cascaded around her shoulders. She adjusted her wrap as she moved, which only seemed to enhance the movement of her hips.

Mangos let his gaze linger on her before resuming his search for Talgon.

Another butler drew his attention by gesturing to one of the couches. "This couch is for the Mongoose," he bobbed his head at Mangos. "And that for the Meerkat."

Each couch sat at an angle, head toward the fountain. They were frames of burnished bronze covered by a thick mattress with pillows to prop up the guests. Each had a small table next to it and a slave behind it.

"Talia will serve you," the butler told Mangos with an elegant flourish of his hand to indicate the tall woman behind his couch, a woman made strong and fit by her labor in Talgon's house.

"Evard will do your bidding," the butler said to Kat, indicating the stocky slave waiting beside her couch.

Mangos tested the couch, appreciating the view of the courtyard and the clear view of the more honored guests. A quick twist and glance confirmed less fortunate guests had a superb view of his feet.

"Mangos!"

The Hand of Bursa, the Bursa's administrative assassin, lifted a hand, and Mangos walked over to him. "There are rumors," the Hand said. "Bardor is taking an unusual interest in you and Kat."

Mangos looked around. "Is that right?"

"Bardor only cares for money, and he makes it in two ways—predatory banking and fencing Rhygir's loot from Alness. Which one do you threaten?"

"Who wants to know?"

The Hand looked over his shoulder. The Bursa reclined on a couch in the corner deepest in shadows. It was impossible to tell if he watched them or not.

"This business with Bardor doesn't involve the Bursa," Mangos said.

"Yes, it does," Kat said, breezing past them.

The Hand turned to watch. "Only she can walk past me like that without my killing her."

Mangos laughed and clapped the Hand on the shoulder. "And I have my own business."

There, the man by the door, the one talking with the short fellow, must be Talgon. He stood almost a head taller than Mangos. He showed his prosperity in his enormous girth that almost hid his broad shoulders and deep chest and his toughness in the strong bands of muscle that even the thick slab of fat couldn't conceal. When Talgon started moving, it would be wise to stay out of his way.

"Time to buy an army," Mangos muttered and started through the crowd.

His movement drew the attention of the woman in red. She moved out of the shadows, and the torchlight danced over her, making her chiffon wrap seem aflame and her wreathed in fire.

He thought their paths would diverge, for he had business with Talgon, and she couldn't possibly have business with him, but she surprised him by approaching and resting a hand on his arm. Her touch was dry and warm.

"I've been told the Mongoose is one of the most dangerous men in Alomar." Her voice was low, slightly breathy, yet rich in tone.

"I can't imagine who would be telling you that, or why," Mangos said. A quick glance showed Talgon still deep in conversation with the short man.

"Tell me," the woman drew close enough that Mangos could feel her heat and ran her hand over his upper arm, "what makes you so dangerous?"

Mangos glanced at Talgon's back. The woman's caress distracted him. He opened his mouth to ask what she wanted but realized that was a very stupid question.

Her hand closed on his elbow. "Show me the fountain." She steered Mangos into the courtyard, pausing by one of the flower-filled urns. "So beautiful," she purred. "I love these flowers."

They were bright yellow flowers, globes, like suns. Mangos recognized them as the same flowers that grew in the mountains west of the Terzol Valley. Beautiful, yes, and very poisonous; did the fact she loved them mean anything?

"Very nice." Even he wasn't sure what, exactly, he was complimenting, but he did know he needed to get away from this woman. Somewhere amongst his swirling thoughts was the belief that nothing in Alomar was innocent. "Very nice," he repeated, pulling his elbow free. "But I'd like to talk to somebody before dinner."

The woman hooked her arm through his and reached up to pat his cheek. "Of course. Business." She took a deep breath, half-turning to make sure he noticed, "My loss. But surely it can wait?"

By the gods of Eastwarn, Mangos thought. "No. I'm afraid it can't." He pulled his arm away and headed toward Talgon.

"Wait," she said, but her footsteps stopped, and he didn't look back.

"Talgon, I'd like a word," he said just as Talgon nodded and shook hands with the small man.

"I don't believe I know you," Talgon said.

"Mangos of Arnelon."

"Ah, yes, the Mongoose." Talgon looked around, surveying the crowd, apparently looking for 'the Meerkat.' "Glad to have you here tonight." He smiled broadly. "Having thieves and adventurers here reminds people why they need to buy *Fedai*."

"Actually, I'd like to buy *Fedai* myself."

"Really?" Talgon tugged at his lip. "Huh. I didn't expect that." He looked down at the man next to him and back at Mangos. "When do you want them?"

"Now."

"That, Mangos of Arnelon, is unfortunate, for I've none to sell."

Mangos felt his stomach go cold. "None to sell?"

"None. Bardor here just purchased all I had."

"Bardor?" Now it felt like Mangos had been punched in the stomach. That shrimp of a man was Bardor? He had pictured a grossly overweight octopus, a man fat on the flesh of others with his hands in a dozen different pies. Bardor looked like an evil child next to Talgon, if the child was bald, wrinkled, and had a chin so sharp it made his face look like a hatchet. "He has five thousand already."

The banker lifted his goblet in a mock toast. "I like to be prepared. If I can't remove the trouble before it starts, at least I'll be prepared to deal with it."

"What of them?" Mangos said, pointing to the *Fedai* stationed about the courtyard.

Bardor laughed, a shrill, 'hicking' sound and waved his hand in front of his face as if Mangos's question had left a funny, but noxious, cloud in the air.

"My house guard are not for sale," Talgon said.

"When will you have more?"

"I have already spoken for those." Bardor stepped very close, though he only came midway up Mangos's chest. He lifted his chin to glare upwards. "There will never be *Fedai* available for you, or that orphan princess either. Your days, and the days of your rebellion, are numbered."

Mangos sat on his couch, glaring at the mosaic floor, trying to puzzle out the situation. He needed to buy those slaves. Kat couldn't build her army without the credibility they brought.

Talia, the slave by his assigned couch, intercepted him. "My Lord," she said, holding up a broad, shallow brass bowl, "I have sea lemons in light syrup."

Mangos shrugged.

"The sea lemons cleanse your palette and prepare you for the next course," she explained. Fishing out a slice of lemon, she held it up for him.

Mangos regarded the dripping fruit, not sure he wanted the syrup on his hands.

Talia smiled, clearly experienced in the protocol of the feast and how to handle guests. She lifted the fruit to Mangos's mouth and fed him. Then, glancing down, she sucked her fingers clean. "Now, My Lord, you are ready for pre-dinner delicacies."

"Thank you." Mangos pushed himself up. He needed to talk to Kat.

He approached the Bursa's couch, where Kat still talked to the Bursa, oblivious to all else. The Hand stepped in front of him and stopped him with a hand to his chest and a gentle push.

"They are busy," the Hand said.

Mangos's irritation flared. "I know that," he snapped. "It's important."

"They," the Hand repeated with emphasis, "are busy."

Mangos slapped the Hand's hand from him and made to push his way past. The Hand snapped his fingers in Mango's face, and a dagger appeared as if by magic. The Hand snapped again, and the dagger vanished.

Spring-loaded forearm sheath hidden by his sleeves, Mangos thought. There was a time he would have feared the Hand, but that time was past. Still, the fact the Hand would warn him like that made him pause.

The Hand nodded. "Now that I have your attention, listen. Kat's calling in everything the Bursa owes her, and the Bursa doesn't like it—he's resisting." The Hand looked over his shoulder at the two in conversation. "If you interrupt now, there's a good chance she won't get what she wants."

Mangos nodded his reluctant understanding.

"Good," the Hand said. "Whatever you needed, you'll have to do it yourself."

Mangos munched spiced fowl, acutely aware of the empty couch next to him. The courses came and went, each dish chased by a slice of sea lemon, finger-fed by Talia, but he had no ideas about buying *Fedai*. The largest band of *Fedai*, after Bardor's army, was Talgon's house guard, and none of them were for sale.

Bardor sauntered past, paused. "The Mongoose and the Meerkat," he sneered. "So little you know, so little you understand."

Mangos climbed to his feet.

Bardor didn't flinch. "Haven't you learned? My information is always good." He snorted. "Crawl back to your couch and finish this farce."

Mangos clenched his fists and jaw.

Bardor laughed. "I am the one who is honored to toast our host. I hope you have a worthy goblet. But I doubt it." He walked away, smiling warmly at the woman in red as he passed. With every familiarity, he plucked one of the yellow flowers and tucked it into her hair.

The poisonous little bitch! She delayed me on purpose! Yes, the flower suited her.

Suddenly, he had an idea. *This is a house of honor, is it?* He pulled the Golden Pearl chalice from his pouch, and while Talia fetched the toasting wine, plucked one of the poisonous yellow flowers. He needed to finish a farce.

He shredded the flower over the sea lemon, taking care to let the pollen cover the floating fruit. Next, he pulled the flame tube from his tunic and dropped it on the ground. He brushed off his hands just as Talia returned and filled his goblet.

"One last entremet, so you can appreciate the wine," Talia said. The pollen blended into the yellow of the lemon, unnoticed except by Mangos. Death. Talia watched him expectantly. He rubbed his thumb over the cool side of the goblet. Life.

He ate the lemon from Talia's fingers.

Bardor raised his hand, turning so everybody could see him, no matter where they sat. "Friends," he said. "Now is the best time of the dinner. This is when we get to toast our host." He made a great show of lifting his goblet from the pouch at his side and holding it up. The gold cup gleamed in the torchlight. Rubies flashed like blood between his fingers.

"Friends," Bardor said, "a toast. To Talgon, may his *Fedai* grow ever more dangerous."

Mangos snorted. *That's a self-serving toast. I drink instead to life.* He started to take a sip.

"And now you pass your goblets to the left," Bardor called.

Mangos froze, the goblet halfway to his lips. Nobody around him drank, instead they did, indeed, pass their goblets to the left. The fat old man to his left held out his ring-encrusted hand impatiently.

Mangos's breath caught in his throat, his chest spasmed as he drew in air that would not come. His throat throbbed. He needed that drink, must have it! *Damn manners!* He started to drink again.

But the old man snatched the Golden Pearl chalice from his hand, and Mangos raised only air. He couldn't even squawk his protest. The edges of his vision already darkened.

Kat lifted the goblet out of the old man's hand, deftly replacing it with a silver chalice. "Did you just poison your own food?" she whispered angrily as she held the Golden Pearl chalice to his lips and helped him drink.

Mangos took in wine, feeling it soothe his throat, opening it again. He gasped, letting wine spatter in his rush to breathe.

Heads turned their way. He didn't care.

"What do you hope to accomplish with this?" Kat demanded.

Mangos coughed, but before he could answer, there was a crash of falling trays. Talia clutched her hands, trying to stop them from shaking, then she started to tear at her throat, her face turning red and her eyes bulging. Her fingernails dug furrows in her neck and blood trickled down her body.

Evard, Kat's servant, stared in horror.

"Give her a drink," Mangos wheezed, holding out the goblet.

"She can't swallow!" Evard protested.

"Give it to her anyway!" Talia was turning purple, and her neck was bloody. Mangos grabbed her and forced her head back. He poured wine into her mouth.

She paused, frozen in her panic. With a gag and gasp she spat out the wine, but then took several labored breaths. Mangos gave her the goblet and she swallowed all that it held.

"What is this?" Talgon stood in the center of a cluster of guests at the edge of the

portico.

"Somebody has poisoned your slave," Mangos said. Kat stood next to him, her eyes darting from him to Talgon.

"There is no point in poisoning a slave," Talgon said, his eyes were narrow, and he looked around the courtyard as he spoke.

"I think she was just in the wrong place at the wrong time," Mangos said.

"Who would do this?" Talgon demanded. He stepped closer, his gaze going to the lemons, then to the crowd around him.

Mangos raised his eyebrows. "Somebody who cares little for your guests or your honor."

Talgon nodded, still looking around. He stooped down to pick up something. He held up an assassin's fire gun. "Yours?" he asked.

Mangos shook his head and waited for Talgon to reach the desired conclusion.

Talgon's knuckles turned white. He jerked his jaw toward Talia. "You saved her. What saved you?"

Mangos held up his goblet. Talgon took it, turning it over in his hand. "What is this?"

"Half a golden pearl," Mangos answered. "Hollowed out and made into a goblet."

"Incredible!" Talgon examined the goblet, wonder on his face. "You could never be poisoned while you have this. I've never heard of such a thing!"

"What chalice is more unique or valuable?" Mangos said. "I do you great *honor*." He loaded the last word with irony, and Talgon flinched. "Let's talk honor and guarantees of safety."

Talgon drew a deep breath and let it out in a gust. "There is nothing more to see," he told the clustered guests, and when they moved away, turned to Mangos. "I know what you want. The only *Fedai* I have are my house guards. There are fifty. How many would you like?"

"All of them," Mangos said.

"You shall have them." Talgon waved Talia toward the kitchens, then shot a swift, malevolent glare at Bardor. "But," and he turned back to Mangos, "With them I buy my honor and your silence. Bardor may hold me in contempt, but I can't afford to cross him. Damn his blood."

Mangos nodded.

"We'll make arrangements when I hire new guards." He thrust the goblet back in Mangos's hand and spun to leave, as if not wanting to draw more attention to their conversation or just wanting to put the episode behind him.

Kat laughed and leaned in so others couldn't hear. "And did you plan to poison his daughter, or did you just get lucky?"

"His daughter?" Mangos glanced at the kitchen door, but of course Talia wasn't to be seen.

"She didn't get that nose from her mother," Kat said. "Talgon wouldn't be the first man to have children in the slave's quarters. He loves her, though he hid it well."

Mangos leaned forward and lowered his voice. "You think it lucky I poisoned his daughter?"

"You didn't," Kat said. "Bardor did—and it was careless of him to drop his fire gun like that. That might have been too clever, by the way. If Talgon wasn't so angry about his daughter, he might have suspected a frame-up."

"It showed Bardor was near the lemons," Mangos said. He changed the subject. "The goblet switch nearly killed me."

"I thought you knew about the chance. The crowd at the first banquet was quite rowdy and free-spirited with their drinking. It's up to the toaster if they call for the switch or not. Sometimes they switch, sometimes they don't."

"Did you get what you wanted from the Bursa?" he asked.

"Yes." Her expression didn't change but her eyes exulted, and Mangos knew she had accomplished something important. "We must be ready to move quickly now."

Several days later, they were ready to move north. They would march, but equipment and supplies would follow on wagons. Jalani, the Alnessi merchant, was only too willing to aid their cause.

Mangos waited in the study to do one last task.

Kat stuck her head in, Grel behind her. "We're ready to march," she said.

"I'm not ready quite yet," Mangos said. "Grel," he called. "I'd like a word."

Grel came in. "What?"

"You won't be going north with us," Mangos said.

Mangos drew his dagger and, with a quick step, drove it into Grel's stomach and up. "Somehow Bardor knew Kat wanted *Fedai*. He even knew to delay me, not Kat, so he could buy them. Somebody told him."

Grel doubled over and looked up, his eyes wide. He looked toward Kat, but she didn't move to help him.

"I talked to the slave who told Bardor about Kat," Mangos said. "She confirmed my suspicions.

"The slave girl gave away Kat's identity because she had no hope," he went on. "But you betrayed the hope that stands before you. This is your *Queen*."

Grel fell to his knees, still clutching his wounded stomach.

"By the gods of Eastwarn, you're Alnessi. You're supposed to be faithful. Three years of burdens don't change that." Mangos snorted his contempt. "Kat deserves better than you. *Alness* deserves better than you."

Grel's eyes held his answer, an expression of sadness, remorse, and helplessness, but also defiance. He opened his mouth, moved it as if unsure what to say, or just struggling to speak. Finally, he gave up with a slight shrug and jiggle of his head. He collapsed completely, reaching out with one bloody hand while he kept the other pressed to his stomach.

Mangos wiped his dagger and re-sheathed it. "Now, I'm ready to march."

Kat nodded, her expression thoughtful. "You are indeed ready."

Jim Breyfogle's Tales of the Mongoose and Meerkat are out now from Cirsova Publishing! Find it on Amazon.com or ask for it wherever books are sold!

https://jimbreyfogle.wordpress.com/

Egg

By JAIME FAYE TORKELSON

A geo-seismic research team is stationed on the strange moon Epsilon Epsilon Six, better known as Egg, a smooth and volatile body that could go at any moment!

It was with infinite sadness that man broke the bonds of his solar system and discovered that he was utterly and unalterably alone. There was no race of wise, bulb-headed grays, no clan of tank-bound super-brains. Man was alone. Alone with his triumphs, alone with his fears, alone with his mistakes.

At the withering news that Goldilocks One was perfect for habitation but devoid of intelligent life, scientists, who promised fountains of otherworldly wisdom, retreated in disgrace to their mansions, built by the wealth of billion-dollar lectures. Presidents and Prime Ministers begged for calm. Rest assured, the experts vowed, Goldilocks Two will bring salvation.

Humanity visited their second golden world and found it splendid: water as clear and cool as a mountain stream; plump, bright berries of delectable taste; hills and rivers as fertile as the Nile Valley of great antiquity. Perfect, perfect, perfect. *Empty.*

There was great shuffling and mumbling and charts; they promised our Exalted Thule would be found among the next stars.

It was not Thule, nor even golden. When mankind finally reached it, it was desolate. From within the ruins of broken rock and acidic seas, they found the remnants of an unadvanced species, their ashen shades locked in perpetual warfare. Flinty spears held in tight claws with terror plastered on faces too much like men to bring any comfort.

Life! great men said. *Life!*

Life was found! In death, unfortunately, but the experts erupted from their seclusion, shaking hands and muttering I-told-you-so's from smirking side-mouths. *Luddite doubters! Only a matter of time before we find something greater!*

Renewed in hope, fresh in vigor, humanity rushed further into the universe, pressing boundaries, secretly fearful they might indeed find a creature in some colorful corner of dark space and rouse his mad fury.

But they found no slumbering old thing, just another planet perfectly suited to man. There was life on this one too, microscopic things. An entire civilization in the palm of a hand, like mold on old bread.

That vigor finally gave up the ghost.

With new resources and widening space, humanity ferried through astronomical oceans, rushing to commit the same blunders that made them seek salvation among the stars.

But man is a dreamer.

Driven into a bacchanalia of scientific triumph, he continues to dash his hopes upon other worlds. Each new Eden filled, like a cornucopia, with good things to eat and drink...

Oscar Ramirez pulled his hands away from the keyboard. He leaned back in his chair and stroked his chin. Greying hairs rasped against his fingers. *Maybe I'm going too hard on the biblical imagery?* Then switching tracks like a train, *or maybe not enough?*

He huffed and pressed his fingers to the keys again, determined to keep going. *First draft,* he reminded himself. *Doesn't even have a title yet.* He sat at attention, sagged, and sighed. Pulled his fingers back again and peered out the plasma window.

Epsilon Epsilon Six, third moon from Tanitar Two, was categorized as frontier. Ramirez and his crew lovingly called her Egg. Her white exterior was smooth and glossy. The luster was a product of the high metallic content in her soil. Unlike Earth's moon, Egg tended towards violence, occasionally cracking off bits of her glossy white shell and sending them ricocheting towards Tanitar Two.

The aluminum mining was good for a while, but after losing a third crew to seismic violence, Epsilon Mining Corporation donated the system to science. If only to salvage their investment with some public relations capital. They evacuated, leaving their mining satellites and ground bases to be retrofitted for research purposes.

Ramirez liked the peace and quiet of Extraterrestrial Planetological research. Geologists were less demanding than physicists and biologists. He set his fingers to typing, jumping ahead to get a sudden glut of words out. *I spent my early years on an Extraterrestrial Outreach frigate; I was at Xanadu Eighteen when we found the mold. They immediately took to patting themselves on the back and enjoying a good old-fashioned elitist's circle jerk.* He missed the Officer's Lounge, though, and their fine selection of brandy.

And, he leaned back in his office chair to peer across the Conchae Maris at the other side of the installation. *Commissioner Beaks.* Space travel left little time for romance. Ramirez remained single, but he had liked Tanya. She was out there somewhere, extending an open hand to empty worlds.

At the other side of the installation, the plasma drill was in ready position, but Engineer Randal Flowers was hesitating. His foreman, Doctor Boris Yesikov, made that harsh pointing gesture of his.

"But Boris, my knees are aching, something's about to rumble," Ramirez murmured, inflecting a British accent and chuckling at his poor attempt. "I don't care if your knees fall off, get in that drill, or I'll bury you under it." He chuckled at his even worse Russian impression.

The activity alarm began blaring, and both men scrambled through the weak gravity and back to the airlock, feud forgotten until chowtime when Flowers would insist that his *knees were never wrong*. The rest of the crew would insist the Commissar resolve the argument before Boris fired them all. *Flowers's knees are never wrong, Boris,* he'd say and then tell Flowers that knee pain was not a scientific method; they would obey the activity alarms from now on. Two weeks later, they'd pick over the same fight again.

The plasma windows turned opaque, indicating earthquake mode. Ramirez climbed under his desk and tried not to think about sinkholes. The installation was sectioned into modules. Each could detach from the rest of the installation in the event of a sinkhole. The only portion lost would be that module. A tragedy, for sure, but it was better than losing all hands. And each mod was equipped with a week's worth of emergency rations and oxygen, for what little that meant.

Luckily, no sinkhole opened. Egg shook and shimmied as if she was about to hatch, but it lasted little over thirty seconds. Later, there would be some aftershocks for a few weeks, each successively weaker until the next "big one."

Ramirez crawled out from under his desk, pulled his chair back and sat. He hit the console, clearing the alert. Nothing outside betrayed anything amiss. He adjusted his shirt and keyed the comms.

"Commissar Ramirez, mod sound off."

"Mod One, clear." Baker.

"Mod Two, clear." Cunningham.

"Mod Three, clear." Graves.

There was a pause. Ramirez was never one to panic. None of the detachment sirens were wailing, but even machines made mistakes. Although, Boris was the kind of man to pick up a fight where it was left off, re-gardless of circumstances.

Ramirez tapped his finger on the comm again. "Mod Four?"

"Yeah, yeah, Mod Four, clear." Yesikov grumbled.

"Mods carry on." The activity alarm blared again, cutting him off.

Ramirez sighed. He was slower getting under his desk this time. Egg rolled, he lost balance, and slammed his head against the desk. Cursing, Ramirez put his hands over his head the way the drills said he should.

The ground swelled and fell, slamming his tailbone into the floor. "Christ!" he spat, watching pens slide off each end of his desk.

His chair slid across the rug and smacked against the bookshelf; it fell back towards him. Ramirez's knuckles struck the bottom of the desk, but this time his tailbone made a softer landing on the rug as another wave rolled through.

He waited a good minute before he tried to move. No one was sounding off on the comms, hopefully because they were just as stunned as he was. *Been a hot minute since you got this rowdy, Egg.*

Ramirez rose and picked up the chair. His books were locked in place by magnets; he collected the pens and threw them into his penholder, straightened, and hit the comm. "Ramirez," he said. "Mod rollcall."

"Mod Two is clear; little shook up, though," Cunningham.

"Mod One, clear." Baker.

"Mod Four." Boris. "Lights are down."

He waited.

Tapped his fingers on the desk.

Thirty seconds went by.

Graves was efficient; she wouldn't fail to answer.

A minute.

Ramirez hit the comm. "Graves, come in?"

Not even static.

He did not let himself panic.

"Cunningham, I'm coming to your position. Yesikov, do you need assistance with the lights?" He didn't wait for a response. "Baker, take two men and help Mod Four." He was met with a cavalcade of *roger* and *copy*.

Ramirez grabbed his jacket and clipped a comm to his lapel. His command console read nothing amiss, but he grabbed his emergency kit anyway. The airlock hissed open, letting him through.

He followed the long, uncarpeted hallway down to the next airlock, tracing the yellow running lights with his eyes. The HVAC system was humming; status lights on the maintenance console were green, indicating oxygen levels were normal.

The airlock hissed as he approached and met Cunningham in the five-way. Cunningham was already plugged into the server outlet, running a diagnostic while his men were removing the paneling around Mod Three's airlock control station.

"No leaks," Cunningham said, anticipating Ramirez's question. "I think it's just the comms."

"Just get it open," Ramirez grumbled, opening his pack and pulling on his air suit. The others were already dressed, and he wasn't about to take his chances.

The diagnostic came back green. Cun-

ningham threw down his tablet. "Prima Servos," he cursed, pushing aside his companions. "Remind me to order Terra-Made from now on." He took a pair of wires out of a clump of cables and hooked them to the mini-source in his tool kit. It clicked on.

The wires sparked, and the airlock lights snapped on, flickered sightly, brightened, and turned green.

Ramirez frowned. Green for oxygen; green for gravity; red for power.

"Are they in auxiliary?" he demanded.

"It's Graves," Cunningham said as if that was an answer. He started pressing buttons on the panel. The airlock whirled, opening both doors with the hiss-pop of a cola can.

Mod Three was dark and loud. The lights were off, Graves and her team were using flashlights. The gravity generator was going, and the HVAC was whirring. Graves was barking orders at her second, Carter, who in turn was barking orders at the rest.

Ramirez clicked on his flashlight and stepped inside. Graves was lying on the ground, penlight in her mouth like a cigar, hands working on the underside of the comm console. "Someone get my mini-source, I think I found our—" she peered up. "Commissar," she greeted. "Mod Four, reporting a power outage."

"Your HVAC is fine."

"It is," she muttered, getting back to work. "I don't know why yet. Loose connector or something." Carter brought the mini-source, she connected and rebooted the comm system. "Mod Three, testing... Mod Four, do you copy?"

"Mod Four, good copy," Yesikov answered, palpable relief in his voice. "Do you need further assistance?"

Ramirez spoke into his lapel. "Stand by, Yesikov."

Satisfied with the comms, Graves turned her attention to the seismic equipment. Cunningham and his crew went to help her team find the source of the outage.

"Did you get any readings before you went down?" Ramirez picked up a chair and sat. He watched her hands glide across the console, snapping switches and hitting buttons.

"I can recover data for a printout," she muttered as the console booted up. "Sure, felt like an eight, though."

She gave the terminal her command code and started downloading the last data packet sent up to the satellite. While it worked, they helped clean up the spilled coffee, broken cups, pens, and paper tossed around the lab.

When the console beeped and voiced: *download completed,* Graves started tapping away, sifting data points Ramirez couldn't begin to understand. She seemed agitated, drumming her mouse while she waited for the print. The printer spat out a ream of paper patterned with dots and lines and numbers. She snatched it up.

The lights were still refusing to come up despite all of Cunningham's finagling. Graves whistled and called: "Carter!" She took the printout to the airlock. Together, the two seismologists looked over the chart, speaking quietly to each other in the harsh blue light of the five-way.

Scientists, Ramirez knew, like doctors,

did that when they didn't want to alarm anyone. He knew the tone well. *No life here, it's a bust. Another waste. What will the President say?*

"Report!" He used his Sergeant voice, saved especially for moments like these.

Graves hustled over and handed him the printout. He examined it, making a show of pretending to know what it said.

"That was a foreshock." Graves kept her voice blunt, unamused by his antics.

"What?"

"At least, I think it was."

Ramirez licked his lips. "What?"

"The computer always runs our data patterns up against previously acquired data—anything seismic from the Milky Way to Alpha Centauri. The pattern is similar to the Yosemite eruption of 2245." Ramirez nodded slowly. He knew that, but his thoughts wouldn't congeal into anything coherent enough to stop her explanation. "It has tonal similarities to the sound Titan II made when the ice cracked open and began liquifying," he nodded again, following. "But it's mostly similar to the patterns Egg made when they lost that third mining crew in the Vaughn Trench."

In his mind's eye, Ramirez watched the mining rig in mid-shift, its nighttime lights glowing so bright he could barely look at it. There was some rumbling because there was always some rumbling, but the boss encouraged the crew to keep working. Paydirt was in mid-collection, once it was hauled up for processing, the transport would take them back to the colony for two weeks' leave. Then the drills came to a crunching halt, metal crushed against rock as dense as titanium. There was a bone-chilling silence, soft creaking, and Egg swallowed the entire rig into a trench so deep the drones they sent down to find the bodies never came back.

Then the rig was his little crew of mild-mannered geologists.

Finally, he managed to spit out: "Wh—when?"

Graves shrugged. "Tonight, tomorrow, thirty years from now?" She started folding up the chart. "I'll recalibrate the early warning system's sensitivity. We'll have plenty of time to reach escape velocity before Egg cracks. Remember, boss, we have way better safety measures than some backwater mining operation. They ignored all signs. Epsilon knew what was happening; they decided to sacrifice the crew."

Sense reemerged from fear. "Right, right." Ramirez scratched his chin, playing the fear like an itch. They weren't some greedy mega-corporation mining until the earth cracked under them. They were a tax-exempt, government-funded scientific outpost. If they left, no harm done, but a few trillion tax dollars lost.

"Okay," he sighed. "Recalibrate the warning system. I'll get Boris and his team over here to help while Baker and I check the escape pods."

Graves nodded and tucked the datasheet into her coat. She and Carter returned to their workspace. Ramirez spoke his orders into the comms, halting all regularly scheduled work and putting everyone on inspection duty.

They spent the rest of the day-cycle running diagnostics until they found the source of the power outage in Module Three and Ramirez was satisfied that everything was back online and unlikely to malfunction again.

He was feeling better by the time the crew met for chow. His foremen were appraised of the situation; they decided to keep it quiet. There was no need to worry the janitorial staff or the nice ladies who made their meals.

During dinner, Ramirez gave some remarks about how the auxiliary coupling between Module Three and Four came loose and burned out a sensor, resulting in a reporting error. The HVAC systems were clean and working properly, and the gravity generators were fine. They had nothing to worry about.

When chow finished, and everyone was splitting into recreational groups, Ramirez ordered a pot of coffee sent to Mod Three. Graves and Carter would spend most of the night working on the alarm system. *And,* Ramirez knew, *Graves likes to see things in real time*; if there was another rumble, she'd want to watch it in real time.

Flowers started a game of poker. Ramirez played a few hands and settled the Boris-Flowers conflict just as it was heating up again, reminding Yesikov that Flowers's knees were preternaturally accurate and reminding Flowers that Boris was his foreman and the chain of command existed for his safety.

It was in these moments, sipping coffee and laughing, that he truly loved his job. Even with Graves's disquieting information hanging over his head, he was glad for the companionship. *Remember that*, he made a mental note. *People like it when professional men got a little sappy with their crewmates.*

Night cycle rolled around, and the crew started filtering out to their dorms. Ramirez excused himself and went to check on Graves and Carter before he turned in.

Mod Three was dark, only a single desk lamp to provide light. Graves was tapping away at her keyboard, a cigarette hanging from her mouth. Carter's chair was empty, his coffee cup unused.

Graves was so focused she didn't hear Ramirez approach. He watched cigarette smoke waft up until it disappeared into the darkness. There were supposed to be a dozen red lights along the ceiling. He counted eleven.

"Graves."

She jumped, taking the cigarette out of her mouth and jamming it into Carter's empty cup. "Hey, boss," she sounded like a kid caught skipping class in the girl's room.

"You need a lot of smoke to set them off." He tilted his head up at the sprinklers.

"Pays to be careful," she sighed. "Wasn't really a secret anyway."

"I don't have a problem with the smoking; just don't turn off my sprinklers."

"And here I was expecting a lecture about smoking on government property. The old Commissar would have thrown me out the airlock." She turned back to her screen, taking information from the graphs and numbers that he could not. "I always thought deep space would help me quit, but—"

"How's Egg?" he cut her off. She was too valuable to alienate with petty rules.

"Active." She pressed a finger to screen, drawing his attention to a line graph. "She's always active—like Earth—you just can't feel it most of the time. But my instruments certainly can."

"Will there be another tonight?"

"I can't predict the future."

"You just did," he pointed at the chart on her desk.

She gave him a sideways glance and went back to her keyboard. "That's pattern recognition; it's hardly prophecy. Like I said, tonight, tomorrow, thirty years from now?"

He sighed. "All right," then, "you almost done?"

"I'll be here all night. I sent Carter to bed; he'll be on tomorrow. He's just as good." Ramirez doubted it. His foremen were experts at the top of their fields, their academic glory days were on the downward slope. The rest were good people, but also the kind that didn't mind being at the ass-end of the universe.

"I'll keep my comms on if you need me."

"Gotcha," she poured coffee and saluted him with the cup.

Ramirez turned in for the night, starting with his first draft. He saved the untitled work to a flash drive and cleaned up the broken bits of a coffee-stained mug thrown from his bedside table. The pillows were flung off his bed, a few pens scattered on the ground, but everything else stayed in place thanks to the prototype magnet system.

When the room was clean, he did his

nighttime routine: some basic stretches, showered, brushed his teeth, flossed, read for an hour.

Due to Egg's short rotations, the installation was timed to automatically simulate the day-night cycle. The plasma windows darkened for night-cycle and brightened to simulate day. Even with all the carefully calibrated day-night simulations going on, Ramirez always had difficulty falling asleep.

He usually lay awake for an hour before he slipped off. It was now a part of his nightly ritual. He spent the time making mental checklists in preparation for the next day. There were thirty-eight people to take care of. A quiet, unassuming group whose worst habits included secret smoking and quirky, uncanny body-part divination.

Easygoing people. Theirs was a humble mission. The humility of *knowing-what-you're-about* translated into a jovial kind of understanding. His time with the Extraterrestrial Outreach Bureau had skewed his perception against most experts. They were always on about finding *a civilization for the benefit of mutual education and service exchange.*

More to save us from ourselves, he used to joke with his secretary.

Ramirez rolled over, laughing to himself. Here, they tested earthquake warning systems, volcanic predictor software, and stress-tested seismic-ready quality-of-life upgrades like magnetic book covers and ultra-pliable plasma windows. On Egg, they were doing *real* work, advancing *real* science, trying to solve *real* problems.

He thought of the graph Graves showed him; for a moment, he could feel the waves of quaking earth rocking him like a baby in the cradle. All was calm. *Thirty years of service to humanity. Twenty years in the Force, ten in the Outreach, two on Egg, and he was most proud of Egg...*

The activity alarm wasn't blaring, more like the soft beep of a gentle alarm clock. The kind that increased in volume every five minutes.

He scrambled awake and snatched at his comm. Instead, he struck it with his half-asleep arm, and it rolled off his nightstand. Ramirez cursed, jumped up, and keyed a command into his console.

"Graves?" he grunted into the microphone. "Graves, you copy?"

"I copy." She answered, sounding sleepier than he did. "Stand by." The alarm clicked off as the rolling ceased. "Just a quake, green across the board. Go back to sleep."

Awake anyway, he searched around until he found the comm somewhere under his bed. He attached it to the console to charge and lay back down. His heart was hammering in his chest. He took a moment to calm down and laugh at himself.

Getting jumpy in my middle age. Back when he was in Space Force, alarms never jerked him awake. Usually, someone had to kick him. He settled; his heart slowed. He rolled onto his side when a snore tore through his throat and he came awake long enough to change position.

Then he was awake again.

Something unsettled him. A soft greyish glow emanated from the opaque windows, mimicking early morning. He looked around the room. It was spartan: a picture of his old unit in the Force, a farewell card from Tanya Beaks; his books were just plain thrillers, a small portion of his collection still waiting on Earth in the bedroom he rented from his sister.

Thoughts of home roused his instinct, telling him exactly why he was awake. When he was fifteen, he had a big, mean rottweiler who turned into an anxious mess whenever an earthquake rolled through his quiet Californian suburb. Sleeping soundly and then suddenly pacing back and forth between himself and his sister, climbing into her lap, jumping down and climbing into his. Settling right back down when the waves rolled through and all was calm again.

He reached for the comm.

"Graves, this is Ramirez."

"Stand by," she answered, wide awake.

He put the comm down and started getting dressed. Putting on his air suit, grabbing his emergency bag, stuffing a few personal items into it. He took his flash drive and slipped it into the pocket of his suit. This book was his nest egg, his ticket to a quiet retirement.

Ramirez's comm blipped, and Grave's voice came over the wire with an eerie tone of finality. "She's hatching." The alarm started blaring—not the simple warning klaxon, but the keening shriek that came with flashing red lights and a slick female voice.

"Attention all personnel, please prepare for immediate evacuation. This is not a drill. Please prepare for immediate evacuation." The message repeated twice before Ramirez was clicking orders into the console, shutting down the announcement so his voice could be heard.

"This is Commissar Ramirez, remain calm—we've done the drills, we knew this day was coming. Make an orderly way to the escape pods. Foremen, be ready for roll-call. That is all." He clicked off the comm, and the alarm returned in full force.

Ramirez followed the running lights to the five-way. He entered the Mod Three lab, where Graves was tapping furiously on her computer.

"Let's go, Graves," he snapped. They didn't have time for curiosity.

"You don't have to tell me twice." She watched paper vomit out of the printer, snatched it up, folded it, and stowed into the pocket of her suit. "We've got ten minutes, maybe fifteen. There isn't much out there to slow the waves."

Ramirez set his watch and followed her to the Mod Three dorms. "All right, all right, let's go!" She started pounding on doors and walls. "It's the big one, kids! Let's go!" She did a quick head count, went to her own room, snapped up her emergency bag, shoving two research portfolios and a picture of her parents into it.

"Ten minutes, let's move!" The crew was already up and moving, putting on their suits, grabbing their bags, making a nice orderly line.

Satisfied, Ramirez left Mod Three and made his way to the evac. The automated systems already had the pods warming up.

He could hear the rumble of their engines, felt it through the steel and aluminum, knew it was probably the quakes.

Eight minutes.

The first crew to appear was Mod Four. Flowers led; Boris brought up the rear. Boris took rollcall, counted heads twice, and Ramirez ordered them to load into the launcher.

Mod One and Two appeared as Boris loaded his crew. They called names, counted heads, then Mod Three arrived.

"All hands secure," Boris said just as Graves was turning in her head count.

"Away," Ramirez ordered. Mod Four's pod took off; the noise was muffled but the rumble shook the installation. One and Two radioed their status. "Away," he ordered, checking his watch. *Five minutes.*

Ramirez followed Graves into the Mod Three pod. The ground swelled up, meeting his foot. Now that it was daylight, the plasma windows cleared. They rippled like water, moving with the rolls. He saw the drill across the Conchae Maris wobble back and forth and fall into the mess hall. Pieces of crushed steel and shattered earth floated off in the low gravity.

In the pod, he sat beside Graves and Carter. The doors locked, the launcher pressurized, then it was up and the ground was falling away.

Ramirez smirked. *Not us; not like you had the miners.*

The way up was bumpy. Launches were always bumpy. The force jostled Ramirez's teeth and made his bones seem too thin and too heavy all at once. He would have drift-ed out of his seat without the harness, and then just as weightlessness took over, he was slammed back against the hard padding. The crew was quiet. There were no tears, no rage. You didn't travel to this backwater with precious items. They were a transient people with a transient job.

Then, they were out of the atmosphere, and he was drifting in his harness.

"This is Ramirez," he spoke into the comm. "Modules, sound off."

"Mod One, clear."

"Mod Two, clear."

Graves spoke into her lapel. "Mod Three, clear."

"Mod Four, clear."

Ramirez smirked, swelling with pride. "Good work, crew." He could hear his own smile through Grave's comm. "Once evac distance is achieved, I'll radio HQ." They knew the drills, but years of experience taught Ramirez that stating it could soothe the anxious. "We have rations for two weeks and enough fuel to get us to Tanitar One if required. Keep comm chatter to a minimum, keep sensors live. I don't want anyone floating into anything."

"Copy," was the response.

Beside him, Graves and Carter were poring over her printout, whispering to each other. Ramirez ignored them.

It took approximately twenty minutes for them to reach total evac distance. The onboard computer beeped; the locking system would allow them out of their chairs. Ramirez hit the release button on his seat, unbuckled the straps around his chest, and pushed towards the front of the pod, floating in zero gravity.

The training received in the Force kicked in immediately. He was almost swimming through the air. He missed zero-g war-games. It was one of the few things he missed about the Force.

Using the handgrips placed around the console, Ramirez forced his body down and slipped his feet into the automatic clamps that would hold him to the floor while he kicked on the artificial gravity. He warned the team, flicked some switches, and felt the weightlessness dissipate as if he stood at the bottom of a pool suddenly and violently drained.

He turned back to the crew, and feeling slightly giddy, raised a thumbs up. Graves and Carter were still deep into their data sheet, but the rest smiled slightly, not so much afraid as disappointed their work was interrupted by the very object of their study.

Reassured, Ramirez radioed the other pods. "Pod Three, gravity enabled. Pod sound off."

"Pod One, gravity enabled. Ready for comm path." Baker.

"Pod Two, gravity enabled. Comm path set." Cunningham.

Quickly, Ramirez flipped another series of switches, extending the pod's comm relay. The ships were designed to stay near each other in the event of rescue, ensuring all four were found together. To do that, the pods relied on a long-range comm relay that pinged their SOS off each other, making it easier for a passing ship to triangulate their location. Baker had explained the system to him back when his assignment began, but he'd long forgotten how it actually managed to work.

"Pod Four?" Ramirez asked, feeling only slightly concerned.

"Pod Four...vity enable..." the message was marred with static. "Hit by debris...all hands...can't extend...comm...usted."

Ramirez cursed. "Baker, could you make that out?" He didn't wait for an answer and instead called Pod Four back. "Pod Four, message garbled. Repeat?"

Boris's clearly irritated voice came back over the comms, still raspy with static but easier to understand. "Gravity enabled," he grunted. "Relay was hit by debris. Long range not possible from Pod Four."

Frustrated, Ramirez yelled into his comm. "What was that bit about all hands?"

"All hands safe."

Relieved, Ramirez ordered all comms open. "I'm going to send out the SOS. Baker, we'll be fine with just three?"

"So long as Pod Four remains close. I advise we burn some fuel and couple with Four. Pod Two is nearest."

"Agreed," Ramirez said. "Do you copy, Pod Four?"

"Copy," Yesikov grunted, his short-range audio was clearing up now.

"Pod Two?"

"Prepping engines," Cunningham responded.

"Once coupling is secure, switch to support power. I want nothing but HVAC, internal floor lights, and emergency beacons."

"Copy," they answered at once.

With that, Ramirez finished linking up their long-range comms and extending Pod Three's relay. He began broadcasting their SOS message. Protocol expected they wait thirty-six hours before burning fuel towards Tanitar One; HQ would receive their first broadcast in three hours and help would arrive in six to eight.

Must be some cards around here somewhere? He clicked off the gravity generator and was about to release his feet when Graves came floating towards him. She grabbed his shoulder. He pulled her down into the clamp beside him.

"I'd appreciate a chance to look at her."

"The satellites should have captured her end, Graves."

"Sure," she didn't smile. "But it's not every day you get to see the broken wreckage of a small exomoon." She smirked then, but her voice was tinged with something—*ominous*, he decided.

He shrugged and peered back at the crew. Everyone but Carter was waiting for the window. Carter was sweating, furiously studying the data sheet. "All right," Ramirez said. "For a few minutes." He called their intentions over the comms and opened shutters.

Ramirez's mouth fell open.

Stardust.

After college, he and his buddies romped around Arizona for a month, hiking, camping, and studying the stars they were about to journey into. Laying face up in the desert, watching stars and satellites float by, was a poor approximation of what he saw now. *Like sitting inside the heart of a star.*

It was all surging, swelling, floating like jetsam on the ocean tide. The aluminum-rich crust glittered in the light of the system's sun. Egg was a rogue moon, a little scrap shifted further and further away from the galactic interior. Ramirez loved her. She was beautiful, with jagged edges of broken crust, bits of earth the size of frigates, some larger than the Super-Cruiser he had served on all those years ago.

All this raw material would make its way back to its origin. It would feed the star that drew it in, would dust the wide, shallow seas of Tanitar Two, and burn in the hydrogen-rich atmosphere of the blazing gas giant that made up Egg's nearest neighbor.

He felt himself choking up. Shivered, *book material.*

Once they were rescued, his little platoon would return to their universities and write their research papers; they'd settle like space dust. Ramirez himself was getting old. He'd finish his book, publish, maybe hunt down Tanya Beaks?

Or, he mused, eyeing the chestnut-haired scientist beside him, *ask Doctor Hanna Graves if she'd like to get a drink.* Her home academy was the Interstellar University of Titan; that was close enough to Earth.

Graves was studying with a wild intensity, her eyes worked back and forth across the scene, taking it all in. She looked down at the instruments and started activating some. They were no longer waiting for rescue, but back in her laboratory.

"Graves to Yesikov," she said into her comms.

"Copy," Yesikov responded. "We're almost done with the coupling."

"Forget that, look out the window."

"What?" Ramirez hissed. "What is it?"

Carter came floating over with a few of the other senior scientists. They started crowding around the view, their eyes flicking back and forth between the scene outside and the instruments.

"Commissar?" Boris said over the comms.

"Just do what she says." Then he turned back to Graves. "What is it?"

"I'm not a geologist." She eyed the console, waiting.

Scientists, Ramirez found, could be annoying when they stepped out of their fields to opine on things they didn't know. But they could be downright dangerous when they decided to stay in their lanes.

"If it's an emergency," he began, unable to face her because of the clamps. "I need…"

"Hellfire!" Boris cried over the comms. "Graves, transmit me that data."

"We better turn off our comms," Graves said, taking the data sheet, feeding through the scanner and transmitting it to the other Pods.

"What are you talking about?"

Graves couldn't turn to look at him, but he saw her eyes reflected in the monitor. Her eyes flared, bright and watery with fear. "We've always jokingly called her an egg," she whispered. "We've always said she was going to hatch—but," she started laughing, "more things in heaven and earth, Horatio."

Ramirez swallowed bile. "Does anyone want to explain what the hell she means?"

"I don't see any signs of actual geological activity," Boris began, halting, subdued. "She has no molten core."

Ramirez swallowed and reasoned. "She's a dead planet, then?"

"We've always theorized her with a cool, but active core, especially in light of her geothermic activity." Graves folded the readout and shoved it into her suit. "I don't see any signs."

Flustered by his own lack of scientific knowledge, Ramirez peered out the window. A chunk of broken crust was floating by, its edges jagged and torn, like a piece of concrete broken up by a jackhammer. It told him absolutely nothing.

"I don't understand," Ramirez couldn't work enough moisture into his throat; the rest came out like a hideous croak. "What are you saying?"

"She's hollow," Carter muttered, the first words Ramirez thought he'd ever heard the man say. "Jesus, Mary, and Joseph, protect us."

"How is that possible?"

Before anyone could answer him, Baker's voice came over the link. "Super-Cruiser inbound."

"Super-Cruiser?" Ramirez gasped, bowels churning. "How—we didn't get any light-speed alerts." He reached for the hailing beacon.

Grave snatched his hand. "Don't hail it!"

He pulled free and puffed his chest, outraged. "And why the hell not?"

"Because it's not ours."

"That isn't possible." His blood turned to ice water. He spent years in Outreach. He knew. Man was alone.

Graves pointed at the sensors. "No one jumped into this system. Think about what Carter just said. Hollow. Oscar, Egg is hollow."

Ramirez was physically incapable of thinking. His mouth opened; his tongue was limp. He closed his jaw, and his teeth clicked, jarring his numb face. His arm hurt where Graves had grabbed him. Graves was staring at him, waiting for him to make a decision.

"Shut it down," he wheezed, his mind slowly rebooting. "Shut it down."

She didn't wait for him to start the command sequence and did it herself. "You heard the man," she said into the comms. "Go dark."

The other Pods didn't copy. They blacked out.

And they were utterly and unalterably alone.

Graves closed the shutters.

Humanity has dreamed of this moment. Ramirez thought of Tanya Beaks, getting caught up in her enthusiasm back at Xanadu. Would she have hailed the unknown craft? Call out to them? Begged them to come save them from themselves?

No, the thought stabbed his reasoning brain like a knife and twisted. Self-preservation would win the day. The lizard brain that lived deep in his cortex, that told his ancestors to fear the snake and fight the stranger, took control like a tyrant. It brutalized his reason, beating it into submission, breaking the last vestiges of his innate curiosity. He sucked in a breath, sweat welled up in his clenched fists. He reached for his heart; it was thumping wildly, trying to escape. *No, she wouldn't, because we don't want this. We think we do, but we might just be small fish in a real big pond. Food for the bigger, meaner things with no qualms about their place in the food chain.*

Did Columbus fear the dragons he might find when he launched from Spain? Was he surprised to find men? Or was that his truest, worst fear? To find something like himself?

The clamps holding Ramirez's feet were released with a hiss, and he felt himself floating away. He was clutching his heart. Graves was shouting about the first aid kit. *You're having a heart attack.*

Carter brought the kit. Graves forced asprin and water down his throat while Carter attached the heart monitor's self-sticky nodes to his chest. The machine beeped erratically, picking up his heartbeat. It began counting, giving directions.

We just did this drill, two weeks ago. They didn't turn on the gravity generator. Instead, they did what he would have told them and pulled him into the medical brace. The clamps held him down.

"Clear!" Graves threw her hands up as the defibrillator's alarm warned and delivered the shock. It began to beep steadily. With every successive beep, Ramirez felt the covering haze melt away.

He took in air, completely unaware that he hadn't been breathing. Graves, red-faced and sweaty, sighed a brisk, "Thank God."

Metal groaned above them, the defibrillator flew out of Carter's hands and knocked against the side of the pod.

"Grab onto something!" Graves released the clamps holding her feet and grasped at the handles around the medical brace.

The pod rocked back and forth; metal creaked the way it creaked on Egg during a quake. His people scrambled to find holdings. Beneath the tense beep of the heart monitor, Carter was praying. Graves pulled the sticky nodes from Ramirez's chest, and the monitor flatlined and died just as the pod's proximity alarm began to flash silently.

Gravity swelled in like the sea, pulling everything back into the hard world of earthbound physics. The heart monitor crashed to the floor, cracking plastic and bits of aluminum. Someone fell from the ceiling, slamming his head into the console, and lay still. Trapped in the med-brace, Ramirez couldn't see who it was.

Beside him, Graves flicked the clamp switch, but he was too weak to get up. "Weapons," she whispered and then yelled because there was something outside screeching against the hull, trying to pry the hatchway open.

He could see it in his mind. A vicious, scaly beast with claws curved and wicked as scimitars, teeth long and sharp and poisonous. *Here there be dragons.* Ramirez chuckled and finally named his book.

Graves helped him up. "Handguns," he pointed weakly across the pod. "In the supplies."

The noise stopped. Quiet seconds ticked by. There was scuffling above them. *More monsters,* Ramirez thought. *More dragons.* With a shrieking of steel, the hatch was peeled away like the ripping and tearing of flesh under the teeth of a gluttonous beast. Ramirez looked up to see the face of his devourer.

The face that looked back at him was like his own. A nose. Two ears. Two bright blue eyes. A mouth full of teeth made perfectly for an omnivorous diet. A mop of lightly greying hair. The beast had two legs, two arms, and one head. It wore a form-fitting spacesuit with strange insignias and letters embroidered on the chest.

"*Yldneirf?*" It spoke out of the hole that looked just like Ramirez's mouth and it sounded like a man.

Utterly and unalterably alone. Ramirez gripped at his heart and broke into wild peals of laughter.

Jaime Faye Torkelson lives in central CA. She's an autodidact most passionate about writing, medieval history, and philosophy. This is her first published work, but hopefully not her last. She can be reached at the.salon.at.elfland@gmail.com.

Search Pattern

By WILLIAM SUBOSKI

A strange woman seemingly miraculously cures a man's terminal cancer! His son has devoted his life to data sciences, but can he follow the clues to track her down?!

When I was twelve years old, my father was dying of cancer; I still don't know what kind. My parents tried to shield my younger sister and me from the diagnosis. For a time, there was cheerfulness, and I was too young to recognize this false optimism. The doctors espoused positive mental attitude—"We're going to beat this!"—and my parents wanted to believe it. So there was a lot of humming and glad-handing and fake laughter and false conviviality.

Which all ended one day when they came back from the latest doctor sortie. They were silent and dour. As I said, they tried to protect us from the reality—so we were never told what had happened. But as an adult, I believe that that day they learned that my father's cancer had become metastatic and spread throughout his body. They were quiet and morose, that day and the next, and this dark mood only slowly and slightly lessened over the coming weeks. Hopefulness had been erased by the inevitable.

After that, Dad didn't work anymore. He had been off and on, missing many days, but after that visit, he tired too easily. His physical appearance started changing ever

more rapidly. He lost weight, and his eyes sank into his face. He lost muscle in his arms and legs and slowly became a stick figure. For the first time in my life, my father, who had always been so loud and brash and bigger than life, now seemed a shrunken shadow of himself. This lurching scarecrow terrified me. It was almost as if he were an old shirt, with his color fading from each repeated wash, until he was drab and threadbare and worn, and soon to be thrown away.

And for the first time, he spent time with me. He had always tossed a ball around, and we did things on family vacations. But usually he was too busy to spend much time with my sister and me. It was confusing. I liked spending time with him even as he faded in slow motion. I felt guilty about it. I felt that simply by being with him and being happy, I was betraying him. How could this make me happy? And yet it did. I have learned since then that life is often this perverse, giving a small compensation while exacting a crippling toll. I have learned since then that it was not my fault—I was just a kid who liked spending time with his dad, no matter what. It was wonderful and awful both, and we were all preparing for

139

the soon-to-come day when he would be gone—he most of all.

And so it was that one Saturday we had ridden the city bus from our neighborhood to the downtown of our small village. Mom had given us a list, an itinerary of many errands within a few blocks of each other. She had not wanted him to go, but he had been insistent, as firm as a man struggling to stand can be. And Dad was very tired waiting for the bus, even at eleven a.m. after a full night's sleep. There was no bench, and so he sat on the curb. He seemed disconsolate and so thoroughly defeated. When the bus appeared down the street, he slowly rose as a weary old man would. I saw the light dimming in his eyes. It wouldn't be long.

That day we spent most of the time resting. He would walk a block, then find a bench and sit. He started apologizing for holding us up, and my guilt almost paralyzed me.

"Dad, it's okay…"

"No, Jimmy, it isn't, it really isn't…" and his eyes moved back and forth as if searching and his voice broke, and for a moment, he almost wept. My dad was going to die, and there was nothing I nor anyone could do about it. He sent me to do the rest of the errands alone. He would wait on the bench, he said. I hurried away, confused, afraid, not wanting to leave and also wanting to run as far and fast as possible.

When I returned, he seemed a little stronger. We shared a sandwich, and he was silent again. He seemed too tired to speak, but he tried. He would smile and even try to

laugh. We made our way to the bus terminal for the trip home. It was late in the afternoon, but it was summer and the sun still bright. Dad waited on a bench on the platform, and I went inside the waiting area to check the schedule. His head slumped down, and his eyes closed.

When I came out, a middle-aged woman was stopping as she walked past my dad. She wore a long skirt patched in grays and blacks, a puffy blouse, and a gray shawl or poncho over her shoulders. When I first saw her, she seemed hidden in the folds of her clothes. She stopped and looked down at him and said, "You aren't doing too well, are you?"

"No, ma'am, not well at all." His voice was a dry whisper. His eyes didn't open.

She leaned forward and put her hand on his forehead as one does with a child to check a fever. She ran her hands lightly across his face the way a blind woman might, then she bent over and took his hands in her own. I saw her squeeze them tightly, and he opened his eyes and looked up at her.

I was frozen in place. It felt like a dream. I didn't even consider moving. As she squeezed his fingers, their linked hands glowed different colors, yet all of them were golden, lighting the shaded platform, the best gold of the finest sunset, the richest gold of the best autumn, a gold that had never shone before. I stopped breathing. The air hummed electric, yet there was total silence. I saw them lock eyes with each other. The air smelled of ozone and apples. It was a moment, only a moment, a tear formed in the corner of my own eye. I blinked and it was gone.

She gently laid his hands on his lap, and she stood straight.

"I think you will do better now."

And she hurried away, but she was limping slightly as she did, and she coughed when she turned from him.

Death takes everything from us, in creeping steps; each death is a thousand cuts. First, our freedom of movement slips away, then independence. In time, for tasks we did for ourselves we must wait, while others warm our soup or wash our clothes or simply tie our shoes. And in time, all dignity is taken, lost to time. The French say death is female, la mort. I say death is a harridan, a virginal maiden gone awry, a spurned and unrequited lover who knows no mercy in reprisal.

I am now forty-six. That was thirty-four years ago. My mother passed away in her sleep last year. My father is still alive and living with my sister and her husband. He looks after his grandkids and is strong as I ever knew him, and stronger than that day of magic. His forearms seem bundles of thick cords, and his step has a determination that intimidates lesser men.

In the days after our Saturday trip, his face grew fuller. He stopped losing weight, and his tiredness faded. A few weeks later, he was loud and brash again, laughing easily and often. My mother smiled again. I did not realize that all her smiles had stopped until they returned again. That day of the next doctor's visit, they came home, hand in hand, skipping along the street. Laughing. All traces of cancer seemed to be gone.

My father was a veteran of Viet Nam. He was injured and rotated first to a hospital and then home stateside. He has never talked about his injury or his time there. I know that he was months recovering, and at one time, his degree of recovery was uncertain. But in time he did almost fully recover, and by the time I knew him, he had only a small limp, more pronounced on cold days. But after the golden hour, that day at the bus station, he never limped again.

I had my father back. As he recovered, we grew more distant again. I saw less of him. But there was a change. He did still spend time with me, much more than before. Not only was he alive but we were close.

And as I grew, we grew apart again, but not in a neglected way. Instead, I matured, and the father-son dynamic became more friends, more teammates, as can happen in the best families. I went on in school, and I studied mathematics and statistics. I aggressively pursued government contracts. When I was unable to find computer programmers with government clearance, I learned coding.

I started a company. It was a means to an end. We found correlations, things that go together, apple pie and ice cream, and things that don't, anchovies and chocolate pudding. I barely noticed, but as I wrote programs, always refining the searching and sifting algorithms, we discovered details, foods and lifestyle choices that seemed to either cause or prevent illnesses or diseases. I barely noticed. But my company was publishing papers, and money poured in.

We set up a subscription service—a crude website. We would post results, ideas, data fragments; our phones rang off the hook, so the website was just a way to save time. I didn't pay attention at the time. But so many companies signed up for the feed that the subscription revenues covered our operating expenses. It was never about money. It was discovery, exploration. It was a search.

A young man named Marty joined us. He began to monetize the fallout. Bank accounts swelled. I have a vague recollection of hearing that cancer rates had fallen as much as fifteen percent. The preliminary website had been buffed and polished, then split into fragments, fissioning into entirely new slick specialized informational entities. I kept developing my software. Spontaneous human combustion is real—who knew?

One day, driving home, I stopped at a corner store and saw my face on the newsstand. The text on the magazine cover read, "Obsession Personified." Who are they talking about? They don't know me. I bought it, and the facts were mostly correct, but the conclusions... They seemed to be fill-in-the-blanks. They couldn't get a nice prepackaged explanation, so they made one up. Who cares? I am a normal person. I visit my sister and father a few times each week, have dinner with friends once or twice a month, and even watch the odd sitcom. But it was a nice picture of me, and they said nice things.

One passage stays with me: "With the rapid growth of deep analysis have come serious research monies. The temptations for corruption had become commonplace, yet independent audits have found the Cetus Institute to be remarkably scandal-free. The creation of the overseas development grants seems almost to be a manner of surrendering an embarrassment of riches, and yet those grants have themselves yielded increasingly impressive results. In recent years, ten million people have risen from poverty as a direct result of Institute grants. The employees of the Institute, more accurately described as adherents, seem scrupulously honest and singularly devoted to their cause."

How to succeed in business without really trying, or something like that. But what does money mean if a loved one is dying of incurable cancer? We skate through life, pretending that our daily concerns matter and mean something, but we are all mere players, ants at a picnic, until a shadow falls and a shoe lands and life ends. I will not apologize for acting with purpose.

At the age of thirty-eight, I had the Holy Grail—unrestricted access to Social Security medical records. I could cross-reference this database to any other and look for patterns. I look at a polished piece of rock and know in an instant if it is granite or limestone, simply from a pattern. Computers cannot see. Programs are blind. But this is what is needed, glancing at a thousand million million data points and knowing in an instant.

There is no way to even describe what we found—we found so much. I asked Marty for some numbers. This is what he said: there are 8,700 patents that cite our research as primary (we don't waste time securing patents). We have some 43,000 corporate newsfeed subscribers. Each day our researchers produce six to eight new papers or significant memoranda.

Years ago, a businessman-explorer named Steve Fossett disappeared when the airplane he was flying did not return. The very intensive search for his crash site found eight previously undiscovered crashes—some decades old. The other crash discoveries gave comfort to the families of the missing, but the search for Fossett continued.

Intensive searches make chance discoveries inevitable. And just as the hunt for Fossett later widened, with upwards of 50,000 people all scrutinizing high-resolution aerial photographs, until the entire possible crash field had been visually if remotely examined, so too my programs ran, searching and shifting and shuffling, again and again and again...

Serendipitous finds become certain. Months became years. There are no ghosts. Let me rephrase that. I suppose I am almost a scientist, so I should be precise. There is no evidence of anything like ghosts. People forget that the story of Lavender Lily was actually printed in the Reader's Digest in the 1950s. Roswell was a weather balloon. Perhaps I have resurrected the Renaissance idea that if one knows enough facts, one becomes God. Maybe I have; maybe it's true. Oswald acted alone.

I was searching, reaching blindly in the darkness, seeking an explanation of how a woman could grasp another man's hands and create a golden glow, and afterward, he would be cured of a deadly cancer. Neither my father nor mother had cared. They were happy of the miracle, as I was. But someone walked among us who carried great power. In this broken world of Tikkun Olam walked a woman able to lay on hands and hold back death.

And despite the intensive searching, Fosset's crash site remained undiscovered. Almost a year after he went missing, twenty-eight friends conducted a foot search, again, no results. It was not until a few weeks after that that a lone hiker found some identification cards that led to the nearby discovery of the downed plane. I thought often of this as I searched, how it is not effort but luck that leads to the discoveries—Fleming and penicillin.

Six years ago, I started receiving invitations to various state dinners. I declined, but Marty and some of the others attended. We developed a scalable water purification device—desalination, also—that we sell at cost. We have no patent; our research is online and public. But companies pay us to consult on design, and we have expanded, and we profit. Cholera has virtually disappeared. Cheap potable water from the oceans allows the irrigation of deserts. The economics of the world are changing, reshuffling, as Africa modernizes through agriculture and plenty.

And as everyone has enough food, the need for war has lessened. Trade relationships are being forged. Instead of fighting over scraps of land, former competitors are working together, building bakeries to add value to new wheat crops. Even as erstwhile world leaders still try to use fear to motivate their electoral bases, the world has become better. The struggle for security has been won, scarcity has been defeated, and prosperity rules the day.

My breakthrough came three years ago. These most private searches are not published. I have a small staff, and we maintain utter discretion. There are people with gifts. There is a familial thread, in a certain group of people, the second-born of every female receives a gift. This is predicated upon the first pregnancy being stillborn. This is a necessary condition for the gift. Given this condition, it is always the second born, and it is not Mendelian genetics. This bears explanation; there is no genetic mechanism to ensure that one child and only one child will express a trait. And yet this gifting descends through a form of inheritance.

Finding this has been difficult because the gifts vary so widely. The software looks for "odd occurrences," and when it finds one, it seeks a surrounding pattern of similar occurrences. The familial link did not emerge until over two hundred such clusters had been identified. Only then were there enough data points to start linking individuals.

I have names. I have found individuals with rare gifts, and in time, I will approach them. But that is still in the future. For now, I seek only one woman from thirty-four years ago.

These names are not stored. I will not allow them to fall into the wrong hands. Over

the course of my lifetime, my vision has changed. Or perhaps simply evolved. No government, no agency, will be given these names. No agency will ever be allowed to learn of these gifted people. None of my staff, only myself, know of them. I would trust Marty, and others, with my wallet, but they will never know of these findings. The names are encoded. I will never reveal them.

I knew the what, at least I thought I did, but I still didn't know who. My software can access only digital, and only a fraction of the world becomes digital. No one but you will know that your cat doesn't mind water, or likes to sit on the dryer during its cycle for the warmth. The health of the cat, certainly, from the digital records, and even his or her preferred brand and flavor of food is digitally accessible through your purchases. But unless you take a picture and post it online, I will never know if your cat is black or white or Cheshire.

This is the challenge, riddles within riddles, patterns within patterns. Trying to assemble a gray jigsaw puzzle with many missing pieces in a dense fog. Long ago, I reconciled myself to failure, that despite these efforts, I might never find her. I can live with that. We have done great things, Marty and I and the others. I have had a good life, and I am grateful. But I had to try.

It has taken three years since I learned of the gifted ones. Even with a target, it has taken three years to find a particular person, to learn her name and address. Tomorrow, I will travel several hundred miles, and the day afterward, I will approach her and try to talk to her. What happens after that depends on her.

I sit on a bench. This is an older neighborhood, brownstones with staircases that lead up to doors a level above the street. It is a beautiful neighborhood, small trees adjacent to the curb, a wide sidewalk, and a sedate pace of life. I have been on the bench for an hour. I bought a kielbasa and soda pop from a street vendor. I now sit with a newspaper on my crossed knee, a few doors down from Mary Janis's entrance.

I am absorbing the neighborhood—developing a feel for it. It is busy but relaxed. Residents wave to and greet each other, and also the delivery drivers on quotidian rounds. It has a pleasant feel. If it were a pie, it would be apple, heavy on cinnamon, with a large scoop of creamy vanilla ice cream. Although I am a stranger here, in the last hour, three people have made pleasant greetings. I understand why she lives here.

Less than another hour later, she emerges. She pauses at the top of the steps, looks up and out, and takes a deep breath. I cannot guess her age. She smiles, the patchwork woman, blacks and grays, then she carefully descends the steps and limps away from me down the sidewalk.

I wander away shortly afterward. I find a small bistro and have an overpriced sandwich and mediocre soup. In contrast with the bench and neighborhood a few blocks away, this meal feels dishonest. Someone is counting the celery stalks and weighing the carrots in this soup. Quality has fled, and the soup is enumerated only in arid dollar signs that are paltry ciphers. I taste again the bitter lie of heartless capitalism.

The next day I am waiting closer to the time she emerged. I am on the closest bench to her staircase—only a door away. I play with my phone, seeking to look busy, and almost miss her when she emerges. I wait until she is still a few steps up, then stand and walk toward her.

"Mrs. Janis?"

She looks up, surprised. Despite the friendly neighborhood, names are rarely used, and she wasn't expecting me or anyone. She looks at me and squints, examining me, does she know me?

"My name is James Sheridan. I am with the Cetus Institute. I wonder if I might—"

But she interrupts me. She starts to smile, a knowing smile.

"I know who you are. You are the founder of the Cetus Institute. Don't be shy."

Her smile blooms across her face. She seems to be silently laughing.

"Little Jimmy, from the bus station. You certainly have grown. I saw you here yesterday."

Her next words are Graham crackers and marshmallows and freshly mown grass, and gasoline from a pump and a dusty street at the start of a summer rain.

"It's good to see you, Jimmy."

I called for my car. We rode around in the backseat with the partition up and the windows slightly opened. Mary seemed to appreciate the privacy. She expressed no apprehension.

She was retired. She had worked most of her life as a nurse—no surprise there. She was careful. She used her gift lightly and would change jobs often. She would always try to use it unknown to the recipient, often when they were asleep. She told me she would often address smaller issues, arthritis in a piano player's hands, hearing loss in the elderly, heart murmurs in the sickly. She tried to use it so that no one knew she had.

She had been careful. She did not want to be abducted, by the government or by the wealthy. This was a large aspect of why she had been so hard for me to find. She was clever and covert and watchful. But despite this, she trusted me from the start, treating me as she would a loved nephew or a long-time friend.

"Your father was hours from death, Jimmy. I broke my own rules. He was so young and in so much pain and… I couldn't walk past. I couldn't."

"Did you limp before you laid hands, Mary?"

"Yes," she said, a hand gesture waving away my concern. "That was an old injury. I fell when I was a teenager."

"I think you just lied to me."

"Jimmy, how could you say such a thing? How harsh you are, how cruel!"

Her head dipped and a small smile spread across her face.

"Okay, I lied. Honesty isn't everything it's cracked up to be. And now you will feel forever guilty, and there is no reason to feel bad at all. I knew what I was doing, and now I am going to have to lay hands on you to take that away. This is your fault, Jimmy!"

And she burst out laughing, and I told her about the dishonest soup.

"Well, here's another fine mess you've gotten me into."

We sit on a bench in a park up from a lake. The air is still, and the lake is a mirror. My car is parked a hundred feet away. There is no one else around and we have been talking for hours. Oddly, I never imagined what would come next. I planned, I hoped, to find Mary, to speak with her, but I never addressed the question of the afterward.

Obviously, we will stay in touch. As relaxing as this day has been, I want to know more. The developed scientist in me wants to learn about Mary's abilities. What are the limits? Is it magic or science or something else? Could it be bottled, recreated in another person, or device? But none of that is what brought me here today.

"You acquired the limp when you cured my dad?" She nods. "Why didn't you ever cure it in yourself?"

Her voice has a mournful tone.

"I am the only person I cannot heal, Jimmy." She pauses. "And I think that will bear on something you will ask me, sooner or later." She pauses again. "Light healings do not affect me. But in the worse cases, I suffer. Your father—he was so sick. I needed all my concentration not to die myself, and the limp is permanent. So…no, Jimmy, I can't heal the world. That is what you were going to ask, isn't it? I could only die trying. I think this is the beginning of a beautiful friendship. But it really doesn't matter, anyway, if I heal the world. Because," she raised her hand and lovingly stroked my cheek, "you already have; you just haven't noticed yet."

The day was late. Mary was tired. I would see her again the next day, and we have been in close contact since then. I pressed the money into her hands, a stack of one hundred hundreds. She resisted, but I insisted.

"Treat yourself, Mary. These are mere leaves, pieces of paper. Buy yourself a new pair of shoes, go out to a fancy dinner, give $500 to charity, get your bills current. Whatever you wish. Let me know when you need more. And look after yourself."

We were on her street, and the car pulled over and came to a stop. We had been holding hands. I had enjoyed that afternoon. It had been more than I could have ever hoped. She squeezed my hand.

"Thank you for finding me... for spending half a life looking. But why did you bother?"

"Something I had to say to you, Mary. Something very important. Something that had to be said."

It was already dark out, but I still saw the questioning look on her face.

"Thank you."

Bill is an aspiring fiction writer with a background in computer programming. He is still trying to decide what he wants to be when he grows up. Born in Indiana, Bill is a transplanted Hoosier living as a Buckeye by way of Canada. Contact Bill at WSuboski@yahoo.com.

My Name is John Carter (Part 15)

By JAMES HUTCHINGS

Though my captor was mute, and our words took a
  route
from one brain to another directly,
and I should, I admit, have felt awed—truly, it,
if I'm honest, did naught to affect me.

I heard speech, clear and plain, and replied with
  the same,
just as if it were here and could hear me.
As—some detail it shared being vague—I prepared
to give voice to some trivial query,

My intent was conveyed in some noise that I made,
I suppose, or some twitch of the eye
that my captor detected, which might be expected:
I never once claimed to be sly.

And what patience it had—and a lust-maddened
  lad
is a relative font of that virtue—
was completely destroyed, just as sure as that boy
will break hearts, resolutions and curfews.

Though the pedant may squall, I shall nonetheless
  call
what it wielded a voice of derision,
and I would have propounded, had it not been
  bound
with the crust of a world for a prison

That it angrily paced. If God gave it a face,
I'd imagine it bearing a glower.
In one tenth of a second, its thoughts, so it reck-
oned,
went further than mine in an hour.

To converse at my speed was a burdensome deed,
a gazelle keeping pace with a glacier.
'Twas a bird born to soar made to limp on the floor
and, in short, an affront to its nature.

It declared it would cease sending thoughts in small
  pieces,
like one who gives food to a baby,
but send swiftly instead—and, uneasy, I said,
"Will the weight of your psyche not slay me?

"Will my human-sized brain not collapse with the
  strain,
as an infant might perish from choking?"
"Very likely, O stranger, but I face no danger,"
it said, and I doubt it was joking.

There was never a palace held tyrant so callous.
No nation hailed god-king so haughty.
Not a heart was so hard with such blithe disregard
as within the cold creature that caught me.

Though the tyrant rejects any thought of respect,
you can only reject what you know,
while my captor no more knew of human rapport
than the desert knows midwinter snow.

Then my brain seemed to fill with an alien will,
and I thought that my head soon would burst.
I've been punched, bit, and stabbed, and my pri-

148

vate parts grabbed.
Of all bodily pains, this was worst.

And the pain inside swelled to a foretaste of Hell,
and the desert before me grew blurred,
and the memories were shared, and I knew then
    and there
what unapt, clumsy vessels are words.

On the day mute Mankind learns to speak mind to
    mind,
snakes will walk, and the blind be unblinded.
We must pour what we think into speech, into ink,
never knowing if any will find it

or take heed. All is wholly beyond our control,
as if we were some chieftain or pharaoh
doomed to helplessly wait on an embassy's fate.
Will they meet with a welcome or arrow

or take flight, or betray, or fall sick on the way,
or be slain, or their passage forbidden?
So a phrase we deemed good oft is misunderstood
or a point we thought obvious, hidden.

How uncertain and slow! What a labor to sow
and how scanty a harvest we glean!
With a thought, and no need to write down or to
    read,
I beheld all my captor had seen,

and I figured at first that the stars must have burst
and each speck become lurid and bloated.
Stunned to silence, I thrilled to a sky over-filled
like the sea where Leviathan floated.

And the black of the night turned to glittering
    white,
and each spark grew—or, rather, came nearer—
and they fell to the ground, and the land all around
was as clear as your face in the mirror.

This unnatural day was a splendid display
till the light of the visitors faded,
and in each, tall and grim, a dark figure within

made it certain that Mars was invaded.

In this dream I possessed neither clothing nor flesh.
Disembodied, I floated in place,
but I found I could move, and my progress was
    smooth,
though I went at the half-hearted pace

of a ghost, pale and gaunt, when the joy of the
    haunt
has long vanished, and he must morosely
make the rounds of bleak halls where no visitor
    calls.
I examined a newcomer closely.

Clad in animal skin and sepulchurally thin,
with hair long like the mane of a lion
and a face grave and lined, he did much to remind
    me
of Inca, and Aztec, and Mayan.

Dejah Thoris's kin, then, had had their beginning
on some other world, like my captor,
though if this were mere chance, or a mind more
    advanced
than my own would have thought of some factor

that predestined the spot they would meet, I know
    not.
Still, this vision did much to explain
how there came to be born, far from Earth, folk
    with forms
like to mine as two handfuls of grain.

Was our motherland Earth? Or was that but a
    berth
on a journey whose start none remembered?
Were all worlds made a pyre for humankind's fire,
some blazing, some ebbed to the embers?

Nor was I to be shown how these people had flown
through the void between worlds, nor if I
rediscovered the same, long-lost art when I came

to Barsoom, and if so, how and why.

I was never to find out these answers. Mankind
lives its days as if wrapped in a cloud,
and who hears of the sky, though the tale be half
    lie,
has learned more than nine-tenths of the crowd.

But I learned that these first men on Mars had
    been cursed
by misfortune, whose nature was this:
some precaution not taken, or signal mistaken
when sailing across the abyss

meant that some had been scathed by the journey.
    They bathed
in the blistering Sun's naked glare,
and for them this wrote doom in the seed or the
    womb
sparing them, but condemning their heirs,

for to be thus defiled meant a monstrous child
and such offspring were murdered or chased
where a hideous frame could cause parents no
    shame.
They were first of the ghouls of the waste.

And, as time was compressed at my captor's be-
    hest,
so a century passed in a minute,
and the stately parade became frenzied cascade
that I might see the patterns within it.

I learned why 'twas opined that the first of Man-
    kind
had been crafted like tools on a lathe
by some alien breed, moved by sloth or by greed,
that they might have a species of slaves[5].

They were slavers, 'twas true, and great scientists
    too,
yet withal they were nothing but human,

though their scholars and priests called all other
    folk beasts
and their own kin, Barsoom's only true men,

and their holy book stated that they had created
all others to work as their chattels,
but that book was a liar, its gospel no higher
or nobler than imbecile's prattle.

Call me cynic or wise, I was not that surprised,
for, since Cain raised his arm to his brother,
what the world does to men is not one part in ten
of what men will inflict on each other.

---

*James Hutchings lives in Melbourne, Aus-
tralia. He releases Western, noir and science
fiction-themed music on YouTube as Good-
Looking Corpse.*

---

[5] *See Part 8, Spring 2020.*

Notes

Things are going a million miles a minute here at Cirsova, it feels like.

It's January when I'm writing this, so not everything is set in stone yet. Did the Mongoose and Meerkat Kickstarter succeed? I sure hope so! We're either fulfilling by now or at least getting ready to.

Even I don't know what order that my future self has put all of the upcoming projects in... But here are some of the things you have to look forward to:

Wild Stars VI – We just wrapped this one in the Winter 2022 issue. We'll have a collected edition soon, hopefully with some bonus content! I mean, we usually have bonus content, don't we?

Sky Dance of Winter Fire – Michael Tierney has been working on an experiment with AI artwork, bringing his decades of experience as a professional artist and digital art restorationist to create a strange fantasy romance in words and pictures.

Small Worlds – Misha Burnett brings us a brand new collection, featuring several previously unpublished stories, including an all-new Erik Rugar adventure!

Mighty Sons of Hercules – Paying homage to classic peplum adventure, Cirsova Publishing is putting together an epic anthology of Sword & Sandal stories from some of its top authors!

A Bad Case of Dead – Just because Mongoose & Meerkat is ending doesn't mean we don't have more Jim Breyfogle for you!

Soon, we'll be bringing you this enchanting romantic adventure about the undead! This one is sure to be an all-time favorite alongside stories such as The Princess Brides and Stardust!

Next issue, we'll be taking a break from Mongoose & Meerkat, but don't fear! We'll still be running the final two installments serially for those of you who have been following along in the magazine [though I really hope you've ordered volume 3].

If you're enjoying The Gold Exigency so far, Constable Conrock's first appearance was actually in a bonus story [first published in The Multiversal Scribe in 1977] we included in the collected edition of The Artomique Paradigm, so you might want to pick that up!

There is probably waaaay more that I needed to be covering in these notes to you guys, but again, it's January, and I can't predict how things will have shaken out by March!

As of the writing of this column, two of the three Illustrated Stark books are back in print. If I wasn't lazy, I probably got the third one back on Amazon sometime before the end of January, early February if I dragged my feet.

Also, farewell to our copy editor, Xavier, who is stepping back after the fall issue! We thank him for his years helping to make Cirsova as good as it has been!

P. Alexander, Ed.